OVERTAKER TERRITORY

PRAISE FOR DAWN OF THE TRADE (DOORMEN 1)

"*Dawn of the Trade* grabs you from the first page. A compelling story you shouldn't miss."
    –Brian Drake, author of the Sam Raven series'

"An exhilarating, high-stakes crime story with twists and turns from start to finish."
    –January Bain, author of City of Lies series

"Jarrett Mazza writes in a distinctive style that hits like a punch in the gut and yanks the reader into a vividly realized blend of thrills, excitement, and compelling characters. DAWN OF THE TRADE is a great debut novel, and I look forward to seeing what the author comes up with next!"
    –Best-selling author, James Reasoner

"Following in the footsteps of *Roadhouse*, Mazza's *Dawn of the Trade* is all action. It tells the story of a man with a code who makes himself at home with a community of like-minded warriors: the Doormen. The night club setting–NYC's the Conquistador–is so atmospheric that it's a major character all on its own!"
    –John Corr, author of *Eight Times Up*

"Jarrett Mazza has written one hell of a good book with *Dawn of the Trade*. His protagonist, Jon Haze, a tough-as-nails former marine, is the kind of guy you'd want next to you when your back's against the wall. This one has it all: excellent writing, fabulous action scenes, intriguing plotting, and best of all, it's the first in a new series. Do yourself a favor and pick up this first Doorman novel. You won't regret it."

–Michael A. Black, author of the *Trackdown* series

OVERTAKER TERRITORY

DOORMEN
BOOK 3

JARRETT MAZZA

ROUGH
EDGES
PRESS

Rough Edges Press
An Imprint of Wolfpack Publishing
1707 E. Diana Street
Tampa, FL 33610

roughedgespress.com

Paperback ISBN 978-1-68549-734-7
eBook ISBN 978-1-68549-733-0
LCCN: 2024941980

For Mom.
Always there, always prepared.

OVERTAKER TERRITORY

PROLOGUE

THEY CAME AT NIGHT. THE MEN IN SUITS proceeded into The Conquistador like wolves approaching a wounded calf. Blood had been spilled here. The scent of death was still palpable. The predators—the OverTakers—entered the club, and the Doormen waited.

"Remember, no one is to speak unless spoken to. These men are not your friends, do you understand?" Addison Krowe's orders to his brothers were clear. His brigade of loyal bouncers were positioned behind them. "Understood," said Danix. "Not a word."

The Doormen were in their standard uniform and were combined into a single unit. They were a phalanx primed for an attack. In a straight row, after surviving the Showdown against the Fallen Sons, the guardians of The Conquistador had fully accepted their fate.

They were more than just nightlife security.

No, what lay here was the infamous and much-sought-after ciphers.

Their treasure was a key, the key to all nightclubs across the world!

The Conquistador wasn't a site exclusively designed for dancing, drinking, music, or fraternizing. No, it provided the precious *access* so many wanted and would do anything to obtain. And after nearly four decades of assembling as much as they could, Addison and Larry were guarding this secret, protecting it from the very people who had invaded their club now.

Waiting for the right moment or the right use of their primary resource, Addison thought the time was now. He thought this, and then Michael Irons and the OverTakers arrived.

"Where is he?" Among the OverTakers, one man stood with his shirt unbuttoned and was wearing no tie. Before Addison Krowe, this man's eyes were stone-cold.

Almost the same age as The Conquistador's cooler, the OverTaker leader was part of the replacement crew. Once thought of only as a bodyguard, as well as the boyfriend of Jon Haze's mother, Michael Irons stood tall before Addison as something else entirely.

His gaze gleamed the sweet ambition of conquest.

No more club. No more secrets. No more Doormen.

"Stop talking," Addison snapped at Irons. "You know where he is."

Irons smirked.

He was selected as the new security. If The Conquistador did not pass its review, then Addison and Larry would lose control of their precious club. They would be stripped of their rank and ownership, and everything else they valued would be gone forever.

If this happened, then a change in leadership and security would follow.

The Doormen would be gone, and Michael Irons and the OverTakers would take over.

A new age, with new rules and new management, would supersede whatever came before. It would be an ugly and messy transition, but it would be the future of The Conquistador.

"We'll see. Gentlemen, let us begin our conquest, shall we?" Irons proceeded.

Under the Nightclub Oversight Commission, The Conquistador was now subject to a review of its standards and practices. Its rules, laws, and new ways must be taken into consideration. Once it was over, the club would either pass or fail and the Doormen would be pushed aside, reassigned, and redone. The OverTakers would proceed to bring their review. They would either concur or they would deny.

None knew the outcome.

Addison Krowe was the club's official spokesperson as well as its attorney. He had been since he tied the knot with Larry Thomas's daughter. Addison rarely spoke about his wife. He didn't because he couldn't.

Family was best left out of business.

While currently tied up in a legal battle, Addison's chief strategy when deciding how to go forward was to cooperate. He cooperated while also devising a new plan for himself as well as his fellow Doormen.

He opened the doors and had no choice: he let the enemy in.

The OverTakers had fully infiltrated The Conquistador, and Addison had a few words for Michael Irons. As the head of his own brotherhood, Irons didn't reveal his true identity and motive until after the Showdown. A master manipulator, Irons gawked at Addison.

"Don't make the mistake of thinking you own this place," said Addison. "You might be the one in charge for now, but your authority is decided by the *Overseer*. And you know who he's *really* loyal to."

"Sure, I do. Sure, I do."

The OverTakers were once thought of only as bodyguards but were now under the leadership of Mr. Irons, a man whose reputation was that of a lion. He was well known in this industry but his image went deeper than how he appeared. He was a man who knew things, knew people, and he was also part of the guild linked to the highest level of authorities among the nightclub world.

His plan since the beginning was to infiltrate and disrupt The Conquistador. He wanted everything the club had and sought to acquire its *ciphers* for himself.

Everyone wanted the club ciphers because everyone wanted access—*unlimited access*.

Like he stated from the beginning, the OverTakers would decide the fate of The Conquistador as they were the organization hired to replace the Doormen. With all this in mind, Addison Krowe, as well as the rest of the Doormen, understood that what lay ahead would be their greatest challenge to date.

After the Showdown, everyone thought it would end in their favor.

The Doormen won. The Fallen Sons lost.

Everyone thought this. They assumed it was the truth. And yet, as Addison was beginning to see now more than ever before, thoughts were not truth. The only herald for truth was action. It's exactly what the Doormen were prepared to do now.

They were prepared to take action.

"What do we do now?" Danix asked Addison.

Until now, Addison felt like he was alone. When the other bouncer spoke to him, Addison flinched and remembered where he was and what he had to do.

"We find Jon," said Addison. "We have to find... *Jon.*"

CHAPTER 1
HOME AWAY FROM HOME

THE TRUTH HITS THE HARDEST.

There is no doubt about that.

Jon had taken his fair share of beatings throughout his life, but none hurt as much as this. He'd been punched, kicked, whacked, pounded, choked out, and stabbed. And, whenever Jon believed there was no other pain he could endure, another one emerged that took him completely by surprise.

And, when Jon thought he couldn't take more, he always did.

For Jon, the pain he was experiencing now served as a reminder that everything he once thought was true was actually a lie. Jon had been lied to, yes, but he had also lied to himself. When Jon jumped in his mother's car with only one luggage packed, his emergency bag, he drove and kept driving. Before leaving, Jon sent his mother a text and told her he needed to go and not to try and contact him.

He would be *out of reach.*

And so, Jon could only imagine what his mom was

thinking now. When Jon's mom learned the truth about Michael Irons too, a man who once brought her so much happiness and joy, her heart was broken same as her mind. Michael Irons was a man who pretended to actually care for Jon's mother. Such warmness didn't come often for a woman her age.

Therefore, it would seem Irons's only intention was to use Jon's mother so he could get close to Jon. Irons wanted to get into Jon's mom's life so he could pretend to be something he wasn't. He would do this so he could learn more about Jon and The Conquistador.

While Michael had only scratched the surface of what a club could do, after he earned Jon's trust, he made a significant move in the right direction. It was only after Jon came to Michael Irons for advice that the head OverTaker had granted Jon the tool that would lead to his downfall.

The dart was poisonous and *illegal*, yet Jon didn't know this, no.

No, he was set-up, double-crossed, and left to fail.

Rex MacIntosh, who was the leader of the Fallen Sons, in the end, was not working alone. Someone else was pulling the strings. Someone else was helping this renegade clan to bring the Doormen down. At the very top, had to be someone skilled. It had to be someone who had not only extensive knowledge of nightlife security but also someone who possessed great knowledge of security in general. It needed to be someone who was educated and wise. And, while the Doormen were focused on beating the Sons in the Bouncer Showdown, they were immune to the other sinister forces lurking in secret. And, if they couldn't fight their enemy in the dark, where they operated, then how could they beat them in the light? What light was left now that its brightest one was out? What was the point of being a bouncer if all it had prepared you for was what *not* to do during dangerous situations?

How could Jon be loyal to an institution so flawed and untrustworthy?

What did he have to gain, and what did he have to protect?

When Jon left Queens, he drove across the bridge and entered New Jersey. His choice to leave New York was spontaneous to say the least. He didn't have an idea about where he was going or why. He just knew he couldn't stand to be where he was for a second longer. Jon needed time to think, to breathe freely, and to think of nothing.

He ignored all his text messages and ignored all his phone calls too.

His mother was likely panic-stricken. She was likely a toal wreck. Jon was less concerned about her and more concerned about the person who was attempting to contact him. She was Jon's newest person and someone he couldn't stop thinking about, especially now.

Kya was the only one Jon needed to contact since leaving The Conquistador and removing his crest. Crests had changed since the time of the Fallen Sons. Jon only removed the one sewn to his shirt. There were others that the other Doormen had that he did not. Nevertheless, to him—to Jon—that was enough. Kya sent Jon not one but four texts in the days that followed.

Nearly all of them were the same.

Where are you?

Why did you leave?

Can we talk?

Please.

Although Jon refused to answer any of them, he found himself mystified by each and every one. After all, it was Kya who was the first to ask Jon the all-consuming question he could not escape from.

She was the one who said it first: *how well do you know the club where you work?*

At the time, Jon dismissed this question, and it was not because he was dismissing Kya. No, it was because he didn't know enough to answer her. Therefore, it was easier just to avoid talking at all. Jon pretended like he was working for a pristine institution, the best nightclub in the entire city of New York, because that's what he was told. So, Jon kept telling himself this story over and over until it became true. Jon insisted it was. Then, he learned why The Conquistador was considered the best.

There was more to its story, and it was a story Jon loathed thinking about.

Kya didn't join Jon in his exile. She couldn't because she didn't feel as strongly about it as Jon did. Part of Jon believed his reaction was emotional and he didn't actually want to leave.

Jon just didn't have it in him to stay. And, since there was no place in the city he could go, Jon decided to go far away. He adored New Jersey, actually. Some people had nasty things to say about the state and its residences, but Jon liked how it was family-oriented as well as the versatility offered by its various cities. Jon

appreciated the wide demographics, and most importantly, he liked its silence. There was only one reason
for why Jon was traveling there now.

His former lieutenant lived there. He was Jon's
friend, his confidant, the person Jon went to for advice.
And Jon needed his help, now more than ever before.
Lieutenant Albert Daniel, or as Jon and the Marines
called him: *Lieutenant Dan*.

It was an obvious nod to the *Forrest Gump* character, but Jon's Lieutenant Dan earned this title. Like
Gary Sinise in the film, Jon's Dan was also thoughtful
and to the point but always kind. He was actually the
last person Jon spoke to before he left the Marines.
Back when Jon attended James's funeral, Dan was there
too. When Jon couldn't sleep, he called to speak with
Lieutenant Dan. When Jon was unable to leave the
tragedy that had taken his leg and part of his life away,
it was Dan who told Jon what no one else would.

He kept their interactions simple by informing Jon
of three simple words:

"Feel the pain. Feel the pain."

When Jon heard this, he stopped resisting all the
suffering that had a place in his life. He thought he
could resist it like he did an enemy. After James's
funeral, Lieutenant Dan spoke with Jon in the car,
alone.

"Let it in. Let it hurt."

For so long, Jon was under the impression he could
beat his pain. He wanted to bury it like you bury other
things that are too heavy to carry. You find a way to
throw it all into the ground using as much strength as
you have, and then you just let it drop into its grave.
You grab a shovel and toss in the dirt. You do this until

all of it is completely submerged and gone forever. This was how Jon once thought he could combat the trauma and the suffering he had endured. The club helped. The job helped him to cope and to heal. Jon wanted all of this. Then, he realized that this was not the way to handle it. The only way a person can overcome their own pain is to face it head-on. Only then does the pain die.

Jon understood how this was possible. He learned this well before he began working at The Conquistador. The club was just one way Jon was handling the side effects of war. When at the club, Jon had a purpose. Jon had a role and he had a job. For so long, that was enough. After the Showdown, it brought Jon to the precipice of a new kind of pain.

In the military, it was pain that came only as a result of loss. However, at The Conquistador, it grew because of deception and secrecy. Jon only thought he knew who he was and what he wanted. He thought he was on the right side and now, he was lost and wreathed with conflict and uncertainty. And it was for this reason that Jon had to consult the only person who could help him now.

Lieutenant Dan lived in Jersey with his wife.

They used to have two sons, but both died in the war. This was one of the many reasons why Jon trusted Dan as much as he did. He wasn't some life coach who could provide advice to people without actually understanding what they were going through. Dan understood loss and pain better than anyone. He understood because he had suffered through damn near all of it. Dan was not just a platoon leader, he was also a preacher.

In fact, the latter was his most profound characteristic.

When Dan's enlistment ended, he returned to his former career. He used what he lost not to become bitter or dismayed, but to lead and to provide hope and truth to people who needed it. Jon loved this about his former lieutenant. He loved it so much because Jon was a person who did need it, who did and always would need hope.

Jon marched along the path that jutted across the lawn outside of Lieutenant Dan's bungalow. A tastefully decorated home, Jon had journeyed to this house before.

Always, he was pleased with how it made him feel. It was homey and warm. Jon hoped to someday own a house like this one. He wanted to move out of his mom's, and sometimes, Jon didn't believe that would ever be possible. He was twenty-five now and could see himself living at his mother's for still another five years.

He hated how it had to be this way, but that was Jon's reality.

He thought maybe he could explain this to Dan as well.

He knocked once, patted down his thighs, and slid his hands down his chest. He flattened his crinkled shirt and did his best to appear *presentable*. For what reason? There was none. It didn't matter how Jon looked. In the eyes of a man like Lieutenant Dan, Jon would always be the same, and that way was *brother*, that way was *friend*. The door opened, but Jon was not looking at his lieutenant or fellow Marine. Instead, he was looking at a woman with red hair dressed in a silk blouse and wearing pearl earrings.

"Hello?" the woman said, charmed by Jon's sudden arrival.

"Uh, hello. And you are—"

"Dan's wife," added the woman. "Maria. Not sure if you remember me."

Jon thought about all the previous encounters he had with Dan, if he had crossed paths with his wife before. From what Jon could recall, there were no instances whereby he met Maria. Even at James's funeral, he didn't remember seeing her there.

"Sorry," Jon said. "My memory is not all that great, but it's nice to meet you. I'm—"

"Jon," said Maria. "I know."

"Right," Jon replied. "I'm sure Dan told you I'd be coming by."

"He did. Now, please. Come inside. He's waiting for you."

Maria stepped aside but held the door open. The house smelled of roses, and the foyer was hardwood and clean. A crystal chandelier hung above Jon's head. The living room looked like a photo from a catalog. After Maria let Jon into her home, he searched for his lieutenant.

But he didn't see Dan anywhere.

"Thank you," Jon said to Maria. He was being polite, but a woman liked Maria deserved more than just manners.

"He's in the living room, waiting for you," said Maria. "But can I get you something to drink if you'd like?"

"Uh, no. No, thank you," said Jon.

"Okay then." Maria raised her hand and gestured to the living room she mentioned earlier.

From where Jon was standing, he couldn't see Dan. He presumed he wouldn't until he looked at the two love chairs facing a serene fireplace. This seemed more like Dan's style.

"Dan? He's here, no worries." Wasting no time, Jon was left to wait by the fireplace. Once inside, Jon did manage to see more of the love chair facing the flames. Seeing a man's arm and a hand holding a glass filled with a transparent liquid, maybe white wine? Still, Jon leaned in to have a closer look.

"Sir?" Calling to his lieutenant, the face of a battle-hardened man with gray hair and a clean scar across his face came forward.

"Jon Haze," Dan said. "I see you're here. Thank you."

"Yes, sir," Jon saluted. "Thank you for agreeing to meet with me."

"Always," Dan said. "Please, sit."

Jon sat in the chair opposite to Dan. Sitting primly, Jon folded his hands across his lap.

"Thanks. So...I know I asked to see you on such short notice, but I needed to. I figured you might be the only one who would understand."

"Like the friend that I am," Lieutenant Dan replied, "I am, and always will be here, to listen to new allies and old ones."

"I appreciate that," said Jon. "Really, I do, sir. Appreciated."

"So, why is it that you felt the need to see me of all people?"

"Because...for as long as I could remember, you've always been the one who could help."

"What did I say to you back in the Corps?" asked

Dan. He drank more of his wine while sitting in front of the crackling fire.

"I know what you said," Jon answered.

"Tell me again," replied Dan, "just so I know for sure you heard me correctly."

Jon never refused an order, not from a commanding officer. This was also his old way of thinking. Now he learned that taking orders for the sake of taking them was not always the answer, right, or true. In fact, it hardly ever was.

"No one can help everyone," Jon recited. "First, you must learn to help yourself."

"Right," said Dan. "Exactly. By coming here, I know something is troubling you, and you require the help of your wise old master to get you through it."

"Yeah," said Jon, "You could say that."

"Then go ahead, lay it on me," commanded Dan. "I didn't let you come down here for nothing, now did I?"

"I left the Marines," said Jon, "because I lost someone important to me. Then, I went home, where I thought I would find my way back, and I took a job because I needed work, and I hoped that it would help me get back on track to give me a purpose and a mission. I wanted that because I thought that's what I needed."

"And?" asked Dan. "It didn't?"

"It did, but then everything changed," said Jon. "I thought I was doing good work, protecting people and working at a good institution, but...things weren't as they seemed to be. Most of it, from what I understood... well, it was all just a lie."

"A lie?" said Dan. "How so?"

"Well, I didn't know what was true," said Jon, "and what wasn't, what was right and what was wrong. And, when I can't tell the difference between the two, then that's my signal to walk away and never look back."

"So...it's only when you realize things weren't as *you* thought them to be," said Dan, "that you turn your back and abandon your duty."

"It's not abandoning if the team you serve is bad."

"Well, that all depends," said Dan.

"On what?" Jon sardonically asked.

"If the organization really is bad," said Dan. "I mean, people thought we were bad too, remember?"

Jon nodded. He remembered.

"And sometimes we were, no doubt, but our hearts always stayed where they needed to. We tried to have empathy, Jon. We had honor, and we were in those cities because we were trying to help the people who were trapped inside of them. It wasn't all just about following orders. Most often, it was about doing what we thought was right, especially when the conflict began to dwindle and things started to really change. We were still trying to do what was right, because see, there are two groups of people in this world," said Dan, "the people who say a system is broken and others who know the system is broken but still try to fix it."

"Who cares whether you try to fix something or not? Everyone tries, few succeed, so what's the point?" asked Jon. "What's the point if you have to lie to get it done?"

"I think you just answered your own question," said Dan.

"You lost me," said Jon.

"Trying to do what's right *is* the point. Actually, it's the *only* point. World isn't a simple place anymore, Jon. You know this. It's complicated, dark, and twisted. Few are able to navigate its web of inconsistency and deception. Some, you're right, don't even bother to try. Those that do don't always know what the right decisions are. And yet, they just try to do whatever they can, and that in itself is what matters, son. I don't know anything about these people you worked for, whether they were good or bad, but before you pass judgment on anyone, take a second and put yourself in their shoes. Ask yourself, what would you have done, and would it be different, better, or the same?"

"That's just it," said Jon. "I don't know what I would do."

"And if you don't know, but someone else does, and they have a plan, are you really better than they are?"

Jon needed a moment to consider Dan's question.

He reflected on Addison and the secrets that lied beneath The Conquistador. Jon remembered the Showdown, the results of it, and whether or not he would have done anything differently. At the time, Jon was sure that what Addison and Larry Thomas had done was wrong. They had lied to Jon about what the club really was and had put his life in danger. Worse, they were a possible criminal organization, as they had something *precious* hidden inside their precious vault that many people wanted to obtain. Now, after speaking with Lieutenant Dan, what was once thought to be uncertain wasn't exactly uncertain.

What would Jon have done? He asked himself this while staring ahead.

Maybe it all wasn't so simple.

Maybe Jon was too quick to judge. Maybe he did turn his back on his duties, even in spite of the fact he believed in the Doormen's cause.

"You think every man I'd ever taken orders from told me to do what was right? You think every mission ended the way I wanted it to? I have regrets, and yes, there are things I would have done differently, but that doesn't change the fact that when it came to our enemies, we acted better than they would have. We had honor. See, because what was in our hearts was always better than what was in theirs. In the end, our intentions didn't change. We were there to help, and we did, and we were at war because we wanted to serve. Killing is not all that defines us, and I imagine whatever you're wrestling with now, it's not all that defines the place where you used to work either. Contrary to what most people think, it's never an easy path. It's not because if it was easy, so many people would walk it, but as you know now...so few people do."

"It all seems too simple," Jon said to Dan, "when you say it. For some reason, I don't know what to think anymore."

"No, you know what to think," Dan assured Jon. "You're just conflicted. You just have your doubts, which you are allowed to have. Nothing is ever certain. Sometimes, actually, most of the time, you have to stop and try to see as far ahead as you can. Once you do that, well, that's when you have to do what comes next."

"And what does come next, sir?" Jon asked his former lieutenant. The flames danced in Jon's glassy eyes and he could feel the heat on his face. Looking at

Dan, Jon had not changed his sitting position since they came to this room.

"A leap of faith," Dan replied. He finished his drink. "*It's a leap of faith.*"

Hearing this, the conflict and the doubt Dan had mentioned continued to burn deep inside. Yes, all of what Dan said was true, and there was no pretending like it wasn't. And yet, Jon was assured by Dan that doubt was good. Doubt, he thought, *marks the beginning of truth.*

Jon had heard Dan say this once to his unit before they went on mission. It was a long time ago, but Jon remembered. He remembered everything Dan said.

"And how do I know when I should take it? When is the leap real, and when is it only just a figment of someone else's imagination?" After Jon inquired about this, what he said was sharp and sensible. By no means an easy question, Dan placed his drink down on the table.

Fortunately, Dan did have an answer. It was one he'd spoken of since the beginning.

"What does your gut tell you, Marine?" What Jon experienced now was a mild sense of euphoria. "What does your heart tell you?"

A new feeling blossomed deep within Jon and spread throughout his body. What he felt he could not stop feeling, and it was in that moment Jon was awakened. He was so awakened he smiled. He hadn't expressed such happiness at all since he had come to visit Lieutenant Dan. That was his entire reason for being here now. He wanted answers. Now he had them.

"Thanks, Lieutenant. Thank you." Jon tightened the hood on his sweater.

With a newfound sense of clarity, he didn't wish to stay here for more than he needed to. What Dan had provided was enough. Now, all Jon had to do was decide what to do next.

He had an idea.

"Well, I do look after my own," said Dan. "I know you'd do the same for me. Once a Marine, always a Marine."

Jon nodded and grinned.

He pretended like he would. Truthfully, Jon did not see himself to be the same person as Dan was. He didn't have the same level of patience, and he wasn't nearly as kind, at least not at this point in his life. However, what Jon was certain of now was how thankful and appreciative he felt. Therefore, Jon raised his hand just the same and saluted right back. Jon showed as much pride as he could summon at this moment. In fact, Jon was feeling so proud a tear almost slipped out from beneath his eye.

He could almost cry but held back in favor of preserving the moment.

"Good luck there, soldier," said Dan as he saluted. "I know you'll do what's right. So far, you always have."

"Thank you, sir."

"So...I take it you're headed back home then?"

"Better," said Jon. He turned away from the fireplace. He was about to make his way to the door. "I'm going back to where it all started. I'm going back to work."

Jon had never been more serious about anything in his life. He had rid himself of his crest and disavowed himself from his duties as part of the club's elite bouncing brigade known as the Doormen. But now, it was time for Jon to get it repaired. He was ready to find his way back, and the entire time, Jon knew there was only one way to prove this.

"I'm going back to fight."

CHAPTER 2
THE FIGHT BACK

WHEN JON LEFT HOME, HE DIDN'T SAY A WORD TO anyone about where he was going.

Having officially ex-communicated himself, Jon's mother, Kya, and Addison were all left in his rearview, in a matter of speaking, that is. When Jon said to his mother, *he would see her soon* and asked her *not to contact him*, it was because he needed *time alone*. But, looking back, Jon realized how wrong this was to do. His mom deserved more than those responses. Jon hadn't checked on her, but he should have. It was her boyfriend who set Jon up. Michael Irons, the owner of the elite agency known as the OverTakers, was the same agency now in control of The Conquistador.

He was also a man whom Jon's mother had once cared for, maybe a man she almost loved.

Michael revealed himself to be the puppeteer who orchestrated the club's downfall. Jon's mother's heart had been broken—shattered. She likely hated Michael as much as Jon did. Considering how much they had enjoyed together, in the end, Michael was only using Jon's mom to get to the club.

What Michael wanted was The Conquistador's wealth and power.

Michael Irons desired this but then so did so many others.

And so, the two most important men in Jon's mother's life were both gone.

Neither one told her where they were going. They just...*vanished*.

When Jon made the decision to return home, he said to Dan he planned on going back to work. He wasn't exactly lying. Jon was returning to work but not at the club. Work is often synonymous with *repair*. Jon was working to fix what was broken.

He needed his mother. Like all good sons, he wanted her more than anything.

Jon stepped through the door and was then struck by a wave of cold, almost impenetrable humidity. Whether it was because his mother had turned off the AC or closed all the windows, Jon thought maybe it was the fear chilling his bones. It was uncertainty that was causing his temperature to drop. Jon leaned in to press his hand against his thighs. Afraid to call out to her. Normally, when a door opened, a chime followed. Once the chime was hard, Jon's mother would call out to him.

Today, no one called.

No, there was nothing waiting for Jon when he stepped through the door. It wasn't often that Jon's house was overwhelmingly quiet. He considered this part of his punishment, which was what he deserved.

What did Jon deserve? Well, that's what he was here to discover.

"Mom?" Calling out to his mother, Jon's heart sank.

He tried fighting his nerves. Jon was fighting the kind of wrath his mom was sure to unleash when she realized her son had come back home. Jon waited for the expected raised voice, the vicious shouts, and the constant repetition sure to rattle his eardrums. Jon looked around as he proceeded through his living room. Everything there looked fresh and clean. Jon heard footsteps after calling his mom a second time. He followed the sound, which led out the backdoor and into the yard. Listening to the sound of tinkering glasses, Jon pushed through the door and stopped near the patio furniture. Jon was slow, gradual, *careful*. He wasn't sure how to approach her, but what was most strange about his mom was she was sitting.

Resting on the sofa, shoeless and with her legs crossed, Jon's mom didn't move when she saw her son. She was reading a book in cold, shunning silence. Donning her reading glasses, she smiled at Jon, though it was not her most pleasant one. It was given only out of obligation. Jon's mom couldn't pretend she was not happy to see her son, but then she was also disappointed too. Jon recognized his mom's look of disappointment. In the twenty-four years since his birth, a mother's look of scorn did not change.

It did not alter. And, when Jon observed it now, his mom shivered as she stepped.

"Hi, Mom," Jon said. He was cautious about how he approached. After all, he did leave her.

"Jon," she said. "You're here."

"I'm here," Jon said with a nod. "I'm home, and I'm happy to be back."

Jon's mom nodded, but her smile quickly turned to a scowl and then into a sulk. She frowned as she fought back tears. Jon's mom glanced away from her son and looked at her book. The struggle was obvious. Jon believed the best way to fight it to keep talking—to explain.

"You were gone a long time," Jon's mom said.

"A few days," Jon replied. "Yeah."

"But you just left," said Jon's mom. "You just...left."

"Yeah," Jon said. "Sorry."

"Is that all you have to say? You're sorry?"

Jon's mom's reaction was justified. It was also very predictable. Such a passive-aggressive way for a mom to respond. Jon could have printed it on a card they just handed to their kids.

"I am, but I had a lot of thinking to do. I just had to do it on my own."

"On your own?" Jon's mom posed to her son a sharp yet necessary inquiry. "Explain to me why whenever anything happens to you, you always think it's something you have to do on your own, without telling me or anyone?"

"Because my fights are my fights," declared Jon. "You know what I need to do to win them. I buck up and I push forward. This time, I just couldn't involve anyone else. You weren't the only one I left behind."

"But I was the only one who needed you here, especially when..." Betsy Haze's eyes began to twitch. Looking away now, what Jon's mom was thinking about was the man Jon hated most of all. When he left, Jon didn't think about Michael Irons. Jon left his mom alone with a man who hated him. Why did he do this? How could he?

Where was Irons, and how did the relationship with him and Jon's mother end?

All were crucial questions, but Jon didn't even tell his mom what happened at The Conquistador. He hadn't mentioned the Showdown or how Michael had a significant hand in hurting The Conquistador. Jon didn't know where to start. He began in the best way possible. For him, it was to start slowly and easily.

"I'm sorry about what happened," Jon said to his mom. Although it was now starting to sound like more of a confession. "I'm sorry things didn't turn out the way you thought they would."

Among all the details Jon provided, his mother nodded and gulped to contain her sorrow. A heartbreak can only mend with time and with words. Jon needed more time to talk to his mom, not only about her future, but about his too.

"I'm sorry too," said Jon's mom.

"So...he's gone?"

Jon's mom nodded. "You think you're the only one who knew what happened?" Jon's mom asked her son. "What happened at The Conquistador...it's everywhere."

"What do you mean?" Jon asked.

"All over Instagram and Google," Jon's mom clarified right away. It was like she was waiting for her son to ask about this. "All are talking about how the New York club will be reviewing its standards and practices. And guess who's leading the parade?"

Jon didn't need to ask to know the answer.

Betsy showed Jon her phone. It was playing a video of Michael Irons. He was elaborating on how his company was now put in charge of security at the club. He said this would be the case until The Conquistador had successfully managed to pass its forthcoming review.

Jon glared.

"Have you spoken to him at all?" This question Jon feared most of all.

"Tried," said Jon's mom. "When you left, I tried talking to him about what happened. I had so many questions. I mean, all I did was text and call, text and call, but when he just kept asking where you were, I had some feelings. It wasn't until I got another visitor that I began to see what really happened."

"Another visitor?" asked Jon. "Who?"

"Who else?" Jon's mom asked. "Addison."

"Addison? Addison came to see you?"

"He did," Jon's mom said to her son. "Yes, he did."

"And?" said Jon.

"And he told me everything," said his mom. "He told me the truth."

Jon scoffed while he was simultaneously embarrassed by what was said.

Obviously, trusting Michael was a mistake. But this was Jon's mistake. He was the one who made the decision to use the dart gun during the Showdown and so, Jon should be the one who pays for it. Jon had not yet paid this price, however. Instead, he turned his back on his friends and family and he just walked away.

"Michael...he set me up," Jon said to his mom. At

this point, he was sure she knew. "He set me up and he lied."

"I know. Addison told me," said Betsy Haze.

"Addison?" asked Jon.

"Yes," said his mother.

"Is that all Addison told you?" Jon's cheeks began to change color. He hoped Addison didn't tell his mother everything. There was too much to tell. The Conquistador acquired these gold ciphers that few knew about and yet so many were fighting to obtain. This was true, but so was Addison's declaration that there were fewer people to trust with this level of access. It was a long and complicated backstory, and Jon understood why Addison didn't inform his mother of all the details.

Jon neglected to do this as well.

He didn't want to explain to his mom because then she would know just how much was at stake.

"Yeah," he said to his mom. "There's more to the story."

"Well, then I guess it's up to you to fix it, right? You came back for a reason. I hope you know what that reason is."

Jon considered this reason. He reflected on why he made the decision to come back. He once thought it was because his decision to leave was too emotional and impulsive. It was this way because Jon felt betrayed. He felt like he'd been lied to. He remembered what Lieutenant Dan said to him, though. No one serves a perfect organization, but acting on principle is what drives any cause forward. Keeps it alive, real, and worth fighting for.

It's actually the only way for any cause to go forward.

Acting with honor and being true to one's creed, that's the obligation of all Doormen. Jon's hands combed through his hair and sweat wet his palms. Jon perspired whenever he was feeling anxious. Jon felt this way when he first stepped through the door. He was feeling better now, albeit only slightly.

"I came back," said Jon, "because I still have a battle to fight. There are still brothers who need me. Michael might think he has a better group behind him, but he definitely doesn't have what I do. He doesn't have loyalty, unity, or the truth that binds a band together. The Doormen have each other's backs, and that's what makes us the best bouncers out there. I forgot that when I left, but now I remember."

"They need you, Jon," said Jon's mom. "They really do."

Jon scoffed. What his mom said was flattering, but Jon questioned whether it was her talking or if it was Addison.

"Is that what Addison said to you so I'd come back?" Jon asked his mom.

Casually, Jon stood from the couch and stepped back toward the door.

"No," said Jon's mom. "That's your mother talking. Now go upstairs and get some rest. You're going to need it, and now that is Addison talking, because he's expecting you tomorrow night, he said."

"Tomorrow night?"

"He says report in as usual and don't forget to bring your shirt."

"My shirt?" Jon asked, confused.

"Same one you always wear. You're still a Doorman, aren't you?" Jon's mom began to reveal a slight yet enchanted smile. "Like Addison said, *once a Doorman, always a Doorman.*"

Jon thought this no longer applied. Seeing as how much his mother had given to Jon and to the club, she was one too. She was a Doorman, and she always would be.

CHAPTER 3
THE OLD LAWS

After The Conquistador's practices were called into question, a comprehensive investigation was to be conducted as per the Commission's request.

All Doormen knew of this, and all of them abided by the Commission's orders.

It began with looking into the club's standards and protocols, and this was the first time in its history whereby it was being reviewed. Under the Keeper's oversight, the OverTakers were to be installed as the club's new security unit. The Doormen were still on the floor. They could still bounce and dismiss people, yes, but they were only allowed to deal with patrons verbally, not physically. Anything else was to be dealt with by the OverTakers alone.

Addison was still the club's cooler, yes, but he was forced to surrender his power to Michael fucking Irons, someone Jon would now refer to only as *Irons*. As a result of Irons taking Addison's position as The Conquistador's newest head of security, he was the one who made all the decisions. It was Irons who decided how to deal with the club and its guests. According to the Keeper, the standards and practices of The Conquistador were somewhat outdated. Someone like Irons had newer knowledge about how a club like this should operate. Using his experience as a protection agent, Irons's expertise was more current and therefore deemed as more valuable than the Doormen. Irons's entire operation was comprised of older men, midforties, and all highly skilled and quite capable under pressure. What was observed among the Doormen was these new men were also very arrogant. Though they were smart and had an aptitude for crowd control, they did not know how a club was *supposed* to work, specifically how The Conquistador worked.

It was a place built on principles: equality and access to everyone who wanted it and who was willing to follow its rules and respect its boundaries. It was not an exclusionary establishment, but was one which tried to make room for everything and everyone.

Hence, why it was considered *the best*.

Due to this fact, much of the power and authority once possessed by the Doormen was gone. Stripped of their power, Danix, Li, Owen, Addison, and even Kya had lost all their autonomy. This was not only the source of their aggravation. It placed them in a vulnerable and dying position. They could not protect themselves. The Doormen's reach was limited and, as a result, they were losing who they were and everything they stood for.

And there was nothing anyone could do to stop it.

Jon was never more willing to eat fear than he was

at this moment. The time was almost eight o'clock. The doors to The Conquistador would open soon.

When they did, Jon would be there.

He was ready to walk right through the front door.

CHAPTER 4
BACK TO BUSINESS

SEPTEMBER WAS A MONTH JON WAS QUITE FOND OF.

To him, it always felt like more of a rejuvenation than New Year's. It was an awakening, and Jon always enjoyed the feeling of starting something fresh. It was this feeling that fueled his return. What Jon wanted was a new start, a new beginning, and he would have it.

Returning to The Conquistador, the outside of the infamous nightclub had not changed significantly since Jon's departure. There was still a spotlight, and Jon watched as limousines and other luxury vehicles glided along the curb and deployed their many illustrious guests into the entrance. All present and accounted for, the VIPs were given top priority. From what Jon could see on the sidewalk, the lineup was shorter than usual.

Everyone who arrived in expensive cars was given immediate access.

Everyone who was younger and wearing less jewelry was sent to wait in line.

Although this did not seem like a huge detail in the eyes of the average clubgoer, to Jon, he noticed it right away. The Conquistador was one of New York's finest establishments because of its willingness to cater to people from all walks of life.

Larry Thomas was always adamant about serving every single person equally.

Everyone was gold when you came to his club, Larry had once proclaimed. Jon didn't understand this, but now he did. Larry didn't just want to help the super-rich. No, The Conquistador was an experience that could that should be accessed by as many people as possible. Nevertheless, it did *not* appear to be this way now.

And so, Jon was irked by this discovery.

He noticed Jamal standing by the door at the head of the line. Jon examined his old friend's appearance. He hadn't spoken to Jamal since the Showdown. Jon followed Jamal on Facebook and Instagram. He even liked a few of his posts. Still, Jon had not reached out to Jamal. Seeing him now, looking so miserable and unfulfilled, Jon understood well what was happening. He should have been there for him. Jon should have been there for his friend.

And yet, Jon was here for Jamal now.

Jon watched Jamal lift the rope as three men in suits and three girls hanging off their shoulders walked in. More entered, and Jon realized his ability to gain access would be difficult. Men entering The Conquistador were required to wear collared shirts and classy shoes. Women were given more leniency. They didn't necessarily have to wear dresses. The practice of being sexy was unavoidable. Jon was not sexy, not now. A way into the club under these circumstances would be difficult. Jon still didn't have his crest. This technically wouldn't prevent access. If he were to enter without Doormen approval, then he was trespassing. It would be an unlawful entry, and thus, Jon could be bounced by anyone inside. Still, the only reason why Jon wanted to get into The Conquistador was because of Michael Irons.

But Jon wanted to give Irons a message.

So, Jon stood on the sidewalk with his hands in his pockets and stared dead ahead. He felt like he was drawing too much attention to himself. A grown man standing idly by while people lined up across the grand entrance to the city's best club was all too strange. Jon watched Jamal look in Jon's direction.

Jon ducked and squatted.

Sliding along the sidewalk, Jon proceeded to the vehicles parked close to the curb. All were luxury cars: Lambos, McLarens, and some solid Benz models to go along with the other.

Jon marveled at these vehicles.

Also, he did not have a way into the club, not yet. He hated the method he had to use, but it was the only way.

Jon raced across the sidewalk and minded his surroundings. A trio of girls hopped along, and Jon could already hear the music thumping from the grand building. Being the first week of college, most of the people Jon should encounter were between the ages of twenty and twenty-eight. This was a common age for The Conquistador's clients.

None fit the profile now. Undoubtedly, the club patrons were older and also the same race. Jon presumed there were new policies on things like *face control* and *weaponry*. The OverTakers likely specialized in some of these new tactics which were formerly unbeknownst to the former Doormen.

Jon hurried toward the fire escape. Most buildings with fire escapes had the typical steel ladders but this was not how The Conquistador's functioned. There was a ladder, but it was not accessible. Unlike others that were reachable, this ladder was fifteen feet from the ground.

This was only Jon's estimated measurement.

When Jon hurried to the side of the building, the ladder was located at the very back. If Jon hadn't been an employee for as long as he was, he wouldn't have found this ladder. Addison said it was only there because the city demanded its existence.

It didn't mesh well with The Conquistador's overall feng shui.

Jon continued to blend in. The space surrounding the nightclub was jampacked. Jon had only seen the club this busy on a few occasions. This was definitely a day worth remembering.

Marching toward the back, Jon looked over his shoulder.

He felt like he was being followed. There were surveillance cameras positioned along the building's exterior. There was more than Jon recalled. Fortunately, Jon knew where all the cameras were, and he also knew...how to avoid them too.

Jon's back was pressed to the wall. He looked up. The Conquistador's camera system was the best money could buy. Always, there was someone watching, which most of the time was Addison. Jon thought about what Addison was doing now. If he was in his office watching the cameras or out on the floor, Jon hoped he was still somewhere, doing his job.

As Jon looked at the ladder, he made a move without thinking. He leaped and he somersaulted. Jon hit the pavement harder than intended and jumped up toward the ladder above his head.

Like Jon had estimated, the ladder was fifteen feet from the ground.

He thought this was the right number, but having only seen this access point on a few occasions, he realized how off he really was. The ladder was not fifteen feet at all! No, it was closer to twenty, and when Jon planted his feet, he was prepared to jump. Relying on the spring of his prosthetic, still Jon's ability to leap was weaker compared to others. This new model, however, offered more spring and more resistance. Jon hadn't jumped with it before. But, with there being a first time for everything, Jon figured now might be the best time to try.

Channeling all his energy into his legs, Jon flexed his shoulders.

He could not jump twenty feet, and he didn't plan on trying. What Jon wanted was to jump up onto the dumpster and then jump up to the window. Then, he would swing and he would hook onto the ladder. Jon came across the dumpster and glanced at the window next to it. All the perceived pieces of Jon's plan were in place. Jon had somehow managed to transform himself into a parkour legend.

Now, he did have some experience in this area, though not much.

Stepping back, Jon sprinted toward the dumpster. With a hard jump, Jon's prosthetic was solid enough to propel him forward. Now leaping onto the trash bin, Jon pushed off the ledge and soared in through the window. Throughout this entire stunt, Jon did his best to stay relaxed. Although it was practically impossible for him to do this, Jon did connect with the dumpster's ledge. Succeeding here, Jon now had a clear path to making his next move.

On the window sill, the glass was tinted, like the stained-glass windows found in most churches. These windows in The Conquistador were done solely for decoration. This proved beneficial for Jon. When he pushed off the sill, Jon flew up to the ladder like a precarious mountain climber.

But, with the metal being so close, Jon could already feel it within his hands.

Looking up, the inches between Jon's palms and the steel began to shrink. Jon bit his lip and grazed the slick steel. Clutching the metal, Jon seized the bars with all his might. In the gym, pull-ups were Jon's favorite exercise. Right now, he could lift his body weight up and above the bar with minimal effort. Definitely helpful. Jon pulled and jumped onto the ladder. Holding and releasing his grip, the more noises Jon made, the more attention he drew.

Damn.

Addison did mention the fire escape once to Jon.

"*Not the most noticeable,*" he had said.

It was near enough to one camera in particular because this one didn't oscillate as well as the others. This meant it could see the fire escape but only partially.

Jon repeated these words as he climbed. "Only slightly. Only slightly."

Now Jon's strength was undeniable, as was his skillset. He was a solid climber and scaled the ladder like a fireman breaching a burning building. On the roof, Jon cut past the air vents and bulging pipes. He passed the windows overlooking the space beneath and had no trouble navigating where he was.

One night, he and Kya actually did come to the roof. Jon said he wanted to watch the sunrise with her. Kya agreed, and their decision to do this happened after a long and brutal night. What they both needed then was a break. What Kya needed, however, was a cigarette. Jon lit one up for her at the time. He still did not forget the location.

Still, the door could only be opened from inside The Conquistador.

Unfortunately, outside was where Jon was now. And yet, he recalled what Kya told him.

"The door's a little finicky. Don't tell Addison about it, just in case we want to come up here again."

Jon hadn't heard the word *finicky* before, but he could grasp it in context.

When both he and Kya parted from the roof, Jon remembered her banging on the side of the door with a closed fist. Doing this, the vibration forced the door to unhinge. While it was only partially opened, Jon could fit his entire hand in and prop it open that way.

There were worse things than sneaking in through the roof, so it was not an urgent fix, not according to Danix. Still, having seen Kya do this, Jon was capable of doing it himself now.

With a clean slam into the rooftop's door, it popped. Pulling the doors aside, Jon stepped in and had officially entered The Conquistador. Jon had entered along a series of staircases, each one narrower than the one that came before.

Jon moved like he was bouncing. In more ways than one, he was.

Still, what Jon had to do now was keep a low profile. So, with his head down, the Marine glimpsed only where he could without being seen by anyone.

The Conquistador was exploding tonight.

Everywhere Jon looked, he could see guests dancing and drinking and powering up to the beat of the thundering music. On any other night, it would be a good one. The music was booming, and the shots were slinging. There should be extra security on the floor, and Jon knew which territories were which as well as who usually occupied them on a night like tonight. He was still far up in the second level, but was in the corner, where no one could see him.

This level usually belonged to Danix, but he was not here now.

In fact, none of the Doormen were on the floor. Everywhere Jon looked, he saw new guys. He saw men who were gray-suited and with radios looped around their ears. What was most strange was how they were dressed. All of them were wearing jackets with batons holstered underneath. Jon recognized the handles.

These men weren't Doormen, not at all.

No, Jon knew employees of Irons, and that's exactly who these men were.

They were OverTakers.

This brigade of new bouncers were likely on the lookout for Jon and possibly operating under new legislation. Things like *problem-solving*, *counter-action*, and *communication tactics* were all different under this new brigade.

The Conquistador was changing.

Right now, however, Jon was just a wanderer. He was just another guest moving around the club inconspicuously. He scoped the region and passed by a few tables and booths. He was not a man looking for trouble, and yet, as Jon had learned while working the club, the person who's not looking for trouble is usually the one who finds it.

Given Jon's choice of wardrobe, he was only just a bum in a classy joint.

For the people who were all about class, this was a quick way to get confronted. Jon didn't have time for petty run-ins. He wanted to see Kya. He was looking only for her. To find her, Jon went to the railing and tried to get a solid look at the floor below. The club was so packed that Jon could barely move without brushing shoulders with someone close by. It was busy but only by one group of people: old, rich, and rude.

Jon still walked with his head down and stayed close to the balustrade. He hid behind two conversing men and leered.

He couldn't spot Kya in any of her usual locations.

Often, Jon would stand close to where she was working just so he could get a glimpse of her. While some might find the act invasive or creepy, it would be true if Jon and Kya *weren't* together.

But they were together, or...they used to be.

Now, they were just coworkers. Actually, they weren't even that anymore.

Right now, Jon wanted to saunter down the steps, pull her aside, and tell her everything. Jon wanted to tell Kya where he went, why he left, and how much he missed her. He wanted to tell her all of this but knew he would not be allowed to say a goddamn word.

Jon had to remember his cover and the reason he was here.

He had come for him, for Michael Irons, and was here to deliver a message.

Jon parted from the railing and thought of another route to take. Where Michael Irons was among the plethora of security was unknown. Therefore, Jon would need to keep being subtle and careful as he steered clear of all nearby bodies. Head down, Jon shifted to the left and then to the right. Minding his surroundings as much as he could, Jon felt a bump on his shoulder.

He didn't even bother to look up.

Any chance to reveal his face was to blow up his spot and draw more attention to himself than necessary. Low profile was still Jon's game. Feeling a bump, liquid spilled down Jon's shoulder. Jon thought nothing of it. After being doused by this liquid, which Jon identified as vodka, he heard grumbling from a nearby booth.

"Jesus Christ," a voice said.

Jon's back was turned. He didn't bother to look until he felt a pop, and this time, it hit his other shoulder.

"Fucking guy, watch where you're going, you asshole!" Jon turned to see the not-so-sharp tool. What Jon saw was a crew of six people huddled inside a booth. There were three men and three women, and they weren't a young crowd like those Jon had bounced before. No, this group was older and looked like parents.

The men were pudgy, not fit, and certainly not intimidating. Yet, their clothing was damn fine. Jon knew fabrics as well as expensive gear, and all of these men were covered in luxury, so he wasn't about to start trouble. Then, another idea entered his mind. Since the OverTakers were armed, what if one of them had an itchy finger?

Police improperly discharged their weapons all the time.

Was such an outcome likely here and now?

Jon recalled Addison's advice. He was curious about where Michael was? If a situation gets too out of hand, there's no telling what might happen next.

Was this situation capable of getting just as out of hand now?

Jon didn't know for sure, but at least he could read the message loud and clear. Jon looked back at the people near the booth. They marched after Jon, but he couldn't care less at this point about what they did or wanted to do.

"Hey!" Jon yelled.

After raising his voice, Jon had the attention of everyone standing around him, especially the women. Jon might be young, but he looked strong. And, seeing as how he wasn't afraid, this irked the men straight away.

"Who the hell just spilled a fucking drink on me?! You!" snapped the man sitting to the left. "You bumped into me!"

"No," Jon said. "I didn't."

Jon pointed his finger into the silly man's face. He was now ignoring everything he learned as a bouncer. Now Jon was purposefully trying to start some shit. He had never done this before, and to do it now actually felt kind of satisfying.

"Hey! Who do you think you're talking to?!" The other man stood up and so, Jon was now facing down two guys by himself. He was not intimidated or afraid. In the end, this was exactly what Jon wanted to happen.

"Nobody!" Jon yelled back. "I'm talking to a fucking nobody!"

"Fuck you! Do you even know who the fuck I am?"

The man now screamed inches from Jon's face. He was so close Jon inhaled the fool's stinky breath. Jon refused to have someone speak to him like this, especially someone standing so close.

And Jon hated proximity.

The usual strategy for dealing with this brand of boorish behavior was to put your hand up and place it near the yeller's chest. Jon continued to ignore every rule taught by his mentors. No, here, Jon was not a bouncer. He was a bad boy looking for trouble.

"No!" Jon was barely heard over the music. "I'm looking at a really dumb asshole!"

The man eyed Jon, puzzled and dismayed.

Before this man could process what was about to go down, Jon went to work. He started with a clean shot to the man's nose. It was a decent jab, one Jon had been practicing prior to his departure.

At home, there was a tree in Jon's backyard marked by a wooden plank. Over and over, Jon would strike this plank until his knuckles bled. He would do this every day, and every day, he would try and hit that very same mark. All of this was a tip provided to Jon by Danix. He told Jon he needed to stop pulling his punches. It was damn good advice because Jon damn well wasn't pulling any of his punches now.

With the amount of security occupying the second floor, the entire club looked overpoliced. Then, there were only so many OverTakers. Their presence was just too substantial, too grand.

Jon saw men in suits as far as the eye could see, and he understood how they would be here any second. The man Jon punched was now called *Punchy*. Punchy snarled, and Jon replied with a solid push-kick into Punchy's chest. Sending Punchy back, Jon was content with his response.

"You asshole!" The insult was spewed by a woman sitting in a booth.

Jon, however, was still surprised by the age of all the guests. They were in their forties and Jon assumed people from this age bracket would have a different way of handling confrontations.

Evidently, Jon was wrong. *Way wrong*.

The woman threw a full glass at Jon while the angry man, who Jon called *Grumpy*, began to make his move. He swung at Jon like he was swinging a sledge-hammer. All the notorious Marine had to do was step out of the way. And, once Jon dodged this blow, he hit back with a roundhouse. Hitting this man in the chest, Jon knocked the wind out of Grumpy and then watched as he descended to the ground. By then, the entire section was in chaos. People were standing around, pointing and watching.

Jon didn't have time to pay attention to any of this.

Once he dealt with Grumpy and Punchy, it was only a matter of time before Dopey, who was the third man, decided to join the fun.

Two OverTakers stormed onto the scene. They pushed innocent guests aside and marched like robots. Absent of expression, these men were without the affable qualities that made bouncing more about conversation and charm rather than blunt force. When these men made their moves, Jon took a big step back. All he wanted to do was see how the OverTakers did their jobs. As soon as they made their way onto the scene, Jon's plan was motion quicker than expected. While most of his attention was on this Dopey fella, something changed in the fight that not even Jon saw coming. The girls stomped after Jon. With their hands ready to claw at Jon's eyes, they gashed the Marine's face.

It was then the OverTakers began to close in.

"Whoa, whoa," said Jon. "Take it easy."

"Fuck you, you bastard! You hit my fucking husband! Fuck you!"

With his hands up, Jon did his best to stay clear of the blows.

The women were pissed. This Jon was used to. Still, they were strong. As their long nails zipped past Jon's face, Jon remembered how the Doormen handled female customers. It was very different from males.

"*Never hit them.*" The rule was number one, yet Jon couldn't quite get behind it.

He was no woman-hitter, but females can break the rules and be dangerous just as much as men can, no doubt. They were capable of violence and rage, and sometimes would attack a bouncer, or worse, bombard them with at least ten to fifteen haphazard whacks to the face.

Jon witnessed this before. He was witnessing the same thing now.

"*Optics*," Addison had once said to Jon. "*The last thing anyone wants is to go to a club that's too rough on women. Remember, violence is not our game. We're in the word business.*"

Such advice was provided to Jon during one of his very first shifts. He remembered it and so, he obeyed it now. While each strike missed Jon's face by inches, his ability to move in a complete circle did keep him in a good place. In the midst of keeping away, Jon threw his hands into the air and surrendered.

Jon did this just as the OverTakers arrived on the scene.

Stepping in between Jon and the fighting females, the men in suits did their best to keep the women at bay, but they were spunky, no doubt. The OverTakers were looking for a fight. In fact, they were aching to give these girls a good throwdown. They wanted to get their hands dirty. Jon was actually surprised by how badly they were doing in this fight. Using only hostile language, they barked and they pushed.

"I said stay back!" yelled one OverTaker.

"Fuck you!"

The OverTakers were cops working a bad neighborhood. They were officers who believed any force was justified and necessary. Jon's original plan to provoke excessive force was now in motion.

Before the girls reacted or did anything, one Over-Taker removed his retractable baton.

Ejecting the combat stick, he went on to do something Jon didn't think would ever happen at The Conquistador.

The OverTaker raised this baton and smacked the woman in the face, knocking her down.

"Ah!" The people close to the scene didn't pull out their phones.

It was as if they didn't have them.

Who the hell didn't have their phones? Maybe they did but chose not to remove them fearing something worse might happen. After the woman was hit by this OverTaker, he looked at her with a grim, unfazed expression.

Like an android obeying its protocols, this Over-Taker was designed to preserve order, and that's exactly what he was going to do. After hitting the first woman, the second woman screamed and charged. Jon kept a close watch on the unfolding situation. In an attempt to defend her friend, this woman raced. And, while the first OverTaker clearly used too much force to knock the first woman, the second one proceeded anyway.

The OverTaker snatched and squeezed the second woman by her arm and held her tight—*too aggressively*. Looking her up and down, Jon pulled. In that moment, the woman became trapped.

The OverTakers had taken her for a brutal ride, and Jon, who was not a Doorman anymore, didn't like witnessing this kind of terror and abuse.

This was not what bouncing was supposed to be.

The other patrons were ordered to stay back as the OverTakers took care of these women. Dragging them toward the stairs, they lifted them to the doors. It was a disturbing sight to witness, but most of the guests looked unaffected. No one was interfering in order to stop what was happening. To Jon, everyone seemed desensitized and unfazed. It was almost like they were used to this new kind of security, but all of it made Jon want to retch.

So, he refused to stand by and let it happen. This was, after all, *his fault*.

"Hey! Let her go!" Jon trudged at the two Over-Takers both pulling the women.

By now, these women had stopped screaming and accepted their fate. Jon knew he had absolutely no chance against these men but decided to act anyway.

"Stop!" Jon shouted as he darted toward one of the OverTakers. But, before Jon could reach any of them, he was hit with a foot to the face.

"Gah!" Struck down, Jon landed on his back. There were only so many people who could summon such an impressive strike. It could be either Danix, Addison, or Michael Irons.

And goddamn it, Jon thought, it was the last person he wanted to see.

"Easy there, friend. Business is being handled, yes?"

Jon should have been knocked unconscious. The kick was incredibly clean and deadly accurate. Jon rubbed his jaw as he lay on the floor. Later, Jon looked up at the man who now had complete control over the nightclub. Standing in a three-piece gray suit cut from a glittering fabric, Jon gawked at the one who betrayed him, *the man who lied to his mother*.

"Is that what you call what's happening here? Handling business?"

Jon looked ferociously at Mr. Michael Irons. Now Jon's hatred for Irons was palpable. Still, he was rattled from that bloody kick, which hurt like hell.

"As you know," Irons replied, "this club is now under new management. We're here to do things our way because the old ways, well, they weren't working. This club was out of control."

Jon scoffed. He would never characterize The Conquistador as being out of control, but apparently, that's how Irons saw it.

"And beating up on women," said Jon. He crawled back to his feet. "That's the new way too, isn't it?"

"We're adopting a zero-tolerance policy here now," said Irons. "No more poor behavior will be tolerated, allows us to get rid of the riff-raff and enhance the club's clientele. It's the future, and the future is now."

"The future?" Jon asked. "Is that why you lied to me, lied to *her*?"

Her was Jon's mother, Michael Irons's former lover.

"Lies?" barked Irons. He smirked at Jon while also looking him up and down. "You really want to talk about *lies*? This entire building is built on deception, with people pretending to be something they're not. No, if anyone really knew what The Conquistador had in its possession, then they'd know why this place needs better protection."

"And the Commission is going to allow you to do what you're doing?"

"The Commission cares only about order and nothing else. It cares about the future and whoever is going to take them there. And, whether you want to accept it or not, I am the future."

"You?" said Jon.

"Me," said Irons. "And to think, you could have been a part of it. You could have got on the faster train, but instead, you chose to stay on an older, much slower one. And still, you chose to jump off. Actually, you don't even have a job anymore."

Jon cracked his knuckles. What Irons spoke of now was the truth. Jon was a deserter who had abandoned his post. Ever since leaving, Jon felt angered by what The Conquistador had become. Michael Irons and his OverTakers were now running the show. They were preserving the club in the worst way possible. They were slowly shedding the Doormen from the premises so they could gradually take over, yet although Jon knew all of this, he didn't know it was *this* bad. He didn't think it would come to this. With such brutality rising, the OverTakers were moving in, and yet, Jon had come back because he wanted to come back.

Now Jon could see he wasn't here because he wanted to be.

He was here because he *needed* to be.

"You're lost," said Irons. "You're lost, with nowhere to go. In fact..." Irons raised his hand and gestured to some of the other OverTakers. Two jumped to attention and scurried after their lord. "You were involved in a fight," said Irons. "You disobeyed our policy, and therefore, we are well within our rights to take you out."

"Is that so?"

"It is," Irons said to Jon. Looking at the Marine, Irons's smugness was palpable. There was nothing Jon could do against an OverTaker, especially if they were using weapons to get the job done.

And yet, Jon's fury had reached significant levels. Actually, he was fuming. He felt as though he could fight anyone, so he rose up but didn't take his eyes off the OverTaker lord. Jon wanted to punch Irons hard in his face. Sometimes, the price of pride is the same as the price of blood. Standing up for oneself and defending one's honor can coincide with getting your ass kicked.

Jon believed this. He always did and he always would.

"No," said this new arrival. "This man works for us."

Us. It had been some time since Jon was included as part of a group. Hearing this simple word approved his status among the brethren he had recently abandoned. Although Jon was hurting, when he heard the voice of a friend, it brought him back. Feeling returned to Jon's face and he was able to stand on his two feet. Danix Slade stood in front of Jon, arms crossed, and looking ahead at the OverTaker leader.

After Danix stepped in, Irons's gaze narrowed and he placed his hands on his waist.

"Is that so?" Irons asked Danix.

"It is," said Danix.

"Then if he's with you," said Irons, "bring 'em to where he belongs. You know the new rules now."

Danix said nothing. He turned to look at Jon. Danix offered his hand but the kindness wasn't necessary. Jon was already standing. The Marine thought the offered hand was to help Jon up.

He didn't realize it was done as a way of welcoming him back home.

"Thanks." Jon didn't know what Danix might say.

He had his back turned on the Doormen and was still not employed at The Conquistador.

And yet, none of this seemed to matter. Once Jon shook Danix's hand, the hulking bouncer pulled him close and looked him dead in the eyes.

"Come on," he said. "Let's get off the damn floor."

CHAPTER 5
THE DEAD DON'T BACK DOWN

JON SPECULATED ABOUT WHERE DANIX WAS bringing him to.

Prior to his encounter with Irons, Jon was in another section of the club. As Irons said it at the time, he said: *"Take 'em to where he belongs."*

Jon didn't understand this. Then again, he questioned whether he was supposed to?

It had been nearly a month since he left the club and chose to walk away. Now under new management, there was no telling just how much had changed since Jon's departure. Therefore, Jon didn't press or ask any questions.

He simply followed Danix and said not a word.

"Need some ice for your face?" Now in a part where the music was quiet, Jon looked around at what he saw. The booths he passed by were now occupied with other servers. All were sitting on the laps of their patrons, snuggling up to the various customers. Jon saw them breaking several previous club rules. Servers were never to be touched, grabbed, or groped. And as Jon walked with Danix, this was all he could see.

"Uh..." Jon was distracted by all this change. If he were to refocus, he wouldn't be lying if he said that an ice pack would feel real good right about now.

"Here," Danix said.

Before Jon could answer, Danix handed him his pack of ice. Jon grabbed hold of the freezing brick and pressed it to his jaw. Goddamn, this felt good.

"Thanks," said Jon.

"Right on," said Danix.

Going on, Danix and Jon were all the way at the club's "South Side". Still patrons in this part, it was mostly the part of the club designated for quiet time and conversation. The only way you were allowed to sit here was if you paid extra or you had a yearly membership. It was a place known officially as the *Smoking Lounge*. The lounge had a quiet bar and played a little music. Generally, it was reserved for the club's older customers, which were few and not many. Nonetheless, some did frequent the section. And so, where Jon was being taken to was the section next to the former quiet area.

There was another dance floor. It was known as the Annex.

Due to this being separate from the main floor, back when Jon worked, this was where the bouncers would take drunk customers. Here, Danix stopped before a thin door with green paneling. Directly next to this bar, Danix pounded the door.

"Where are we?" asked Jon. Danix lowered his hand and waited for the door to open.

"A safe place," Danix replied.

Jon waited. On the other side of this somewhat hidden door, the tinkering and shifting of metal was heard. After this, a small compartment opened.

"Yo," said a new voice.

"It's us," Danix said to the face in the opening. "Open up."

Jon squinted to see if he could recognize who was on the other side. As of now, he could not. He hung back and waited for the door to open. Jon was reminded of the speakeasies back in Chicago—those secret underground hideouts that would dish out alcohol and were sometimes used for gambling.

What had happened now was the Doormen had clearly gone into hiding.

Obviously not fulfilling the same duties or expected to perform the same tasks, here they were, the best bouncers in the damn city hiding like criminals. As the door opened, Jon was struck by an aura of nuanced light. Like a candle flickering in the dark, Jon couldn't imagine that this was how the room was lit.

Maybe it was and maybe it wasn't.

Danix moved and Jon followed. Stepping in, Jon stopped when he saw the person guarding the door. It wasn't Li, and it wasn't Addison. It wasn't Owen, and it wasn't Jamal.

Damn, Jon thought to himself. Who the hell was this guy?

"Duncan, this is Jon Haze. He's a Doorman too, like us. He was hired right before the takeover was put into effect."

"Right," said this Duncan guy. Jon hadn't met until now. "Nice to meet you, man."

"Thanks, you too."

Duncan shook Jon's hand and the Marine looked at this new friend and ally. Duncan looked to be the same age as Jon. Tall and blonde, Duncan was also surprisingly thin, like a Dutch soccer player. Handsome, Duncan shook with a firm grip. The way he treated Jon, he probably didn't know his story.

Duncan didn't know why Jon left The Conquistador.

Now in the room, it wasn't long before Jon saw some familiar faces. Li, Owen, Divine, and a few of the other "Conquistador" classics were all lined up. They jerked their chins at Danix to greet him.

Jon was now hiding.

Still, he was embarrassed to be here. He had to keep reminding himself he was still not a Doorman. Everyone still had their crest. But Jon? No, he had nothing.

"Hey, what's up, Danix?"

Li greeted Danix next. He was wearing his usual uniform. However, in the time that had passed, Li's appearance did change. His hair was longer. He now had it tied into a bun. Still, he looked damn good, damn badass and cool.

"Hey," said Danix. "How's it going back here?"

"We got a few on the floor, but most of us are in here. Don't worry," Li said. "We're in the clear."

"Good," said Danix.

At this moment, Jon had a number of questions, one being: *why were they hiding here, in this place?*

"Jon! You're here!"

"Yeah," said Jon, unsure about what to make of this newest interaction. "I'm back."

"Nice to see you."

Li welcomed Jon with a big hug, to which Jon returned the gesture in the same way. Jon was happy to see Li. In fact, Jon was happy to see everyone, all the Doormen.

"Jon, what's up, man?!" Next to see Jon was Jamal, the big-ass Doorman with a heart of gold. He was the very first person Jon met at the club. Jamal slapped hands with Jon and pulled him for a shoulder-to-shoulder embrace. Jon was always completely absorbed by Jamal's huge body. However, like Li, Jon was happy to see him.

"Hey, Jamal. Nice to see you, man," said Jon.

"You were gone," said Jamal. "Jesus Christ, man. You just upped and disappeared."

Jon's eyes shot down to the floor. He was now abysmal. Jon couldn't look at Jamal without feeling like he wanted to crawl under the table.

"Yeah," he said.

"Well, he's back now," another voice emerged. Appearing from behind Jamal like he was stepping out from behind a curtain was none other than Jon's main man. It was Owen. Like Li, Owen also looked different. Always shorter than Jamal was, Owen's hair was longer and curlier than Jon last recalled. He also looked bigger, like he'd been lifting some serious weights and packing on some serious muscle. Like Li, Jon was impressed. More than this, he was happy.

Jon was damn happy to see his friend Owen.

"Owen, shit. What's going on?"

"Not much, brother," said Owen. "It's good to see you, though. Real good. You're back."

Owen gave Jon a firm handshake. Owen didn't pull the Marine in for a hug. Their greeting was more professional than anything else. This didn't matter to Jon. He was just happy to see everyone, and oddly, everyone seemed happy to see him. Whatever the reason, Jon was grateful. Why the team wasn't mad at Jon had to be a result of something Addison did. He might have spoken on Jon's behalf, explained why he was no longer present and why he wasn't working anymore. Maybe he gave a good reason, at least that's what Jon's mom alluded to back at the house.

"It's real nice to see everyone," said Jon. "For real."

"Yeah, well, as you can probably see," Owen said to Jon. "This place isn't exactly home anymore."

Hearing this, Jon nodded and frowned.

"I did."

"We're no longer allowed in the main section of the club," said Li. "Ever since the OverTakers, this new security came in, the Doormen are not the main line of defense anymore, as you can see. We've been reduced to standing in the background, near all the fucking hideaways."

"I can see that," said Jon. "It sucks, and I'm sorry."

"Yeah," said Danix. "But it has its benefits too. No one checks in on us. Floor stays quiet and we got a system in place," Danix explained. "Some are on while others are off, which gives us plenty of time to plan and think."

"Plan?" said Jon. Finally, he heard something that he hadn't in a while.

"Plan for what?"

"Our *comeback*."

While Jon stood with his friends, the moment the word *comeback* was mentioned, everyone stopped looking at him and directed their attention toward the new speaker.

Jon automatically knew who it was.

The boldness and the confidence clinging to the response could only belong to one person. Addison stepped out from the back of the room like he was the star of his own action movie. Until now, Jon hadn't seen or heard from Addison.

In fact, Jon had completely ghosted everyone here.

But with Addison choosing to come forward, Jon anticipated a punch to the face or some other emotional response. After all, Addison was the one who saw Jon last. He was also the same person who revealed the truth about The Conquistador. It was for this reason that Jon had chosen to leave. But, when Jon saw Addison, he pretended like all of the other encounters with him didn't happen. During this awkward moment, Jon liked believing none of them did.

"Hello, Jon."

"Addison," Jon said with a heavy breath, like he was trying to hold back embarrassment, regret, and a fair amount of fright too. Honestly, he didn't know what kind of a reaction to expect from his boss and friend. "It's...it's..." Jon scrambled to find the words. He couldn't find any so he stammered on like a child.

"Nice to see you," Addison said as he offered his hand. By doing this, he had in fact skipped over Jon's past decision and made way for a new beginning. Jon was conflicted about what he had done but he was learning how to accept it. In time, he would see it was wrong but necessary. Jon thought now he shouldn't have left the club knowing what happened to everyone. At the same time, Jon was deceived. The Conquistador was a foundation built on lies, and yet, Jon couldn't turn away from it. He refused to turn his back on the men who were now all standing next to him.

"When did you get here?" Addison asked Jon.

"Not long," Danix was now answering for Jon, which was different but not too strange. "He actually got a preview of what the OverTakers are doing here."

"Yeah," Jon said to Addison. "Not good."

"An understatement." Danix was clear.

Jon had another look around the room. From what he could gather, everyone was present and accounted for, everyone except for one person.

Jon had no idea what he was going to say to Kya when he saw her.

He could barely speak to Addison, let alone her. Jon's eyes shifted. He tried to take in as many faces as he could, but this was no time to take attendance or to search for anyone in particular. No, now was the time for action. And, in Jon's mind, it was a time for some serious action.

"So...what do we do? What's happening?"

"Couldn't you tell?" said Owen. "We're in fucking hiding."

"Well, not exactly how I would put it, but..." said Duncan. "However, since I started, yeah, it's been pretty much that."

"We work in shifts, some are out there"—Li pointed in the direction of the dance floor—"and some are in here," he said. "But what we're trying to do is figure out what to do next. It's tough, very tough. They have eyes everywhere and they've doubled security. They're watching our every move and we aren't allowed to bounce like we used to. OTs watch everything now."

"Yeah," said Danix, "not to mention they've changed damn near everything, including clientele, entrances, even who's promoting what events or what it is we're doing. Whole scope has changed."

"And where's Larry in all this?" asked Jon. "It's still his club?"

"Until the review is completed by the Commission, his hands are fucking tied," said Danix. "He also can't be seen governing this place. Since the OverTakers put in a report to the higher-ups, old leadership is irrelevant. The Conquistador has been labeled as *red* so it's under new management now."

"Shit," said Jon. What was occurring at the club was beginning to become that much clearer. "What the hell does red mean?"

"It means we're fucked," said Owen. "At least, for now."

"Does the Commission know what the OverTakers are doing, what Irons is doing?"

"The way they see it," said Li. "We were the ones who let this club get out of hand. Customers were getting away with too much and running things the old-fashioned way, and now the Commission thinks it didn't work. Now, they want to rebuild, and Michael's been telling them that's exactly what they're doing. They've pushed us toward the end of the line while they move to the front."

"Word is out," said Li. "And it's everywhere. The Conquistador is compromised. It's corrupt and it's ripe for a change, or so that's what the world has been saying."

Jon curled his hands into fists and glowered. "Bouncing the bouncers," said Jon.

"Exactly," said Danix. "*Bouncing the bouncers.*"

"Soon as there's an opening, we're gonna step in, though," said Danix. "Our plan is to show the Commission that the OverTakers are brutal and not here for the right reasons. Tonight, we almost had our first show of grace."

"Almost?" asked Jon.

"Well, we would have been able to help those women, but our priorities changed at the last minute."

"Why?" Jon asked again. The women mentioned by Danix were beaten up and needed help. "What happened?"

"Someone else needed our help instead."

Jon's head swayed and he didn't know who Danix was referencing. "Who?" asked Jon.

"Who do you think?" Addison spoke up from the back of this dimly lit room. He looked at Jon with his arms crossed and seated on a cheap, wooden fold-out chair. *Goddamn*, Jon thought, *this room is fucking old.*

"*You,*" said Addison.

Jon couldn't help but feel both bashful and guilty. His inexplicable arrival came at a price. The Doormen couldn't move forward because Jon was inadvertently *in the way*. He didn't expect this to happen, but then it did. "I'm...I'm *sorry.*"

"Ah, don't worry about it," said Owen. "It's a small process. It takes time and well, we're outmanned. This club has turned into one giant fucking chessboard. We're all just pieces now, and we're trying to find ways of moving around. Doing the most with what we have, well, things are going to come up along the way."

"But our plan hasn't changed," said Danix. "We're going to push the OverTakers out. We're gonna out bounce them, and we're going to draw enough attention to what's happening here that the Commission will see the best hands...are still our own."

Jon gave a stern nod like the Marine that he was because this...this made sense to him. It also sounded like a spectacular plan.

"This Michael Irons fuck might be a slippery one," Danix went on to explain. "But we'll get 'em. We'll beat 'em at his own game."

Jon's tongue rubbed against his teeth. He was humored by Danix's description of the OverTaker leader. No one knew just how slippery Michael Irons was more than Jon.

"Yeah," said Jon. He needed a moment to take in everything he was informed of so far. He considered all the pieces in the Doormen's new plan. Actually, this comparison was best demonstrated by two Doormen in a jousting contest. They were two well-equipped and well-trained knights storming after one another, trying to knock the other off the horse. Although this was not exactly what was happening now, it was similar in a way. The Doormen were charging after the OverTakers in an attempt to see who was better. Who would knock the other off the horse first. It would be a rough and brutal face-off.

It was going to make the recent Showdown look like child's play.

Jon looked at the door and around the room again. If there wasn't a plan, then it was up to Jon to create one. He considered a lot before returning to The Conquistador.

Jon understood the next step. He embraced it proudly.

"Yeah, we do," said Jon.

"What?" said Danix. "You gotta plan?"

"You forget," Jon said. He stood up and looked at everyone present in this secret *Speakeasy* room located in The Conquistador's South Wing. "I knew Michael before anyone else did. I know what he's capable of, but more than this, I know what he's *incapable* of."

"Yeah?" Owen piped in.

"Yeah," said Jon. The Doormen didn't blame Jon for what happened. It was Jon who knew Michael, but it was Michael who manipulated and toyed with the Marine, pushed him into places he wasn't supposed to go, and this was why there were here now.

"All right," said Danix. "So...whatta y'got?"

"Yeah," said Jamal. "Hit us, Jon."

"Well," Jon began to elaborate. He hadn't actually phrased what he was thinking until this moment. He knew about the three principles that the Doormen had to use against their enemy, the OverTakers. Now was the time when Addison would tell everyone about what these principles were and how they could be used in this great battle for supremacy. "The OverTakers can only review our protocols and procedures," Jon said. "To them, it's a question of safety, security, and who can do a better job at upholding this place's reputation."

"Right," said Li.

"Okay," replied Jon. "So, as long as we keep this place safe then we're still doing our jobs. Part of our expectations is we're creating a safe and welcoming

environment, which we were doing until the Over-
Takers interfered and took the club out of our hands.
From what I can see, this place doesn't feel as
welcoming."

"No," said Danix. "But it is safer. No doubt about
that."

"True," said Owen.

Less fights were happening now than ever before,
and Jon could see the guests were in line and the Over-
Takers, under Irons's watch, did have this place
completely under control. But it extracted a heavy toll.
Jon was aware of the price the patrons were now paying
in exchange for their safety.

"Yeah, but at what cost?" asked Jon. "The Over-
Takers are using too much fear in order to govern this
place. No one's complaining because of The Conquistador being fucking canceled. They don't know all the
rules the clubs are breaking because the previous
customers have all moved on."

"And yet, this place continues to make money,"
said Li.

"Because its business model *has* changed. I saw how
people are getting in now," said Jon. "Jamal, how many
people are paying for admittance these days and how
much are they willing to pay and who are these people
who are paying?"

"Nearly every VIP pays online, through a membership. Average income customers can't get in, too hard
and too expensive."

"Exactly," said Jon. "Irons's plan from the beginning is to do away with The Conquistador's younger
clients and to turn this place into more of a club for aris-
tocrats, with more upscale and heavy paying clientele."

"If that were the case," said Danix, "there would be no need for bouncers like us anymore. No, this entire scene would be run by men in suits who adhered to the clients and rather made sure they all fell in line."

"Exactly!" Jon exclaimed. Now, it had become clear what the OverTakers' endgame was. It was evident what they were really planning to do to the Doormen as well as to The Conquistador itself.

"We're being exterminated," said Danix. "We're being replaced by a newer form of club security."

"A worse form," said Jon. He spoke the truth like it was his job. "The OverTakers are using their positions of power to control people, not to protect them, and we need to make sure the people see that. They need to know that, while we're gone, this new security that's moved in is not any better. No, their intentions are worse. They're way worse."

"Knowing something and proving it are two different things." At last, Addison had decided to join the conversation. Jon wasn't sure if it was the club's cooler talking or if it was its attorney. Jon wasn't sure which was which at this point. Nonetheless, Jon chose to believe that the man talking was the part of Addison who was his friend.

Now this, Jon could embrace.

"I know," said Jon. "But there's gotta be a way. There's gotta be a way to bring all of this to light."

With all eyes on Jon, the Marine blinked and remembered where he was.

"So long as we're here, this club is still ours. We might not be bouncing," said Jon, "but we still hold controlling interest over this business, including who it serves and who it doesn't."

"But the OverTakers have taken control of all that," said Jamal. "I mean, you saw what that toad Irons is up to."

"And the Keeper supports his decision," said Danix, "because the club is making more money, even in spite of its many drawbacks, its heavy hand...so to speak."

"Yeah," said Owen. "I mean, how do we take the club back? I mean, know the saying: money talks?"

"And bullshit walks," answered Jon. He scanned Addison and contemplated the first move they were going to make against their newest enemy.

"And first order of business, we're going to do what not even a man like Michael Irons would expect."

Having everyone's attention, Jon jumped right into his plan. For the longest time, he was just a soldier. He didn't give orders. Jon only followed them. Channeling the attitude of the two men he respected, Addison and Lieutenant Dan, Jon explained his plan for liberating his friends from the clutches of this madman.

"We're going to use the guests, use the people who are loyal to this club."

Jon looked around and saw how everyone was listening to him. This was how it needed to be from here on.

"We're going to invite whoever we can, anyone we can, and we're going to do the exact opposite of what we did before," Jon said. "We're going to let them run and keep running. In order to beat Michael and his Over-Taker clan, we have to prove to the Commission that they have ulterior motives. Our best bet is to let this place dissolve into chaos and work with the guests instead of working against them."

Jon blinked and let the weight of his plan sink in

deeper. Currently, it was a radical pitch that could lead to both revolution and change. There were many flaws and it was quite chaotic in its design. Yet, it was as Jon said. It was the best plan going forward.

"Yeah, but Jon, they're controlling who's getting into the club. Who's coming in and who's coming out."

"No," said Jon. "They're discriminating based on age and appearance. So, we talk to our promoters, our employees, and we get them to reach out to the exact people who Irons is interested in. And, we come in with one order: *break the rules*."

"Break the rules?" considered Addison, somewhat skeptical of Jon's latest idea.

"You do that and the Takers will be well within their rights to use any and all forms of discretion to neutralize us."

"No," said Jon. "They'll be inclined to use violence and only violence because that's all they've been using. They'll turn this club into an overpoliced fucking regime, and that's all they'll have to show their talent and skill. And, should they do this, then it's only a matter of time before they go too far. And, while they're busy doing this, and we're using the customers to our advantage, it will force Irons to lose control. We do this and we can and will win."

Jon was, in effect, putting his foot down. He was expressing his determination and showing his reverence toward his brethren. Jon was asserting himself as the man he *used* to be. While his crest was gone, the one he wore on his shirt, Jon felt more like a Doorman than he ever had before.

He was back. All he needed was someone to tell him he was.

"Let's go," Addison said to Jon. Walking alongside the Marine, Jon and Addison made their way toward the door. "Time to get you your crest back."

Jon looked around the room and saw countless smiles, each one for him.

Goddamn, Jon thought. *It felt so good to be back.*

CHAPTER 6
NEW DIRECTIONS

The Conquistador closed and nearly everyone went home shortly after the meeting was done. Since Jon was technically allowed on the premises, Addison was required to sneak him up to the second floor, toward his office.

Jon followed.

The entire time he was curious, curious about several things.

He didn't see Michael Irons and didn't know where his office was. Jon was also unaware about what the OverTakers were required to do after their shifts had come to an end. He knew that when the Doormen were done, they had to complete reports about what they observed and if they had broken up any altercations. This was a vital part of the bouncing profession. It protected the Doormen in case any police came asking questions. Jon was curious about this as well as any whereabouts of the person he hadn't seen since his return.

"Where's Kya?" Jon said to Addison.

He stepped up to the swirling staircase. It was almost six a.m. Both had been up all night. Jon's eyes felt so heavy he could fall asleep exactly where he stood. Fortunately, Jon fought to stay awake. He fought because he had recovered a purpose he once thought was lost.

In the end, you have to thank the Lord there's such a thing as second chances.

"Kya?" said Addison.

"Yeah," said Jon. "I didn't see her working. Where is she?"

Hearing this, Addison's reply was only a snort. Jon couldn't tell if it was derisive, like something you give because you were either too shocked or too amused by the question, but Addison wasn't the condescending type.

At least, most of the time, he wasn't. This time, however, Jon wasn't sure.

"I guess you didn't hear."

Jon's ears wiggled a little. "No," Jon said. "I...I didn't. What?"

Addison walked up the stairs, his hand sliding along the railing rather casually. He could have walked faster, yes, but he slowed down so he could tell Jon about Kya, where she was, and why she wasn't at the club.

"Where is she?" asked Jon.

"Well, after you left and the OverTakers moved in, we actually lost a few employees," said Addison.

"After I left?" Waves of guilt and insecurity began to ensconce Jon like a blanket.

"Don't worry," Addison waved his hand. "It wasn't because of you, so if you're thinking you started a resistance or some shit like that, well...you're wrong. People left for their own reasons, and well, I guess you could say Kya had her own reasons as to why she went."

"So what, she's like...not a bartender anymore or what?"

"Nah," said Addison. "Last I heard, she got a job working as a substitute teacher as well as a tutor, which takes up a good deal of her time, as you can imagine. She's busier now. And so, she said she had less time to be here, which is understandable. She stopped showing up about a week ago."

"Shit."

"Yeah, disappointing," added Addison. "She was one of the good ones."

"Yes, she was," said Jon. "She *really* was."

Walking up the steps, Jon's thoughts were now only about Kya. He hadn't kept in touch with her after leaving The Conquistador and Jon knew that was a bad decision. Then again, Jon had been making several bad decisions he was now starting to regret.

This one was headed toward the very top.

"I'm sure you've been talking to her though, right? You were both close, I know."

Addison was a sharp observer. He knew everything happening at the club. And while Jon and Kya did their best to keep their relationship professional and private, it was clear they couldn't keep it a complete secret. Addison seemed to know about it in almost every way and yet, he commented on none of it. Again, as Jon had observed, Addison and Kya did have an odd relationship. And, if there was one person who would pick up on the scent of romance, it was Addison.

"Yeah, we were," said Jon.

"Well, I'm sure she'll fill you in when the time comes."

"Maybe."

"Anyway, you comin' or not?" asked Addison. His static position was noted by Jon, who hustled in shortly after. At the top of the staircase, Jon walked through a narrow hallway and was under the impression he was headed toward another door. Looking at a red door, which was unmistakable, this was the entrance into Addison's office.

However, when Jon walked toward it, Addison grabbed him by the arm. "No, not that way."

Jon's head tilted. "What, this is your office, no?"

Addison's head shook. He was downcast as he answered. "Not anymore it's not."

Jon glanced at the door and then at Addison. The cooler's lips were rolled up into his mouth and he was not looking at the door. All of this seemed to hurt Addison. It bothered Jon as well. This was his boss's quarters. It belonged to the cooler, but evidently, this was no longer Addison's role at The Conquistador.

Addison was now like everyone else. His job had been taken away from him too.

Addison rolled around in a separate corridor and Jon stepped up to another door. Moving in, Addison guided Jon into yet another office much smaller than the last. Absent of any character or taste, it was a typical space equipped with only a desk and a few shelves.

Not much else.

Jon hated being in such a small space. In his mind, he thought Addison deserved better.

"This?" asked Jon. "They put you in *here*?"

"No," said Addison. He moved around his smaller desk. "*I* put me in here."

"You mean, you chose this to be your new office?" asked Jon.

"Why not?" Addison replied. "We're keeping a low profile, remember? And there's nothing lower than this."

Jon had another look around and none of what he was seeing aligned with Addison's personality. Everything was absent of class and sophistication. The room also exuded this vomit-inducing stench. Jon covered his mouth as he sat in the fold-out chair in front of what was now Addison's new desk.

"You can say that again."

Addison faced away so Jon couldn't see what he was doing. He was shifting around a few items and pushing various things aside to retrieve whatever was hidden. Tight in Addison's grip was the box with white trim.

Jon gazed at the box. Addison brought it where the Marine was sitting.

"Certain steps need to be taken before mending a crest, but since you took off your old one, which was only your temporary one—your test crest essentially—now it's time for you to finally get your last one, your *real* one."

"Why didn't you give me one from the beginning?"

"This," said Addison, "is an old tradition." And he said nothing about this afterward.

"Now that you know the truth, it's your choice: stay...or walk away. *Make your choice.*"

Jon gawked at Addison with an affirmed gaze. He made his choice. Jon wouldn't have returned if he wasn't certain about what he wanted to do or who he wanted to be.

"What do you mean?" asked Jon. The crest he had before was a hexagon and crafted out of a very specific piece of fabric. As Jon ripped it off his shirt, all he really needed was a new one to be sewn back on.

Addison rested the box on his desk but the look on his face had now changed. He wasn't disturbed, but was serious as usual. He looked at Jon with his hands pressed against the box.

"You can't just...*give me one?*"

Addison shook his head stoically. "Afraid not. This *is* your last one."

"Okay," said Jon, now nervous to know precisely what the deal was going forward. "So...how do I get this new crest?"

It was only after Jon asked this that Addison removed his hands from the box and unclicked the locks. Now lifting the lid, Jon was desperate to see what was inside. He thought about what it might be, perhaps a batch of new crests or a bracelet or a necklace. He figured it would be any kind of totem that let him know he was still a Doorman. And yet, with Addison behaving in such a cryptic manner, the situation looked grim. Then, when Jon did see what was inside, the interaction had only become grimmer.

"You will," said Addison. "This is the only way you can."

Jon leaned in to get a closer look. Staring into the box, Jon looked at two tools, none of which were what he expected. Truthfully, what Jon was seeing now were two items he couldn't quite place. The first was a steel cudgel the same size as a bedpost. It was black and immaculately polished. The box itself had been preserved quite well. At the edge of this cudgel was another noticeable part of its design. It was so noticeable because the base of the tool was the crest. Now seeing the symbol of the Doormen, it was an unmistakable icon.

Jon gulped and examined this cudgel. What was there in addition to this tool was a mini blowtorch. Small and portable, it was the kind professional chefs used to make fucking flambé or some other dish required to heat quickly. After Addison revealed this to Jon, he didn't require any further clarification. It was now clear how Addison planned to replace Jon's discarded crest. He wasn't going to hand him a new one. No, his plan was to give him something permanent, something that could not be lifted even if Jon wanted to.

"I take this is your way of punishing me?" asked Jon. "I tore off my old crest and now you're giving me one I will *never* be able to take off?"

"This is how everyone's crest is now," said Addison. "Used to be given a lot quicker, but now...it takes a lot for someone to receive their brand. Since we're about to go to war, everyone will be required to wear their mark. Part of the code. As you probably noticed, we're not wearing old uniforms. This is the only mark that lets us know that the Doormen still exist. We do because the marking tells us we do. Now...take off your shirt."

Addison removed the brand as well as the torch from the box.

"My shirt?" asked Jon. He would prefer if this stayed on.

"Has to be somewhere the OverTakers won't see. Secret place no one will know about."

"And where is that?" Jon asked his boss.

"It's where I say it is," said Addison. "Now... roll up."

Addison was firm while Jon began pulling up his sleeves. When Addison asked for something, it was difficult to say no. Undoubtedly, Jon wanted a new crest.

He *needed* this crest. *His crest.*

Jon did as he was told. He removed his shirt while Addison fired up the torch. Jon listened as the flame hissed and inhaled the rancid smell of gas. Jon had never been branded but had heard stories about people who were. It was the activity of biker gangs, cults, and fucking warriors of the past.

It amazed Jon how much his initial perception of being a bouncer was completely wrong.

Jon inserted his crumpled shirt into his mouth. From what he heard, biting down on something was supposed to help. Flexing his back, Addison continued to heat up the brand and then he stepped around Jon. He held his breath and prepared for the eventual pain. Once he stopped hearing the sound of the butane flame, he understood it would not be long before it happened. He waited and gritted his teeth.

With his whole face now flexing, Jon grunted and prepared for what was to come.

"Don't worry," said Addison. "It doesn't take long to leave a mark."

If Jon's mouth was free, he would have told Addison to just get it over with.

Instead, he stayed quiet and felt the scalding metal

searing his flesh. His clamped mouth compromised his screams and he cringed his eyes together so tightly all he could see was black. As he descended deeper into a wretched state of pure agony, the only way Jon could describe what he was experiencing happened when Jon was nine. His hand grazed the stove while it was still turned on. Jon could still remember the pain even now. Yet, the pain inside him today was much worse than it was all those years ago.

Addison pushed hard and Jon could smell his flesh burning. It was more putrid than any other smell he had encountered before. He hoped the pain would end soon, and yet Addison needed to be sure that the mark was permanent.

Five seconds felt like a minute, even longer.

Searing Jon's skin, the crest was now embedded into his back. He couldn't see but he assumed Addison had planted it next to his Marine tattoo. Once it was done, Addison pulled the crest and Jon unclenched his jaw. He let his shirt drop onto his lap and exhaled. It was done.

"How do you feel?"

Jon scoffed. "Felt better."

"Here," Addison doused the burn with what felt like oil, but Jon didn't know for sure. "This will help."

"Thanks."

"Give it a few days and it will feel better."

"Right." Jon slipped his arms back into the sleeves of his shirt. With Addison now back behind the desk, he inserted the brand and the torch back into the box.

"So...what happens now?" Jon asked.

"Now, we execute what we discussed. We get back to work."

"Right," said Jon. "And..."

Jon was about to say more, but he couldn't. From the doorway to Addison's office lay a specter that brought instant tension and fear. An ominous feeling had overtaken Jon and he was afraid. He was *overtaken* by an *OverTaker*.

"Work?" said the specter. "Who said anything about...work?"

By now Jon had his shirt back on. Therefore, the crest he was just given was hidden beneath the fabric. The crest was best left unseen, especially by the man who had abruptly entered Addison's new quarters.

"Michael, good evening," said Addison.

"Hello." Michael was ice cold.

Jon knew this was all part of his act as well as his tactics for dominating the conversation in typical alpha male fashion. Jon glowered.

"Well, good evening there too, Jon."

Irons looked Jon up and down and continued to show his duplicitous grin.

"Michael."

"You're here," Irons said. "Why are *you* here?"

"Because I work here," said Jon. "Or did you forget that?"

"Oh, I never forget anything," Irons replied. Smug as ever, Irons gazed at Jon like he was a pointless excuse for an employee.

Irons was big, no doubt. Ever since the day Jon met him, he was impressed with Irons's size. Seeing him now, however, his stature still continued to impress. More than this, it continued to bother Jon. There truly was no greater enemy than the man standing before him.

"And last time I checked," Irons continued, "you left this club a long time ago. You don't bounce here anymore. You're no longer...a *Doorman?*"

Irons cackled to mock the bouncing unit's name. Jon eyed Irons closely while Addison remained behind his desk.

"No," Addison said. "He still is. He works here again."

"Is that right?" Irons asked. "He works here again, now does he?"

"Yes, he does," confirmed Addison. The brand had burned Jon's back brutally. He could feel it throbbing, for it was a constant reminder of how he never truly left this place.

This was his home.

"And do I need to remind you," asked Irons, "about what is happening at your club? The Doormen have all been pushed to the side, remember? You've all been temporarily overtaken by another organization, *my* organization. Now, we are the ones in charge of The Conquistador's security, which is why we are the main division overseeing all its activity."

"I am aware," said Addison. "But the rules are to conduct a thorough review of this nightclub's policy and procedures and to await Commission approval after the next six weeks. You are in charge of security, yes, but you have no power when it comes to the hiring and rehiring of employees. That continues to fall under the jurisdiction of the old management, which, according to the rules, will remain in effect if *they* are not being subjected to review. Only the security is being reviewed," said Addison. "This is what's happening here. It's managerial, in a way."

"I see," said Irons. Addison had Irons locked up like the lawyer that he was. And, by giving Jon a permanent crest, his status as a Doorman had been officially reclaimed. And there was nothing anyone could do about that.

"And I assume you've told him what's changed?" asked Jon.

"I will," said Addison. "That will be my duty, as all the previous bouncers still report to me. We might not have the same access to employees as we used to have, but we still have the same access to each other."

"Of course," said Irons.

"Will there be anything else, Mr. Irons?" Addison asked. "Or are you going to leave my office?"

Irons snickered. He didn't belong in Addison's office and he definitely didn't belong here with Jon. Both men were done talking, and since Irons had no authority over Addison's decision, there was only one choice left to make.

Irons could politely get the fuck out.

"No," said Irons. "Think I'm good. Have a nice day."

Just before Irons left, he knocked on the doorframe with his ringed fingers.

"Oh, and Jon..." Irons said.

Jon's fury remained as more rage began to burn behind his steady eyes.

"See you around, yeah?" Irons gave Jon a playful wink before moving on.

Jon envisioned his hands wrapped around the son of a bitch's neck. Addison was right there by Jon's side. Arms folded, the cooler stood, and together, he and Jon watched Irons while thinking the same thought.

This guy was a goddamn prick and he needed to get what was coming to him, and he would.

"Jon," said Addison, "we got quite the job ahead of us, and I know exactly where to start."

"Yeah," said Jon. "Just have to find her. You said Kya doesn't work here anymore, right?"

Addison nodded. "Yeah."

"But I still need to see her," declared Jon.

"Why?"

"Because we need her, that's why."

"Do *we* need her?" asked Addison, grinning at Jon. "Or do *you*?"

Jon refused to answer as he walked out the front door. Addison wasn't wrong. Jon needed Kya, and his mistake from the beginning was pretending like he didn't need people but he did.

Jon needed Kya because he couldn't stop thinking about her and because he loved her.

And now, Kya needed to know just how much he did.

CHAPTER 7
OLD THOUGHTS, NEW WORDS

ACCORDING TO ADDISON KROWE, KYA HAD STOPPED working at The Conquistador.

According to him, she was employed as a tutor and as a substitute teacher. When Jon cut himself off from the Doormen, he ceased all communication with Kya, a choice that was now bothering him to no end. And, while this did bother Jon, it didn't bother him as much as it did Kya.

He didn't have the courage to text her or contact her at all.

Jon didn't know where to find her, so he ventured out of his world and into hers.

Jon had met with Kya on the NYU campus before. He had walked her to a class and had even met her afterward for coffee. He didn't know Kya's schedule, so instead, Jon waited outside the regal NYU building, hoping to catch a glimpse of her. Knowing fully well she wouldn't respond to any of his messages, Jon stood for almost two hours. Soon, the doors to the one building opened, Jon's eyes popped. Suddenly, there she was...there Kya was.

Jon's heart sank and he looked at Kya along with two of her friends. Jon believed it wasn't the longest amount of time to be away from a person. Maybe it was now that he had come to consider how long it had actually been. Much could have changed and when he saw Kya now, he could see that so much had. Her hair was longer and darker, like it had been dyed recently. Now dressed in a business suit, Jon could see she looked very professional, almost lawyerly. Though she was a teacher and not a lawyer, Kya could pass for one. When Jon saw her, he marched straight up to her and interrupted her while she was speaking to her friends.

"Kya."

"Jon," Kya replied. She exhaled like she could not hold her breath. "You're...you're..."

"Yeah," said Jon. "*I'm back.*"

Jon didn't know what else to say. He was just as awestruck as Kya.

After showing up so abruptly, Jon had taken Kya off guard and thought perhaps it was best not to say anything more, at least not at this moment.

"Who's this?" A blonde friend asked Kya. She looked Jon up and down like he was a shining star.

"Hi," said Jon. "I'm Jon. Jon Haze. Nice to meet you."

Jon offered his hand and delivered some cordial introductions. He did this even though he had no interest in speaking to any of Kya's friends. He was only here for her, only for Kya.

"I'm Karen," said the blonde. "Kya's friend. It's nice to meet you too."

"Thanks," Jon replied.

"How do you two know each other?" asked Kya's other friend. She was blonde as well, only shorter, and wearing a pair of colorful sneakers. Jon noticed all of this after walking toward the building.

"We, uh," said Jon, not sure about what to say next. "We...well..."

"We worked together." Kya was abrupt and straight to the point. It was clear she didn't like participating in small talk either.

"Well, we used to," said Jon.

"At the club, at The Conquistador?" asked Karen.

"Yeah," said Jon.

"Kya," Karen replied, "how come you didn't tell us you worked with this hot ass motherfucker?"

Jon's brows tensed and he held back his laughter. From what he understood, these girls were all studying to be teachers. He didn't expect teachers to be so blunt and inappropriate, but then this amused Jon, though it didn't seem to impress Kya all that much.

She frowned as she looked at her friends. "Actually, could you two maybe just give us a second?"

"Sure," said Karen. She stepped back and began strolling in the opposite direction. "It was nice to meet you...*Jon?*"

Not sure if she had his name right, Jon smirked before he answered.

"Yeah. Jon," he replied.

"See you around, I hope," said Karen.

Still amused, this Karen girl was the audacious type. Jon wasn't going to lie but he found the quality both liberating and irritating all at the same time. After

Kya's two friends left, both she and Jon stood there, in the same tense silence as felt before.

"So...you're here," Kya said to Jon.

"Yeah," said Jon. "I'm back, actually."

"Back?" said Kya.

"Back to work. Addison brought me back."

"Did he?"

Jon nodded. "Yeah."

"Well, if you're back, then I'm pretty sure you know what's happening. The Conquistador's been taken over. Things aren't how they used to be."

"I'm aware," said Jon, "and that's why I'm here."

"Why you're here?" said Kya. She snorted as she sat on a stone bench outside the building. They were the only ones seated in the resting area. There were four seats constructed entirely out of stone. It was a quiet and quaint space. It was perfect for the conversation Jon and Kya were about to have.

"We need you, Kya. We need you back too."

"Me?" Kya snapped back at Jon.

"We need everyone if we're going to save The Conquistador."

When Jon said this to Kya, her head was turned all the way around. Anytime Kya used a disapproving tone, to Jon, it sounded like flirting. The more cutting she was, the more endearing she became. And right now, she wasn't holding back as she considered what to make of Jon's words.

"Save The Conquistador." Kya scoffed and she shook her head with disbelief. She was utterly amazed with Jon, and not in a good way. No, what she was...was clearly unimpressed.

"Do you actually hear yourself? Do you really hear

yourself right now?" Jon's forehead wrinkled. Of course, he heard.

"Yeah," said Jon. "I do."

"You're starting to sound like you're still a goddamn soldier," Kya said, "like you're back at war, using all these words like *saving* and *we need you*. I mean, goddamn it, Jon, it's just a club! I know that it has its secrets, or whatever, but do you really think the road you're going down is a good one?" Kya's tone spiked as it shrieked. Jon now felt interrogated. "I mean, is that not why you left in the first place?" Kya asked. "You didn't want to serve another power like you did in the war, a power that can lead to dead friends and lost brothers, and also as something doesn't tell them the whole truth about what they're doing or why they're doing it? You left all that behind, don't you remember? And you did it for a good reason, didn't you?"

Jon was silent.

At this moment, he didn't know if he was being interrogated or if Kya was trying to provoke an angry reaction from him. Everything Kya said to Jon, however, was the truth. Yet, everything she said hurt Jon badly. He did leave for these reasons but he came back for the same reasons. Wanting to explain what he learned to Kya—it's not about who you serve but rather *what* you serve. The Conquistador might be a flawed place, filled with secrets and duplicity, yet what it held deep inside was something worth protecting, at least it was for Jon.

Equal access and a place where everyone is welcome? Damn right.

That's real.

Jon knew this to be true, and now, it was time for Kya to know it too.

"Isn't that why you left...me?" she asked.

Jon was racked with guilt and pain. This was the most important question of all. The constant beckoning of questions was not only about the club, it was also Kya too. And Jon had not yet provided Kya with any explanation that could justify his choices or his reasoning.

"I left because I needed time to think."

"*Hmm*, we all need time, Jon," Kya said. "We all need our own time, but most of us just don't take it without first saying goodbye."

Kya's eyes had swelled like she was about to start tearing. She was sad, no doubt, but then Jon was too. Kya fought through her feelings of disappointment and, biting her lip, she began to slowly turn away.

"I should have said goodbye," said Jon. "Yes, you're right. I just...didn't want to make it seem bigger than it was. I needed to just step away and assess, but I didn't think it would hurt people as much as it did. I was wrong."

"You really didn't think it would hurt *me*?" asked Kya. "How could you possibly think it wouldn't? I mean, I was your...*whatever*."

"What?" said Jon. "You were my...what?"

"I was your *girlfriend*, duh!"

Never had Jon heard Kya refer to herself as such. She never admitted to actually being in a relationship with Jon. She never did because Jon had just assumed they weren't *officially* together. Kya moved around a lot, stayed with Jon sometimes, but then there was no talk of any labels, and there certainly was no mention of the whole *girlfriend-boyfriend* thing.

But, before Jon's departure, this was the only word Jon wanted to hear. He didn't hear it then, but he did hear it now. Clearly, it was exactly how Kya felt about him, maybe she did all along. This gave Jon joy, but it almost made him feel overwhelmed.

"But we never...you never..."

"I know," Kya replied. "I know I wasn't being fair to you and that we never really discussed the *actual* status of our relationship, and I know that's on me. Still, I thought we knew each other well enough for one of us to not just turn their backs on the other. That's what I thought, but I guess I was wrong."

"No," said Jon. "You weren't wrong."

Jon was uncomfortable but not upset. Often people assume the two are the same. In this case, Jon was only experiencing one emotion. "I'm just...I don't know," said Jon.

"What?" said Kya.

Jon struggled again to put his feelings into words, to truly express how he was feeling. He was always overwhelmed by uncertainty and anxiety. If he said what was truly on his mind, he was curious as to what Kya might think of it. Considering she was already displeased with everything done so far, Jon believed there was little anyone could hold against him now.

"I'm just not used to people needing me is all."

"You don't think you're needed?" Kya asked. She jeered somewhat as to mock Jon's claims. How he was capable of thinking this had obviously mystified her. Jon could see this, so he needed to clarify.

"Come on, Jon."

"Well," the Marine quickly explained. "I know I'm needed back at work, yeah, and I know I'm needed at home, but I'm not used to like someone else needing me, you know?"

"Someone else needing you like what, *like a partner*?"

Jon nodded. "Yeah, like a *real* partner. Whatever my reasons were," Jon said, "I see now it was wrong. Incredibly. I regret turning my back on the people who were so good to me and who, as you said, needed me. I left them, and I left you too, and for that, I'm sorry."

Jon was doing his best to be sincere. Actually, he was as sincere as someone in his position could be. But, after being confronted by Kya, an apology wouldn't make up for what he did. It wouldn't erase Jon's decision, but still, he had his reasons. And therefore, he would only apologize once. Anything more would imply he didn't give his choice much thought, but Jon did. He had. Still, he wanted Kya to see that he was worried. He frowned and then he reached for her hand. Taking a glance at Jon's fingers, Kya let her former man hold her for a second. The moment between the two of them sank until it became this deep, profound, and real thing. Now that the apology was lent, Jon wanted to speak to Kya about another reason why he was here.

"But I said before that we did need you, and we do. I think we found a way to fix everything, to get back at these guys who've taken over the club. And I have a plan to do that."

"Another plan," said Kya. "You mean, like the Showdown?"

The Showdown Kya had referred to was not exactly a success.

Despite the Doormen's perceived victory, the Keeper informed Jon how he had broken the rules. Now, Jon did have reason to do this, and also, he was not the only one who did. However, it was his choices that spiraled The Conquistador into its now dark situation. Broken rules during the Showdown were indicative of a club's adherence to its rules and regulations. And so, a thorough review needed to be conducted, and this was what led to Irons being elected as the new cooler and what made his OverTakers the new bouncers.

Jon assumed Kya was aware of all this. If she wasn't, then it could mean she wasn't familiar with how urgent and delicate everything was. It's why she was needed now more than ever. It's why he didn't just want her, he hoped and prayed for her.

"This is different," Jon said. "We're going to use the club against these guys. We're going to rely on our own knowledge and our own tactics to strike back at them hard and fast. We're going to show the Commission that we're the better security, and if we can prove that to them, then Michael and his OverTaker assholes will have no choice but to walk away. The Conquistador will be back, *back in our hands*."

"Sounds like...a real plan you got there," Kya said, so disingenuous Jon could almost smell the disdain.

"We just need someone to bring in certain people," said Jon, "like, you know, people who aren't afraid of confrontations or competition. We need people who can force the OverTakers to act out. I mean, what they're doing...it's wrong. You should see what they did to this one girl. They have the whole club latched in between their claws and they're hurting anyone who tries to stand up to them. If we can get them to act with this temperament, they'll go too far and they'll lose it."

"Lose it?" Kya said to Jon. "If the people in the club

are acting like assholes, then you do realize they'll be within their rights to handle them any way they see fit."

"Yeah, but they're supposed to have a better handle on things. Violence is never the first response, you know that. It's like the whole reason why Irons is doing what he's doing. He thinks he can do the job better, and we're going to show everyone why he can't."

"I see," Kya replied, now looking away.

"And that's not the best part of the plan," Jon said. "See, the OverTakers want what The Conquistador has," Jon continued. "What it's hiding," said Jon. He wasn't sure if he should mention the *ciphers* as the club's chief and most desired asset. "But if we can beat the OverTakers at their own game, see...then we can win this way. We can actually defeat them."

"Wow," said Kya, awestruck by Jon's entire narration. "Just...*wow*."

Jon's head tilted to the side. Kya seemed as if she was being disingenuous as well as displeased. He couldn't pinpoint her exact emotional state. He went with what his gut told him, and it assured him his plan was sound.

"I know," said Jon. "It's complicated, but it's still a goddamn good plan."

"No," said Kya. "It's a crazy fucking plan is what it is." Snapping at Jon with cunning disapproval, Jon felt the insult right away. "I mean, *fucking heists*, *taking back*, and *fighting for territory*, do you even hear yourself? I know I asked you that before, but come on, Jon... you have to hear yourself now."

After being barked at for so long, Jon didn't have the courage to say anything more. He already heard himself loud and clear. But he still didn't know where Kya was going with all of these questions.

"You're a bouncer, okay?" Kya said. "You're a Doorman. You're not some goddamn thief or some gang banger or gangster or some shit. You're talking about a turf war here. You know how ridiculous all of that sounds, don't you? And now you want to open innocent people up to dangerous situations, and for what, so you can go back to work and get back at the guy who screwed you over? You're not overseas anymore, Jon! You're not a soldier and this isn't some kind of war! You're not going up against some enemy insurgents, and you sure as shit aren't battling any terrorists. You're just a guy who works security at a nightclub, and that's all, okay! All!"

Jon breathed and needed a second to collect himself. What Kya said cut deep. It was deep because it made sense and it was true.

"But you know about The Conquistador," said Jon, taking a minute to exhale and calm himself. "You know what it's protecting."

"Yeah," said Kya. She avoided talking about this. "Sure. I know and I don't care. Look, whatever the club was or is...all of that has nothing to do with me or with you. I don't want to get involved. The past, the secrets, and everything you're talking about, all of that, it's not what I want. I worked there because I needed a job, that's all."

"So, you never cared about it, you never cared about the club ever?"

"Well, I cared about doing a good job, and yeah, I didn't want to disappoint Addison because he was a good boss and everything. But I didn't start working at his club to be a part of some turf war or some other crazy contest. I'm not going to get into some kind of battle for club supremacy I learned my lesson back at the Showdown."

"And what lesson was that?" Jon asked Kya.

"Oh, I don't know," Kya said, "like I'm done playing stupid and childish games. I'm doing more than just bartending and serving other people their shit. I mean, in case you didn't notice, my real goal was always to become a teacher. I only just *worked* at The Conquistador because I knew Addison and well...it just worked for me at the time. Plus...my sister..."

"What?" asked Jon. "What about your sister?"

"Nothing," Kya snapped back, and she skipped over the subject entirely. "Look, my real goal is to help people and to do it where it matters most. I know I liked my time working at The Conquistador, no doubt. But eventually, I gotta ask myself, where do I want to end up? And no, I don't want to be serving drinks forever."

"You'd rather see it go down then?" Jon asked, resisting Kya's claims. "You'd rather see everyone there go down for the wrong reasons? You'd rather see its powers end up in the wrong hands?"

"Wrong hands?" Kya snapped at Jon, her head thrust back and she guffawed.

She really couldn't contain her laughter and Jon couldn't contain the animosity felt at this very moment. Kya might just see herself as an employee, but what was happening at The Conquistador was still wrong. People were being scrutinized, beaten, and harmed. All of this was because of their choices.

And, when Jon said *their*, he was talking about

everyone who participated in the Showdown. It was Jon, but it was Kya too.

"Jon, this isn't up to you," said Kya. "This isn't something you can just change. It's a nightclub, a nightclub with a deep and complex history, and you can't change any of it because you want to. And if that was your reason for coming back to see me, then I hate to tell you, but...you made a grave mistake."

Jon felt like a knife was being jammed into his neck.

Kya's words cut deep. Jon was already feeling insecure and vulnerable. But, after Kya unleashed her tirade, there was nothing for Jon to do except sit there and think. However, he couldn't even do that. What Kya said, he had already said to himself. He didn't say it in the same way, but the logic was there too.

"I know that this hurts, but if I have to be the one who tells you the truth, even if it's a truth you don't want to hear, still...I have to do it."

"No," said Jon. "Don't be sorry." He looked at Kya and was focusing so much that his eyes began to burn. "You're right. You almost always are."

"No," said Kya. "I'm not always, but see...after you left, I decided to step away and take a break from everything. I had some time to think. I hope you did too, but the Showdown broke me a little. I saw what happens when we go too far and do what we're not being paid to do. I hope you did too."

"I did," said Jon. "I did have some time to think."

"Good," said Kya. "So...you see that I'm right, right?"

"I do," said Jon.

"Then what are we talking about?" Kya replied.

"What are you doing? You know you're not set up for this. Whatever you're planning...*it's too much.*"

"Too much?" Jon barked.

"Yeah," replied Kya. "*Way too much.*"

"So I should just fall in line then?" Jon asked. "I should go back to work and wait for this whole thing to solve itself on its own? Then what, just pretend like The Conquistador is just my place of employment? The people I work with, they're more than just people I know, Kya. I should treat the people I work with as not my friends and not people who are in need of help?"

"Well...no, but—"

"I should just stand back and follow orders, right?" Jon interceded, his tone more forceful and louder than before. He was making a clear point and he hoped Kya would see where he was going with that point. "I should just be a good soldier, serve the cause and not question or see how there's more to things than just how they appear."

"I...I..." Kya sat back, perplexed by all Jon had said. Everything Jon said was not only confusing, it also made him feel quite curious. Until now, Kya had not heard Jon speaking like this. Truthfully, Jon had not heard himself talk like this before.

He was establishing the logic in his plan and he was standing by his decisions.

He was doing this because they were his. *All his.*

"I should just what, *follow?*" Jon asked.

"What are you talking about?" Kya said to Jon.

"You were right. When I left the club, I did have time to think. I went back to where it all began."

"Back to the club?" Kya asked.

"No," Jon said. "No, I went back to the first person I

ever looked up to, my lieutenant back in the Marines. You don't know him because I never really talked about him, but he did talk to me. In fact, he helped me to understand when I couldn't understand a single thing. See, when I left The Conquistador, I thought I was doing the right thing because I didn't want to be part of what I thought was a broken system. But it wasn't broken, see? No, while The Conquistador is not without flaws, what matters most is what it's fighting to preserve, and it's not greed or power. It's access and contrary to what you think, freedom and equality, like our country. When I was a soldier, people didn't know we were fighting for that too. And, just like then, here has value too, and I'm not going to surrender that value to someone who doesn't deserve it. That's what matters most, who we are and fighting to keep one's home safe."

Kya was silent throughout Jon's entire monologue. Now Jon was making a point and it was clear. His choice to return wasn't about his blind loyalty to The Conquistador or its cause. It was about people—the loyalty to Jon's friends and his brothers.

"And who I'm fighting to protect," said Jon. "I went back because what my thoughts were on the club didn't matter nearly as much as my thoughts about its people, and I still care about people. Truthfully, it's just the people I care about. My plan isn't about protecting The Conquistador or its precious things."

Jon didn't even know if The Conquistador had vaults, safes, or anything. He was using the word ubiquitously. Nearly every place of business had figurative vaults and places where it stored its valued secrets.

The Conquistador wasn't any different.

"It's about doing what's right for the people and

preserving one's home, and in many ways, culture and creed."

Jon didn't expect to mention the word *creed*.

He felt it was somewhat of a stretch. And yet, the more Jon thought about it, the more sensible it became. After this, Jon glanced at Kya's hand. Now was Jon's second opportunity for them to connect. Still, Jon declined. He was past all these sappy, saccharine moments that did not add anything to a person's inter-action. No, Jon wanted to finish what he started and also wanted to let Kya know the most important point of all.

"And that's what I regretted most," said Jon. "It's how I turned my back on you, on the people I work with, and that's what the club has always been about for me. It's been about people, about who they are and what *they* stand for, and that's why I had to come back. Because they needed me. Danix and Li, Owen and Addison, and...and you..."

Jon made sure Kya could see him now. What he was to say next was the most important.

"*You* need me." Kya's eyes opened and her head swayed to show her disbelief.

Everything Jon said did make sense. Its truth was undeniable. Jon didn't think what he said would change Kya's mind. No, when Jon said what he did, it was because he wanted to say it. Jon let his mind form the words but all of it was propelled because of what was now brewing inside of him. It was building in his gut, building for too long, and now it was finally ready to be unleashed.

It was ready...because it was real, and you can't contain real...no matter how hard you try.

"So now, all that's left to do is ask one last thing." Kya's eyelashes batted at Jon like they used to back when they were together. Jon liked the feeling it gave and all he wanted was more. Still, he did have more to say. And so, he had to finish what he started.

"Do you need me too?" When Jon said this, he also found himself answering the same question.

In his mind, Jon was speaking for Kya. He hoped there was only one way to answer this.

In a way, Kya already had answered. Already she had discussed how she and Jon were once close, how they were more than just coworkers and were most definitely more than just friends.

"Do you?" Jon asked.

Kya smiled as she reached for Jon's hand. "Yeah, I do."

"Then let's go," Jon replied. "Let's go and let's win."

"Win?" said Kya.

"Yeah," said Jon.

"All right," Kya replied. "Let's *win*."

Leaving the NYU campus with Kya now onboard, the next phase of Jon's plan was about to unfold. Jon wanted to make his way back to his car, but Kya was taking him someplace else. She was leading Jon somewhere, somewhere she knew but he did not.

"Where are we going?" Jon asked coyly, without too much care.

"You want a war, you're going to have to think outside the box, and I have a few ideas of my own, if you're interested? Come on. This way." Kya looked at Jon as he smiled. "I'll show you what they are."

CHAPTER 8
OPENING EYE

JON WALKED WITH KYA ACROSS THE CITY. HAND IN hand, they each stopped at various locations but didn't say much. They were so focused on the moment, and Jon was pleased with just being with Kya. It wasn't until later on, after they walked together for almost thirty minutes, that all of it became clear.

"So...we need to sabotage The Conquistador, now do we?" Kya asked.

Jon nodded. "Yeah."

"We need new clients, people who are going to push the envelope and knock these OverTakers into overdrive, got it?"

"Exactly," said Jon.

"And these new people will need to get access into the club somehow, right?"

"Somehow, yeah. Most of these new clients are rich," said Jon. "They pay at the door and they move right in like they own the place."

"Affluent people with deep pockets and short fuses."

"Pretty much," said Jon. "Know any?"

"Unfortunately, yes," said Kya. "And even more unfortunately, I know where to find them."

Hearing this, Jon smirked. He was not surprised. Kya knew so many interesting people.

"Figured. Where are we going?"

"Chinatown," said Kya. "Ever been?"

"Actually, no, I have not," said Jon.

"Well, lots of nightclubs there, but trust me," said Kya, "this next part of our journey is going to get dangerous."

"Yeah, well, danger I can handle."

"I know," said Kya. "Just whatever happens, I need you to trust me, okay?"

"Do you even need to ask that?" said Jon. "Of course, I trust you."

"All right, but before we go, we're going to need to change a few things."

"What?"

Kya suddenly snatched Jon's hand and pulled. "Come on. Let's go." Guiding Jon away, the Marine slipped forward and began to shuffle along.

"What is it?" Jon asked. Right now, he couldn't pinpoint what Kya was doing while taking him into this alleyway. He had to ask. "What are you doing?"

"Just stand here. Take off your shirt."

"What? Why?"

"Just do it." Removing his shirt, Jon followed Kya's orders.

He enjoyed listening to her. Beneath this one shirt, Jon had on another. He was now wearing a muscle top and looked less put together than he did before. Actually, he was barely put together when he met Kya, so this was not exactly a massive downgrade to his appearance.

"Can't look too proper," Kya added. "Where we're going, needless to say, is the underbelly of the club industry. It's...*different*."

"I thought you said it was in Chinatown," said Jon, mystified with Kya's new choice of direction.

Now kneeling, she yanked Jon's pants at the waist and pulled his ankles. Jon let her do as she pleased. He really didn't care what he looked like, actually.

"Well, it's close to Chinatown you could say, yeah."

"All right," said Jon.

"But Satanists don't exactly have a way of welcoming people who they think are there to hurt them. They like solitude and they also like things loud and messy. They also expect the people who come to their parties to be the same way."

"Right," said Jon. He was concerned about his style. He had almost completely missed what Kya had said to him. "Wait," he continued. He caught up on what was said. "Did you say *Satanists*?"

Kya nodded and stopped kneeling in the alleyway. "Yeah."

"We're going to see a bunch of Satanists?"

"Well, not all of them are," Kya answered Jon, "but some will be, no doubt. See, I have to find Gomez. You want guerrilla journalists or what? Well, this is the place we have to go and these are the people we have to see."

Kya hustled down the alley, and Jon followed her every step. He was intrigued by what she had said. Jon hadn't met a Satanist. Still, as far as a group of people who were completely ostracized, he couldn't think of one that fit into this category more.

Seriously, he thought...*how many Satan-worshippers does the average person actually know?*

"Besides," said Kya, "Satanists are a misunderstood breed. Everyone sees them as these dark, people-sacrificing cults, but realistically, mainstream devil worship isn't about that at all. The only place where actual sacrificing is happening is in fucking Hollywood, in the home of a famous producer."

"Right." Jon was flabbergasted hearing Kya talking in such a different way.

She knew so much about so many things and Jon only knew the basic things. Most often, Jon really didn't know what Kya did, had done, or who she knew or why.

"We just have to get there," Kya said. "Their parties are usually held during the day, which is weird, but I know Gomez can help us. He hates establishments. He's exactly what we're looking for, exactly what we need now."

"Do you think Addison will mind? I mean, don't you think we should run it by him first?"

Kya didn't respond to this. Generally, Addison was the one who privy to the club's clientele. Kya didn't only work as a bartender but also as one of the club's promoters. So, she definitely was significant when bringing new people into The Conquistador. Jon was curious if she still had the skills to welcome potential patrons. When they reached the end of the alley, however, Kya and Jon took a sharp turn and continued the hustle. Where they were going was far. They needed a car. Fortunately, Jon brought one.

"I have a ride. We should take it."

"Fine, but remember, when we get there, just let me do the talking."

"No doubt," said Jon. "You talk."

———

Now in the car, Kya provided him with directions. "*Near Chinatown*," Kya instructed.

Jon now knew where to go. Onto the location, Jon watched as the city became more and more decrepit. He was struck with déjà vu. Such an adventure did remind Jon about where he, Kya, and Addison confronted the leader of the Fallen Sons. They tracked their alcohol supplier, which led to a warehouse and then to a party.

It was here where the leader, Rex Macintosh, challenged the Doormen to a Showdown.

It was for this reason Jon and Kya had embarked on this now dark and uncertain adventure. Now Jon found himself trapped in the more ominous sects within his country's most famous city. Kya told Jon where to park and they stepped out together.

"This is it?" asked Jon.

"Yeah," said Kya. She stepped ahead of Jon but expected him to follow. "This is it."

"Seriously?"

Although Jon was not afraid, he was bothered and he was disturbed. Where Kya had taken Jon to was, in fact, an abandoned factory. Its windows were smashed and rust had accumulated in mutated pockets in various sections within the rotting construct. It was close to

Chinatown, but the complex was secluded. It was a broken, dilapidated building accompanied by dumpsters and a loading dock with thrashed doors and peeling paint.

In this place, Jon felt on edge. He checked all corners and exits. Although he was concerned, Kya was not. She marched to the door and Jon watched her closely.

"Why?" asked Kya. She grinned at Jon while looking over her shoulder. "You scared?"

Jon scoffed at the comment. He loved it when Kya acted playful and giddy.

"No."

"Good," said Kya. "Then let's go get us some disruptors, shall we?"

Jon shuffled up to the stand closer to Kya. The closer Jon drew to this passage, the more thumping sounds of classic head-banging music he detected. The vibrations from a set of massive speakers rattled his senses, and much like the rave Jon encountered months earlier, this new place felt incredibly similar.

Yet, those clients were nothing more than irresponsible high schoolers. Where Jon was going to was a party orchestrated by people whom Kya was acquainted with.

"So...I gotta ask," said Jon, "you're not..."

"What?" asked Kya. "Not...what?"

"You know," said Jon.

Kya stared at Jon and her playful smirk continued to show.

"What?" Kya asked again.

"You know, uh...*uh*..."

"What?" Kya snapped. "A *Satanist*?"

Jon nodded. "Yeah."

"No," replied Kya. "Although, I did dabble in witch-craft a while back," she said, "you know, when I was in high school."

"Really?"

"Really," confirmed Kya.

"So that's why when I'm around you, I always feel like I'm under some kind of spell, huh?" Jon's line was a corny one at best. Still, Kya smiled at the comment as if it had a positive impact. Maybe it did, but then maybe she was just being nice.

"Sure, but when you're in there, just let me do the talking, remember?" said Kya. "I know last time when we dropped into a new location, you did the talking, but trust me when I say these people are not into talking. Still, if you really want to pitch your plan to a particular group of people, then these are the kind you need."

"Understood," said Jon. He had no idea why he was here, what this place was, or what it would look like on the other side, but he stayed frosty while at the same time...curious.

"Gomez is cool, but he's not exactly the friendliest guy around."

"I thought you said Satanists are misunderstood?" Jon replied.

"Oh, they are," said Kya, "which is why they're so unfriendly and careful about who they let inside to their worlds. And, if we're going to ask Gomez for a favor, well...then we'll have to ask it nicely."

"Okay."

"Good," said Kya.

Approaching the door, Kya raised her hand and knocked. Each hit was subtle. Quiet. Normally, a person would pound a door in order to gain entry into such a hiding space, but Kya refused to do this now.

The door opened and Jon looked through a hatch and at a face with red contact lenses and thick makeup drawn across their eyes. This person examined Jon and Kya like the intruders that they were and grunted. "Hello?"

"Here to see Gomez," said Kya. "Is he here?"

"He is," said the person on the other side. "Who's asking?"

"A friend," answered Kya. "*Two* friends, actually."

Jon was pleased to see Kya include him in this response. The two were, after all, together.

"Well, he is here," said the face beyond the door. "But anyone who enters here has to bear the mark. You got one?"

When the obscure doorkeeper asked this, Jon's eyes shifted straight to Kya. The mark he had referred to sounded weird, cautious, and also...very suspicious. If Kya carried a symbol, then it meant she was linked to the group congregated there, maybe?

Did this scare Jon? Yes, in some capacity, it did.

Was he worried? Well, Kya was free to live her own life. She could interact with anyone she wanted, and as she rolled up her sleeve, she scoffed and revealed a tattoo. Jon had never seen this tattoo before. This was the mark the man at the door had mentioned, clearly. On Kya's shoulder was a pentagram sketched in purple ink and containing that one famous eye.

Most people did have similar tattoos, so this was not something that bothered Jon. But, when Kya showed it, the man slid the locks aside and gazed. "All right," he said. "You go."

"So...you do have a mark then?" said Jon. He was doing his best to hide how he really felt. He wasn't going to lie. It felt strange to him.

"Like I said," answered Kya, "I dabbled."

Going on, Jon followed Kya through the door. With the barrier now aside, in Jon's mind, he thought he knew what to expect. He thought he'd see flashing lights, gyrating bodies, and lots of people dressed in dark clothing bouncing around like they were high. He envisioned a rave filled with strung-out fools, not unlike what he encountered many times before. And yet, while Jon did encounter this, it was not quite like he expected.

No, it was bigger. This place was a Vampire's wet dream.

Everywhere Jon looked he could see people in black thrumming to a hard-sounding beat. It was like everyone was hypnotized or possessed, or they were transported to a different realm. Jon imagined that was exactly the point. Strange calligraphy appeared on the walls, and the space looked like a fish market dominated by graffiti and grunge art.

"Where are we going?" Jon asked.

"Like I said!" Kya shouted. "Let me do the talking!"

Jon didn't say a damn thing. The music was so loud he couldn't hear Kya even when she was shouting. Jon followed Kya through the crowd but stayed on his guard. Jon didn't know what to expect from *this* crowd.

Kya said that Satanists were a misunderstood bunch, whatever that meant.

From what Jon could see, they looked exactly as advertised. Dark and grotesque, they eyed Jon like he was a piece of meat. Still, Jon did trust Kya. She escorted him to a staircase positioned across the dance floor. While the music was loud here too, Jon was used to hearing volume at this level but what he wasn't used to was this particular style of music. He couldn't make out any of the lyrics. Whenever words were spoken, all of them were referencing some dark element, whether it be *blood* or *shadow*, and Jon couldn't stand hearing any of it.

Head down, Jon followed Kya.

He had come to the stairs across from the dance floor. Jon hopped along and went to what he assumed was the VIP section. What always amazed Jon was how, regardless of whatever club he was in, there was always a place for the *important people* to sit.

Steadily approaching this level, Jon eyed the man who stood at the very top.

A man on guard had a mohawk and tattoos along his face. He eyed Kya and Jon with a grim expression. On the outside, he looked tough, but Jon had seen much tougher.

When he and Kya reached the end of the stairs, Kya politely touched the guard on his arm. Why she insisted on doing this Jon attributed to her playful ways. Kya knew how to flirt and how to charm. She loved doing this, and Jon could always see it in her eyes. Some people are natural charmers, and no one was more naturally charming than the woman Jon had fallen in love with.

Leaning into this guard, Kya whispered. Due to the blaring of music, Jon couldn't make out a single word. But, once Kya had spoken to this guard, he nodded and stepped aside. He let Jon and Kya go on ahead with little resistance. Jon didn't expect this at all. Neither he nor Kya looked like the rest of the guests, so Jon assumed they wouldn't be allowed to enter. And yet, moving along, Jon was now in a separate space with a torn sofa, a rickety table, and a heap of empty bottles. Also in this section, Jon could see more club patrons. Some were exceptionally younger than he was. Most were female while some males did stand near the center. There was one man standing above the others. He had black hair and donned a tight leather jacket. Jon could only assume this was the leader. He also assumed from his wide eyes that he was the person they had come to see. With Kya standing in front of him, the man in the jacket threw his hands up in an act of pure rejoice and clapped.

"Kya!" The man's voice echoed, still cheery in the presence of Kya.

"Gomez." The man called Gomez sauntered toward Kya while Jon stood back and watched. He didn't know where this interaction was going and was unsure how he felt about it.

Gomez seemed to like Kya, and Kya seemed to like him too.

They were friendly, so Jon believed the two of them were only just friends. Jon watched their interaction as an outsider. He remembered what Kya said. She was to do the talking, which meant Jon had to stay quiet. And that's exactly what he was doing.

"Nice to see you again," Gomez said, still holding Kya's hand.

Kya grinned and slid her hand across Gomez's boney arm.

"Nice to see you as well," Kya replied.

"And you're here!" Gomez shouted. Jon was in awe

of this Gomez's level of excitement. When he thought of Satanists, he most definitely did not think of a guy like this.

"You've come!"

"I have, yes," said Kya.

"Great," said Gomez, "but I thought you didn't come to things like this anymore, you know, now that you're a teacher and all."

"Well," said Kya, "let's just say I'm breaking a few rules here, tonight because I have something very important to say to you, Gomez."

"Important, huh?" Gomez beckoned, rubbing his hands together like sticks.

While Kya was relaxed, now she was deadpan. She was serious. "Yes."

"Okay," said Gomez. His eyes rolled and he looked at Jon. The Marine leaned back. "Who's this?" Gomez asked Kya.

"Oh," said Kya. Jon's presence had obviously slipped her mind for a time. "This is my friend, Jon Haze. Jon, this is Gomez. Gomez, meet Jon."

Jon offered his hand while Gomez just glanced at it. He didn't shake hands. Initially reluctant, Jon continued to remain as non-threatening as he could be. Still, without a doubt, Gomez and those in his company were resistant to *outsiders*.

This was felt as soon as Jon entered their space.

"Nice to meet you," Gomez said to Jon.

"You too," Gomez said, mulling over Jon and then moving in a new direction. "Come on," Gomez said. "We can talk over here."

Gomez walked back to the sofa and joined his friends. Jon stayed close to Kya as she stepped. "So," said Gomez, and he sat down next to some girl who was hitting a bong. "You've come to see me. What is it?"

"Well, it's not an easy request to make, no doubt, but..." said Kya.

"I assumed it wouldn't be," said Gomez. When he sat, the girl with a bong slid aside. Gomez slouched and Jon assessed what he could about this new man. There was something about Gomez that was both suspicious *and* intriguing.

"But the fact that you're here means you still remember what forced us to cross paths in the first place, am I right?" Gomez asked Kya.

"You are," she said.

"And I'm sure your friend, Jon, knows why too."

Grinning madly, Gomez was taunting Jon. It was subtle, but still there.

"Yeah," Jon felt the need to respond. If Gomez was testing to see how well Jon knew Kya, then the Marine was going to pass that test. "She told *me*."

"Did she now?" asked Gomez, still playful and still very cunning.

"Yeah," Jon insisted. "She did."

"And what did she say?" asked Gomez.

Jon ignored Gomez and looked at Kya. In a way, he was asking *her* for permission. Did she want him to say how? Was he allowed to do that?

Uncertain if he was, Jon answered anyway.

"She said she dabbled in witchcraft back in the day," added Jon. "She's got that tattoo, so I guess she was once part of this whole community."

Immediately after Jon said this, a new and more maniacal smile began to form on Gomez's relishing mug. Although this was what Jon assumed, Gomez broke into laughter and felt irked. It was not how Kya knew Gomez, not at all.

"*Hahahaha!*" Gomez's laughter ignited all the others who were in his company. They all looked to their presumed leader with blushing faces as they chuckled along.

"What?" said Gomez, recovering from the mountain of giggles he had just climbed his way through. "You think she's what, a Satanist? Is that what she said?"

Jon sighed and his forehead wrinkled, as he was lost and confused. He then glanced at Kya, who was silent as she sat back.

"She did." Gomez continued to snarl and laugh. He had another drink and then looked at Kya and Jon.

"No," Gomez said. "No, that's *not* how we know each other. I guess you didn't fill him in on the story, huh?"

Kya didn't answer.

"It would seem our relationship is a lot more complex than just that," said Gomez.

Jon's heart sank. He hoped the two were never together. In Jon's mind, they could have been. Now Jon couldn't account for all of Kya's past. He didn't know everything about Kya, just as she didn't know everything about Jon.

"No, she knew me back when I was a student. See, she was just starting out as a teacher, ain't that right?"

Kya nodded.

"Yeah, it was like, what, three years ago?" Gomez asked.

"Four," Kya corrected. "It was four years ago."

Gomez clapped and grinned. "Oh, that's right. Yeah, it was four, had to be. Four years ago."

"I see," said Jon, still lost.

"Yeah, I was seventeen and she was older, early-twenties, I think. Actually," explained Gomez, "she wasn't a teacher so much as she was a *teacher's assistant*, you know, one of those?"

Jon didn't answer, but yes, he did know.

"Yeah," said Gomez, "she worked at this school that I once attended downtown, and well, it's actually kind of a big story, isn't it?"

"I prefer not to think about it, actually," Kya responded.

Kya's frown said more than her words ever could. Jon recognized when she was visibly upset. Clearly, she was.

"Yeah," replied Gomez. "No doubt."

"What happened?" asked Jon. He needed to know more about the story Gomez was describing. There was a reason Kya had chosen to bring Jon here. There was a reason they required Gomez's help, and the story he was now discussing could be linked to all that. It probably was.

"Guess she didn't tell you," said Gomez. "Well, see, the school I attended, the teachers weren't exactly friendly to kids like me. You know, broken, damaged, troubled kids. I wasn't exactly the poster child for good behavior. All the other teachers they..." Gomez gulped and stammered. This next part of the story seemed the most difficult, and Jon understood why.

"Well, they weren't exactly kind to a kid like me," Gomez said, "someone who wore makeup and who liked to draw pictures of demons and liked heavy metal.

What started out as conventional punishment escalated into the kind that left a few bruises, if you know what I mean?"

Although Jon didn't say anything, he did know. He knew it well because Jon had his fair share of bruises as well. Back in the Marines, Jon was the victim of a few initiations. Some were messier than others. He was branded in the calf and was forced to prove his worth in tumultuous and sometimes difficult ways. At the time, Jon was angry. Afterward, however, he found himself feeling grateful. Initiation is the first step toward being welcomed into a brotherhood or a sisterhood bigger than yourself. It was only a conforming ritual meant to test your limits and see what a person is truly capable of. And yet, Jon hadn't experienced anything like that when welcomed into The Conquistador. He loved the Marines, but hated the initiation. Jon doubted this was what Gomez was talking about, or maybe he was. Jon wasn't sure.

"I do, actually," said Jon.

"Yeah, well, no one at the school believed me, no one except for the youngest teacher who worked there." Gomez gave Kya a flirtatious wink. It was then Jon understood the truth regarding their relationship. This was how the two met, and it was why they were still friends today.

"The other teachers refused to help me when I was found crying in a corner, but see, it was Kya who took me for walks and helped me recover. She was so young and I was so young, and she didn't care what the other teacher said. She just didn't want to see a little boy bawling his eyes out."

"The way you were treated was wrong," Kya said.

"Yeah," said Gomez. He had another drink and combated his trauma using the traditional method.

Of course, Jon didn't judge a person for this. The more he became aware of Gomez's story, the better understanding he had about why he was here now.

"Although that wasn't enough," he said, "I might have had someone in my corner, but Kya was still the young, inexperienced teacher, isn't that right?"

Jon watched Kya nod.

"I tried to bring it to the principal's attention," she said, "and she told me she wanted all the teachers involved in the reporting of the abuse."

"But if she was to give a list of names," explained Gomez, "then she'd only be throwing herself under the bus too, see? The other teachers would despise her for talking to a student, especially a bad one like me."

Jon squinted. His understanding of Kya's rationale was now starting to deepen.

The reason for not speaking up did make sense to Jon. Stopping bad teachers was not exactly an easy task. Jon compared all of this to his own experiences. There were several sergeants who liked to play hardball. Now Marines never complained, even after those in charge went too far.

In the end, there was just no one to complain to.

"While other teachers would have told me to tough it out," said Gomez. "Kya here had a better plan."

"Oh?" said Jon, interest piqued. The fact that Kya had chosen to help Gomez provided a warming feeling to Jon. He just didn't know how she had decided to provide him with such assistance.

And yet, he wanted to know.

"Yeah," said Gomez. "Do you want to tell him how?"

Kya smiled at Gomez and glimpsed at Jon.

"I told him the next time the teachers went too far to make sure he had a way to catch them," she said. "Make sure you trap them, get them to do their dirty deeds while being recorded, and that way, if the people who work at the school won't believe you, someone out there will."

"And?" asked Jon.

"And," said Gomez, "let's just say I never had to go to that school or see any of those bastard teachers ever again, none...except for one." Gomez nodded at Kya, and she nodded right back.

Their friendship, from what Jon could see, was rooted in deep and meaningful things. What Kya had told Gomez to do protected him. It was for this reason they continued to stay in touch. It was the same reason why Gomez was here now.

"You find," Gomez said, "that the people who break the rules do it so often that they barely notice anymore. The people who go too far rarely care that they do, and it's why it's a person's duty to make sure their caught and put on display for all to see. It's the most valuable lesson learned while in that shithole of a school, and it's why I continue to remember this truth now."

"I see," said Jon. He looked at Kya as she sat there next to him. It was then Jon began to understand the reason why they were here. Gomez was someone who had completed the task of setting up bad people who do bad things. He made them fall for everyone to see.

It was this same task now repeating.

"And ever since then, I've always kept my eyes open

for trouble. In a way, she saved me," said Gomez, "but also she put me on a new path, for growth and purpose."

"Gomez has his own channel. Instagram, TikTok, YouTube, you name it. Busted Clean, I think it's called," said Kya. "It targets people who abuse their power and captures their corrupt behavior and then shares it online."

"It's a bit of a legal headache sometimes," said Gomez, "but necessary, still. And we research before we move in. So far, it hasn't let us down."

"And who do you target exactly?" asked Jon. He had heard about these so-called *influencers* before, but it never appealed to him.

"You name 'em," Gomez replied. "Dirty cops, educators, and some other plain old scum bags. You give me the details, and if you're willing to pay the price, I'll get your assholes right where you want them to be."

"And is that legal," asked Jon, "to, like, record someone without their consent?"

"It is, if they knew who is recording."

"What?" begged Jon.

"Gomez operates with total anonymity," said Kya. "His channel, and everyone who helps to maintain it, all exist in the dark, in the shadows, I guess you could say."

"Exactly." Gomez raised his hand and pointed at Kya. With his drink no longer in his hand, Gomez was now holding a cigarette and a lighter. This lent more enthusiasm to their enriching conversation.

"I used to think it was a bad thing, being forced to stay hidden, but it wasn't until I met this one over here that I realized its true value."

"I actually can understand that," said Jon. He said this because he really did understand.

Jon lived in the shadows too. First, Jon did when he was a Marine, and now, as a bouncer. It was strange how much in common Jon shared with this surveillance expert Kya had introduced him to. It was a strange yet satisfying encounter.

Jon understood exactly why he was here. More than this, he understood his plan.

"I'm sure you can," said Gomez. Lighting the end of his cigarette, Gomez was clearly being sarcastic. Jon didn't care. Now, knowing what someone like Gomez faced, it was silly to compare their experiences.

Jon stood by what he said and he did understand where someone like Gomez was coming from. Jon also fully believed in Gomez's abilities. What he knew how to do would only prove to be incredibly useful. It would also be, at the same time, absolutely necessary.

"But I know you didn't come here to talk about the past, now did you?" Gomez slyly asked. He ogled Kya. She shook her head, leaned forward, and pressed her elbows hard into her knees.

"No," she said. "No, we're not." Kya squeaked out a semi-audible sound.

"Look, we need you," said Jon. Acting like a prototypical Uncle Sam, all that Jon was missing now was the star-spangled outfit, a goatee, and a solid forefinger. "We need your skills and we need your help."

Gomez mulled Jon over. "You need me?" Gomez asked Jon.

"Yes," Jon replied. "We absolutely need you."

"Corruption has overtaken our place of work," said Kya. "A group of men are abusing their positions and hurting people. We need assistance from those who know firsthand how to bring such forces down, and there's no one out there who can do more than you."

Everything Jon and Kya said to Gomez was meant as a compliment. And, while Jon couldn't quite tell how Gomez felt regarding such flattery, he slouched on the hideous sofa.

"The Conquistador," said Gomez.

Jon squinted. He was mildly intrigued because, until now, Jon hadn't mentioned his place of work, yet Gomez knew about it. How?

"Yes," said Jon. "The Conquistador. How...how did you..." Jon didn't bother finishing his sentence. He didn't have to because Gomez had more to say.

"Lots of people are talking about that place. It's hit social media like a beast," said Gomez.

"What are they saying?" Kya asked.

Gomez shrugged. The news didn't seem to bother him all too much. "Just that the place has gone downhill. It's no longer the cool, sleek club it used to be. New clients and the security are supposedly tight. Everywhere you look, there's someone breathing down your neck. If you step out of line, they hurt you, but still, the club has maintained its position. People still want to go there, they're just...a *different kind of people*."

"And that's who we're trying to stop," said Kya. "It's this new security that has taken the club over. They're trying to push out the old crew, which is us."

"Yeah," said Jon, "and they're doing all of this in the worst way possible. I mean, they think they're creating a more stable place, but they're going too far. So...you see...that's why we need you."

"I see," said Gomez. "You want to go in there, set up

a sting, and bust these assholes by posting their shit on my channel and then hash-tagging their asses into fucking cancelation."

"Pretty much," said Jon.

Kya nodded, as did Gomez. He was with them one hundred percent.

"Yeah, well, you know I like to get back at abusers, but this...this is different."

"How so?" Kya asked Gomez.

"I thought you said you knew what was going on in the club," Gomez said to Jon.

Jon eyed Gomez with a peculiar look. "We do," Jon admitted.

"No, you don't," answered Gomez. "The stories coming out of The Conquistador are bad. People are getting banged up pretty good there. Some are seriously injured, if you know what I mean?"

"There's a risk, no doubt about that," Jon acknowledged. "And that we know for sure."

"Do you also know that legally these guys are wrapped up? Apparently, the club has new laws. They've been granted unwavering powers and privileges."

"Doesn't matter what they've been granted," said Kya. "What they're doing is wrong, no matter what anyone says."

"And we want to show everyone why," Jon interjected. "They need to know."

"Come on," Kya said to Gomez. "You must have taken similar risks at other jobs before, yeah? I mean, all we need is for you to come in with a few others, start some harmless shit like a silly fight or something and then wait for these assholes to pounce and get them like you've been known to do."

"Yeah," said Jon. "And we know you'll get the best footage possible. And, once word gets out, we'll prove that whoever took over the club has led it down a worse path. They all need to go. They all need to disappear."

"Exactly."

"We restore order," said Jon. "Bring the club back to its former glory."

Gomez cackled. Jon thought highly about his plan. It made sense. Everything they wanted from Gomez fit in well with whatever lay ahead. And yet, after Gomez heard this, he smiled.

"Restore order?" Gomez's question was followed by an obnoxious chuckle.

"Yes," said Kya.

"To a nightclub?" Gomez asked.

Jon inspected Gomez as he sat. "Yes."

"No offense," said Gomez, "but restoring order to a place whose sole purpose is to serve people booze and get them so fucked up they dance to bad music isn't exactly known as admirable work, in my opinion. It's not why me and my team set out to do what we do."

"I'm sorry, but I thought you set out to hold people accountable for their actions," Kya interceded. "To stop people who abused their power and who hurt the people incapable of defending themselves."

Once Kya said this, the Satanist-surveillance expert was forced into awestruck silence.

"It's no different," Kya said to Gomez. "In fact, it couldn't be more the same."

Jon's chin moved like he was giving Kya a nod. However, right now, both of them only wanted to hear one thing from Gomez. Before, Jon was just waiting for it. Now, it was Jon who was demanding it.

"Will you help us?" Jon's voice beckoned.

He was running out of patience and also out of time. Gomez was to be the Doormen's ace-in-the-hole. It was exactly what they needed to defeat Irons and his OverTakers. After Jon spoke to Gomez, he wiped his mouth with his wrist.

"I'm in," Gomez said. "I'm way in. Just need to know one thing."

"What?" asked Jon.

He liked what Gomez had to offer. He liked even more how confident and capable he presented himself to be.

"When do I start?" Gomez asked Jon and Kya. Afterward, Kya pulled her shirt against her chest and straightened the fabric.

"Right now," she said. "You start...*right now*."

CHAPTER 9
HERE THEY COME

THE ONLY WAY OUT WAS IN, AND THE ONLY WAY IN was to go through Michael Irons.

Until now, the man who owned his own agency, OT Protection Specialists, which might not have been real—its actual name was OverTakers—was brought into The Conquistador to be an *outside observer* and to introduce a *new bouncing team*. Since its former security was proven untrustworthy, the Commission gave Irons permission to take over as the club's new cooler and install his new team.

Yet, as Irons knew from the beginning, this was not a coincidence.

He has been setting his sights on The Conquistador for some time now. Therefore, to obtain control over the club, Irons had orchestrated a set up by giving one of the bouncers a weapon he was not permitted to use. Then, this bouncer was caught red-handed, which caused a catastrophic failure among the enclave. After this occurred, this one bouncer left the club while the remaining Doormen were stripped of their duties and demoted to a second-rate position within the club itself.

It just so happened that the Doorman Irons chose to betray was the same one he'd been preying on now. To do this, Michael Irons began a courtship with Jon's mother. For the longest time, Jon had come to enjoy being around Irons. But, once he had his mom in bed, Irons lost interest and began pursuing other options. Although all of this was part of Irons's savage plan, it was nothing compared to what he really wanted. And, what Irons really wanted was to have the Doormen completely exiled from The Conquistador. He wanted to become the new head of its security and take complete control over the legendary place. And, if this was something Irons received, then he could also access what was hidden inside the club itself, including the club's most notorious valued items: *its ciphers*.

Irons would acquire the club's greatest treasure, the glory so many wanted.

He would have access—unlimited access—and so he would have power.

While the Commission saw Irons only as a temporary solution, Irons believed he was the planned successor of the club. All he needed was approval from the Keeper and to be told his men were the better security unit. Once this became official, Irons would usurp them all one at a time.

What Irons refused to accept was how The Conquistador was not for sale.

He knew Larry Thomas would never give his club to him or to anyone. And yet, the greatest form of protection for any nightclub was its reputation. The Conquistador was supposed to be the best club in New

York City. Should anything happen to alter this, then the entire business would collapse.

This was but another piece to Irons's plan.

Pushing aside the traditional ways of doing things, Irons had replaced it with his way. Since he was the man in charge of security, he had more authority. And he was using every part of it to control as much of it as he could while he could.

As of now, he was winning.

However, The Conquistador was changing and it was changing fast. Michael Irons was implementing a wide variety of changes. All of them were happening right under everyone's noses, and there was nothing anyone could do to stop it.

What he was overseeing now was only the beginning.

Irons might be in control of security but he also had another trick up his sleeve. In order to ensure Larry and Addison were both gone too, Irons had access to another secret that few knew of.

Larry Thomas might be the owner of The Conquistador but he had not been on the floor in years.

Why? It was because Larry Thomas was...*weak*.

More so, Larry Thomas was dying.

All Michael Irons wanted to do was accelerate this process. What Irons wanted more was to get Larry completely out of the picture by proving he was just as unfit as his Doormen.

Larry's illness made this all the more possible. Larry Thomas was no longer needed because his mind was no longer stable. What was affecting the one great owner of this once-great institution was a disease of the mind. It disrupted Larry's memory and understanding because Larry Thomas was afflicted Alzheimer's.

And, throughout these last few weeks, a great toll had been taken on the great club owner.

Since the OverTakers first came into this, Larry's condition had only worsened. He didn't approve of the Showdown, but he was not in his right mind to do anything. Together, Addison and his wife had done whatever they could to shelter people from the truth. Therefore, Addison had been making all the decisions because he was the only one who knew how to do it.

And it was this one weakness that Irons would seek to exploit.

His security was fine because they were efficient. And they were efficient because they never hesitated. Tonight should be no different. Tonight, Irons invited Larry to come into the club for observations. If there was nothing wrong with him. And, as he had proclaimed himself to be, there was no reason why he shouldn't come and show himself.

Irons was aware of this. It was a power move in order to once again gain the upper hand. With Addison's hands now tied, he was keeping a great secret hidden from the Commission. But this was not a crime. But, should Addison reveal the real reason why Larry Thomas would not be present here tonight, then he would also be exposing another of The Conquistador's secrets.

He would be relinquishing control of the entire club.

Once Larry was on the floor, Irons's plan was simple. He would bring Larry to the second level and he would have him stand there in front of the balcony.

Then, Irons would guide Larry along very slowly. Irons would have the club welcome Larry. He was going to put him in the spotlight, which Larry had not been in for quite some time. He was going to do this without Addison's approval or knowledge, and then...then he was going to let him speak.

While everyone recorded the infamous owner, they would be unaware of his condition.

None knew of Mr. Thomas's broken mind. Still, once he opened his mouth, they would see just how fragile and incompetent he was. Larry's past was also significant. He was a man from a different time. He harbored his fair share of prejudices and outdated ideas, no doubt about that. He was not racist or sexist or any like that, but he was most certainly not a conventional man. Among all the flashing lights and constant noises, Larry's environment would be unstable.

This was all part of Irons's plan.

He would remove Larry, and the best way to do that was to have the owner remove himself. Irons would put Larry on a stage filled with humiliation and despair. The only person who could stop Irons from succeeding would be Addison himself.

And yet, Addison didn't know about it.

In fact, there was nothing Addison was aware of now.

Everything that happened at The Conquistador was going through Irons now.

He was the *new* cooler, so to speak.

There was a lot about Addison Krowe that Michael Irons didn't like. However, what he did enjoy was his taste in décor. Whenever Irons was inside Addison's office, he felt like a baller. Addison's space was not only well decorated, it included top-shelf booze and other luxury items most men adored.

Irons didn't just enjoy it, no...he relished in it.

Irons poured himself a tall drink. Right now, the doors were almost open. Irons had sent for Larry Thomas nearly two hours ago. He said he needed him. He said the club needed him. All he was doing now was waiting for him to get here. Fifteen minutes later, there was a knock at the door. Irons barked at whoever was there to come inside. One of his men, an OverTaker in a suit, stepped in.

"Sir, he's here."

Downing the last of his drink, Irons replied with a smirk so enchanting it nearly put butterflies in his stomach. "Good. Bring him in."

"Will do."

"Oh..." Irons raised his hand to point. "Make sure the Doormen are completely off the floor. Make sure they're all below today," Irons barked his orders. "Setting up the owner of the club would be the nail in The Conquistador's coffin." All of this was true. Once Larry Thomas was out of the picture, all roads would lead to Irons and only to Irons. "I don't want them anywhere near the main levels, is that understood?"

"Yes," said the OverTaker in the doorway. "I will, sir, but they're actually already there." Irons's lips puckered. He let the flavor of the Scotch linger a little longer on his tongue.

"They are?" he asked.

"Went down as soon as their shift started," replied the other OverTaker. "Guess they're getting used to their new place around here, huh?"

Irons should have felt good about this. It would

seem the Doormen were beginning to adjust to the new hierarchy the club had established. Hearing this now, Irons's expression was not one of enthusiasm or happiness. No, rubbing his jaw, Irons was fighting back some unwanted thoughts and feelings. He was battling his suspicions as well as discomfort. "Maybe," said Irons. "Just keep your eyes on them. We did take their club from them, you know? They might seem like they're okay with it, but I assure you...they're not."

The OverTaker nodded. "I understand. We have an hour before the doors open. What do you want me to do with Mr. Thomas?" Irons smacked his lips together again and then he placed the glass down on the desk that was not his.

"Nothing," he said. "Just...keep him out of sight, yeah? He's a crusty old fuck whose mind is slipping. He should be easy to move. Besides, he's so heartbroken about what's happened with the Commission and possibly losing his club, he'll want to get away from everything as soon as possible."

"Right, and what about his son-in-law, you know... Krowe, the cooler? He doesn't know."

Among the OverTakers, Addison did have a reputation.

Everyone who worked under Michael Irons knew of his knowledge, his skill, and above all else...*his past*. He was, after all, *older* and someone who worked at The Conquistador and helped to make it into what it is today. He was smart. In some ways, he was smarter than Irons. Although he'd fallen in line the same as everyone else did, Irons was aware about keeping a close watch.

None of the Doormen were ever to be underestimated, especially not tonight.

"Keep him down below like everyone else. Guard the stairs. Keep a watch, yes?"

The OverTaker nodded. Everything Irons said was clear and direct, the same as it always was. "Anything else?"

"No," Irons finally said. He relinquished his status as the one giving orders. "Goodbye."

The OverTaker left and Irons was now alone.

Behind Addison's desk was the window that overlooked the entire club. From here, Irons could see almost every sector of The Conquistador. The bar, the dance floor, the stage, the other bars, VIPs, the DJ booth, and all the various sections and subsections. All of this was observable from this one standing position.

Despite the panoramic view, Irons could not see absolutely everything. There were some areas of the club not meant to be seen or accessed. Therefore, Irons could not take The Conquistador's most valued treasure until the club was his to behold.

As Irons was remembering now, *rules are rules*.

Seeing his glower reflecting off the glass, Irons was aware how this club was something he had longed to have for a very long time. Should everything tonight happen the way he planned, then it would be his.

It was only a matter of time before it was.

———

Before Larry Thomas was summoned by Michael Irons, Jon, and Kya had arrived at the club and they had come together. Once there, they entered using the backdoor/secret entranceway guarded by Jamal himself. At the time, it was still early. The Doormen, however, were ordered to report to The Conquistador during more unconventional times now. It was strange to be at the club when it was still light out. But, since they weren't the main security anymore, all were required to complete other tasks at new times. Under Addison's leadership, his bouncers were to report for a briefing, that is, to check their outposts and places and grab some coffee before their shift.

Now working in the lower levels, the Doormen's place was the Annex, where the more blasted, untamed customers went. There, he targeted the so-called *others* who didn't quite meet The Conquistador's newest criteria. They worked as bar hands, loading and reloading trucks while dealing with the more *lighter customers*.

They helped servers, cleared the bar, and did some cleaning too.

In the end, it couldn't be more degrading.

Since the Doormen lost their top security positions, this was how they spent most of their time. And so, when Jon and Kya arrived early, Jamal was mystified. Standing on the other side of this secret door, Jamal looked at Jon and Kya, stunned.

He didn't expect them to be here now.

"Yo, what are you two doing here? We don't start for another hour."

Right now, Jamal was wearing a black shirt that extended down below his waist. His head was shaved. There were some new gray hairs growing around his ears and neck. Jon didn't know how old Jamal was, but he assumed he was older than most.

"I know," said Jon. "Sorry, but can we come inside? We need to see Addison right away."

Jamal looked both ways and made sure no one was near. Jon already knew there wasn't.

"Yeah," he said. "Come on, before someone sees."

"Right." Jamal held the door opened and Jon and Kya scampered in.

Hurrying down a narrow staircase with pin-ups of The Conquistador's old days, Jon glanced at these pictures. This was where few went or even fewer had seen. Once they were down the steps, Jon found himself in another hallway just as drab and just as dreary as the one he passed.

It was a long walk to the Annex. Due to the club being empty, it didn't take long for Jon to arrive. He proceeded through a smaller dance floor with a smaller bar. Jon raced. His plan for bringing down the Over-Takers was still fresh in his mind and Kya was here to share it as well.

All Jon was hoping for was to tell Addison as quickly as possible. He was still the man in charge despite not having his original title or his original office. So long as Jon was here, at the club, Jon would always see him as the boss.

"*Owen!*" Jon yelled.

When Jon encountered Owen, he couldn't contain his excitement. He didn't even bother to try. "Yo, Jon, what's happening? What'chu doin' here, man?"

"Here to see Addison. What are you doing here?"

"Nothing," said Owen. "Got a message this morning sayin' someone needed to be here to stack the bar down here. One upstairs is taking everybody's attention. Big night tonight. We're hosting some serious clientele."

"Really?" Addison asked.

"How serious?" asked Kya.

"Not sure," said Owen. "But Taker's will be all over the floor today. That you can be God-certain of."

"Okay," Jon said. A big night at The Conquistador, in whatever capacity, was ideal for the Doormen's current course of action. "Where's Addison?" Jon asked. "We need to talk to him."

"I..." Owen scanned the Annex in search of Addison. Jon was about to look too. When he pivoted, he felt a chill crawling up his arm. It was not a weird or scary chill. No, the chill felt was actually very enticing.

In fact, it was pretty fucking solid.

"Speak of the devil, and he shall appear." Despite lending this ominous phrase, Addison still managed to sound heroic.

Wearing a suit with no tie, Addison's jacket was opened and he was blushing, not smiling.

Was he happy to see Jon and Kya?

Jon liked to think this was true. Jon also liked to think Addison was aware of why they were here and what they were planning to do.

"Addison, you're here?' Addison looked at Jon with his head turned.

"Where else would I be?" Addison replied.

It was true. There was no other place Addison could be other than here.

"Right," said Jon. "Look, we need to talk to you. We should go to the Speakeasy."

"*The Speakeasy*?" Addison said with a grin.

"It's the room in the back," specified Jon. "You know, the one..." Jon pointed at a room near the bar. It was where the Doormen were known to congregate.

Now Jon assumed Addison knew what space he was referring to. He should have, but he didn't.

"I know what room it is," said Addison. "Just didn't hear anyone refer to it in that way."

Jon didn't care. To him, this was the room.

"Doesn't matter," Jon said. "Can we meet there?"

"Yes," said Addison. Jon hurried into the room and held the door open for Kya and Addison. When entering this Speakeasy, Kya touched Jon on his arm. It was her way of thanking Jon. He smirked at Kya as she stepped inside.

The room was dark like a smoking room. Although this was technically the Doormen's breakroom, before it was this, it was a place where people drank and played cards back in the day.

When inside, Jon closed the door slowly behind him.

"Okay," Jon said. "Kya and I have been talking, and well, we connected with someone who I think we can use tonight."

"Tonight?" said Addison.

"Yes," said Jon. "Someone who can help us beat Irons and his gang of bastard betrayers."

"Right," said Addison. Still listening, Jon could see Addison was not enthused or interested. He was downcast, like he hadn't slept in days. Maybe this was the reason why he was losing interest. This didn't matter to Jon. His plan was in motion and he needed Addison on board. He needed all the Doormen on board.

"I have someone who is going to help us," added Kya. "He's a friend. We were talking to him today."

"Yeah," said Jon. "His name is..."

"Gomez," interrupted Addison.

Shocked, Addison's deductive skills never ceased to amaze Jon. Hearing Addison's question, Jon eyed the cooler closely. "What?"

"You knew?" asked Kya, less shocked than Jon. She grinned when she heard Addison's inquiry.

"Of course, I knew. You think this is the first time you mentioned him?" asked Addison. "Kya, you're always quick to speak about those you know. Sometimes, I can't get you to stop."

"And you mentioned Gomez to Addison?" Jon wanted to know when and where this happened.

Was Gomez a closer friend than she let Jon believe?

"Only once, a long time ago, when we were first shut down."

"She said she had a friend who could help. Mentioned him then," said Addison. "I thought it was only a matter of time before she called for reinforcements."

"Then you agree," Kya said to Addison. "He's a good contact to have, yes?"

Addison was by the bar. He grabbed himself a Carlsberg and had a drink. "He's the best."

"So...you know what he does?" Jon asked Addison. "Why we need him."

Addison nodded. "I do, and I knew you would be the one to find him."

"How?"

"Well, friends look out for each other," said Addison, "and I've been looking out for you since you got back."

"You mean, you've been following me?"

Addison took another drink and looked at Jon with little to no expression. "Just been keeping my eyes open." Whenever Addison answered using open-ended phrases, Jon didn't know how to interpret them, whether it was care or something else entirely. Whatever the reasons for why Addison knew, it didn't change what Jon knew to be true at this moment.

And, at this moment, what they needed to do was man up and beat the OverTakers once and for all.

"Well, open your eyes," said Kya, "to take down these assholes who've taken over our club, we're going to need to spring a trap we know for certain they'll fall for."

"Right," said Jon. He jumped into explaining what he and Kya had planned for tonight's mission. In Jon's mind, it was called *Project Overthrow* because he was going to overthrow the OverTaker regime.

"What we know about Irons is he's too quick to react. He likes to use violence first and foremost. He doesn't care about any of the tactics of the Doormen trade."

"Sure does," said Addison.

"Yes," said Jon. "We also know that they have other motives. They don't really care about the club, so they don't really care about its principles of inclusivity, equality, and being a place for everyone."

"No doubt," said Addison, still following.

"They'll do anything to protect their prestigious new clientele."

"And get a little rough with anyone who they think doesn't belong," added Jon.

"Exactly," said Kya. "And there's no one who's more opposite to the new people Irons is letting in. He's different, doesn't belong and so, when they see him, they'll be more inclined to get rough with him. They'll go too far."

"The only way the Takers will get rough with a client is if that client starts trouble. You want to ask Gomez to start trouble for us, for our cause?" asked Addison. "If he does, he'll be taking his life into his own hands. No one knows what might happen under those circumstances."

"Yeah, well, he knew the risks when he signed up for this gig," said Jon. "But our plan doesn't involve anyone breaking any rules, not this time. Our plan involves Gomez going where he's not supposed to go."

"And where is that exactly?" Addison asked.

"Main floor," said Kya. "Near the VIP, where all the older, wealthier clients are located."

"We get him into this section, force the Over-Takers to come, and when Gomez refuses, they'll go too far, and that's when Gomez and his team will start recording. They get these bastards on their phones and then put that shit online, and then voilà! The Conquistador has abusive fucking bouncers running the show, and now we have the proof we need to force them out!"

Jon explained this as best he could.

"And you know how touchy people are with phones these days," said Kya. "You can keep them, but they're an extra charge. It's ugly and it's discriminatory, and not what The Conquistador is supposed to be about."

"Exactly," said Jon. "Besides, Gomez is a solid video journalist. A good one too! Knows how to capture the truth. The plan is to get him inside and then, while acting like any other difficult guest, force these assholes to go too far, like they always do."

"Right," said Addison. As of now, he wasn't quite sold on this plan.

Therefore, Addison didn't comment. His lips coiled and he sipped his beer. Jon knew Addison's mannerisms almost as well as he knew his own. His downcast expression, combined with frequent sighing, all showed how unimpressed he really was.

It was this, or he had a new, better plan of his own.

When Addison replied, Jon found himself instantly reassessing his plan. It made sense at first, but now it didn't.

"There seems to be too many variables here," said Addison. "There's too much that you're relying on to happen that might not. The OverTakers might go too far, sure, but if they hurt Gomez, and he can capture on film, it might be too synchronous, too far-reaching a strategy. Security will be doing nothing but their jobs, and Irons is not the type to fall into a fucking trap. He's smarter than you think. What makes you think they'll even hurt Gomez? You think they hurt everyone here? They might be rough, but they're not insane. And today, given that you're back in the picture, Jon...they're going to be extra careful, more than they've ever been before."

This was the last word heard from Addison before the cooler finished his drink.

Jon rubbed his temples. Although tired and utterly done with all this thinking and considering, he was also beginning to feel more frustration, but not with Addison. No, Jon was angry with himself. This was the only way to stop Irons and prove the corruption happening at his place of work. This was all Jon wanted, but it would be nothing without Addison's accepting it as true. It was not that Jon needed Addison to agree, it's only that he felt better whenever Addison felt better.

Nonetheless, Jon insisted. He stood by his proposition. He was more than willing to defend it.

"They will go too far when they find out who Gomez *really* is."

"And who is he?"

"He's a surveillance expert, and he's young, and I know Michael when it comes to all this. He damn well hates all of it. As soon as anyone sees someone like Gomez getting into *his* club, he'll profile and push aside. But, when Gomez refuses to stand down because he hasn't done anything wrong, Irons *will* go after him and he *will* go too far."

Jon insisted on this rationale.

Emphasizing certain words, Jon believed in what he was saying and what he knew to be true. Gomez was the right person for the job. There was no doubt in Jon's mind about this. He had more to say, more support to give so he continued and did not hold back.

"Gomez knows how to make himself a target. He knows what it feels like to be pushed."

"Not only that," said Kya. "He's also something else too."

A jolt stung Jon's wrists and trailed up to his shoulders. Now, Kya was about to reveal something new, yet Jon didn't know anything else about Gomez. He didn't say more besides what he had said already.

Was there more? If so, what else was there? Was this not enough?

"What?" queried Addison.

"Well, he might be a surveillance king," said Kya,

"he's also something vital to our plan for taking out these bastard OverTakers."

Jon honed his focus. Everything Kya said sounded interesting. It was also valid. Still, Jon was waiting for her to say more. He needed her to say more.

"Do tell," said Addison.

Jon cracked his knuckles and leaned over the bar. He wanted to know too.

"Well," said Kya, "he's also a thief."

"What?" asked Jon.

"A thief?" asked Addison.

Jon's heart pounded. Blood rushed to his face. His hands felt numb. Jon's back was tight. He felt locked up and sore. Kya said nothing about Gomez's other career or if this was even true, or real.

"Yes," said Kya.

"And how exactly does a thief help us with our situation?"

"Because," said Kya, "if there's one group more threatening to our new security team, it's a thief."

"How so?" Addison was now asking more questions, which was suitable in Jon's opinion. He also had lots of questions.

"Soon as he enters the club, Irons is going to ask who Gomez is," explained Kya. "They'll want to know how we got inside and, most importantly, *who* let him inside."

Jon circled back to his original plan. What he had before was good, but what Kya was suggesting now might be better. What Kya had was so golden it was almost platinum.

"Right," said Addison, following along.

"And when they realize he's a thief," said Kya,

"they're going to want to know who let him in and who let him in will be..."

"*Us*," said Jon, already captivated. This plan didn't just pique Jon's interest, it also made him excited and happy.

"And because he's a thief that *we* let in," said Kya, "they'll think..."

"He's here to steal something," said Jon.

"Exactly," said Kya. "They'll attack him based on that one assumption. They'll profile, which is like the biggest no-no in the bouncing world."

"Classic set up. Classic foil. Classic trap." At this moment, Jon was exhilarated.

All he wanted to do was reach out and wrap his arms around Kya and never let go. If there was ever a time when he wanted her so badly it hurt, it was now.

"It's after that happens, he'll go too far, and then Gomez will catch these bastard red-handed. It's a great plan and it's going to work."

As assertive as Kya was, Jon was looking only at Addison. He hoped his expression would change from firm to pleased, but then after Kya outlined their new course of action, Addison's face remained the same as it was before.

He was still not convinced.

"Look, I know how it sounds, Addison," Jon said. "Believe me, this plan isn't going to work without everyone in it with us, and everyone...means you too. We need to stop Michael. He's a liar and he'll do anything to see this club fall into his hands. We need to find him and stop him while we still can."

"His hands, huh?" Addison said to Jon. "You mean the club you left, didn't care for?"

Addison's job always was The Conquistador.

It was about him protecting everything it stood for, especially *its secrets*.

The Conquistador was Addison's life because he'd spent so much of his life preserving its position as the best club in all of New York. He also had a way of solidifying it as more than a club, but a brotherhood.

Sometimes, Jon felt like it was too close to a cult.

Having already distributed his fair share of guilt, Addison had a way of testing the loyalty among Doormen. As soon as you began working, you were volunteering to protect something for all time. Jon didn't see this as his future and yet here he was, making sure that it remained one.

"The club...you left?" After Addison said this, Jon remembered what Lieutenant Dan said to him a while back. It was the something that validated the reason that Jon decided to come back in the first place.

"I'm *still* here."

This was the best response Jon could give at this moment. He wasn't sure if it sounded sensitive or legitimate or neither. Still, he believed every word. Jon hoped Addison did too. Always, he hoped Addison trusted him and believed in his truth. Like so much else, Jon didn't know if this was the case.

Still, Jon pretended like it was.

"All right," Addison said. "Then let's start planning. Let's beat these bastards once and for all."

CHAPTER 10
THE SHUFFLE SWEEP

EVERYONE WHO WORKED FOR THE CONQUISTADOR was part of its online group chat.

Generally, this was how everyone communicated with one another. It had been some time since Jon joined. He sent a message that he and Kya both received. They read it at the same time.

> Everyone report in at 8 tonight. We're going to war.

The message was Addison's and it gave Jon goosebumps, but the good kind. It had been some time since Jon read the word *war*, but the word had a specific meaning for someone like him. The word meant it was time to fight and that's all Jon wanted to do.

─────

With time to kill, Jon and Kya didn't know what they were supposed to do.

There were only a few hours until their shifts and neither one wanted to go back to their respective homes. They were hungry and amped, with lots on their minds and much time to settle in and think. They stopped in Manhattan to grab a quick bite from a pizza parlor they were both fans of.

They talked, yet it was Kya who invited Jon back to her place.

When she asked Jon if he wanted to, he almost choked on his slice.

Until now, Kya never asked Jon to come to her apartment. They spent most of their time eating at restaurants, meeting up for casual dates, and enjoying each other's company in more conventional places. But, should someone ask you to come back to their place, the implications can be intense.

Sometimes it was for a drink, for a coffee, or tea, or some other beverage.

Yet, whenever a girl asks you to come back, it could be for other reasons—physical reasons. Jon couldn't be sure why Kya asked the Marine to come back now, but he chose not to assume. Playing it cool, Jon shrugged. "*Sure.*"

"'K," said Kya. "Let's get going then."

Kya took Jon's hand and pulled him down to the subway station. Kya was so joyous she sauntered while Jon hurried to catch up. He was also excited. Jon didn't want Kya to know how excited he was but the ride to Kya's, he felt, would be short and easy.

Jon continued to review all the different times whereby Kya had referenced the place where she lived.

Jon had only driven her there. Not once had he

visited. While he was looking forward to seeing it, as soon as Kya suggested it, Jon's heart began to race. He could feel blood rushing to his face and then down to his hands. Suddenly stimulated, Jon wasn't sure what the implications were behind Kya's unexpected request.

Kya, however, hadn't said a single word the entire trip. All she did was smile and peep at Jon. She was waiting for him to smile too. While Jon was smiling on the inside, there was an allure to Kya that was beginning to stir.

It was becoming more intense the closer Jon came to Kya's home.

———

The apartment Kya lived in was decent, but Jon felt anywhere was better than where he lived. He was still at home with his mother in Queens. Though it was a comparably nice living space, it was not exquisite or elegant like Kya's. Her place was clean. It was fashioned with white bricks and included an arched entryway to go along with its Romanic motif. Jon had seen the outside of this building before, but the inside was just as he imagined. Sleek and immaculate, Jon and Kya walked along the clean marble and up to the building's elevator. Still silent, Kya wore jeans and a black top, exposing her naval while Jon's heart beat faster and faster.

In his mind, Jon envisioned what was going to happen.

He had thought of this many times before but didn't know for certain if it was going to happen tonight. He and Kya were an item for almost four months. It was off and on, with some wide breaks in between, but to say they were a *couple* wasn't exactly true.

Jon couldn't help but ask if this was the reason she was bringing Jon to her apartment now?

Was this to make their title complete and maybe something else more official?

When Kya opened the door, Jon smelled rich scents of cinnamon and honey. It was so enticing that Jon began to fantasize about having a big bite from a delicious slice of cake. The kitchen was next to the door and Jon watched Kya stroll to her refrigerator. The appliances, from what Jon could see, were nice too. Truthfully, everything Jon saw was nice. Among spanking new future, in a tastefully decorated living room, Jon liked everything even more when Kya asked him to have a seat on her couch.

"Sure," said Jon.

As soon as he plopped himself down on Kya's nice sofa, the Marine found himself feeling instantly rested and very comfortable. Jon glanced at a picture on Kya's table. It was of a person Jon didn't know, a person he wanted to know but was not yet told about.

"Is that your mom?" Jon was staring at the picture. He held its frame and, like Kya, the woman also had dark hair and the same color eyes.

"Yeah," said Kya. Stepping to the couch, she handed Jon a bottle of water.

"Her name's Amanda, lives in Long Island."

"*Hmm,*" said Jon. "Don't remember you mentioning her."

"Yeah, well, not much to say about her, really," said Kya. "Good mom, smart woman, kind and sweet, you know all that stuff."

"Right." Jon placed the picture back onto the table and drank from his bottle. "You don't talk about your dad much either."

Kya gawked at Jon. With a clenched jaw, Jon could see he plucked on a sensitive strand he shouldn't have. He could sense that maybe it was a bad situation with Kya's dad and he shouldn't bring it up again, so he didn't.

Kya sat next to Jon and nudged so close to Jon that her breast touched his shoulder.

"So...there's a reason why I asked you to come up here," Kya said to Jon.

He trembled. "Yeah?"

"Yeah," said Kya, shooting Jon a flirtatious gaze. Jon continued to quake. "I would tell you," Kya said. She pushed out her chest and popped her breasts as if she knew Jon was staring at them. In all honesty, he kinda was. "But I think you already know."

Jon gulped. He was aroused, no doubt, but still... kept cool. Kya guzzled the water and touched Jon's shoulder. She was gentle, and suddenly, Jon couldn't think of anything but holding her, pressing his body into hers before stripping off all his clothes.

Jon wasn't shy. In fact, working at The Conquistador had boosted his confidence by ample amounts. No longer was he the short guy he was back in high school. He was now a former Marine, badass, jacked, and someone who knew how to fight. He lost some of his leg but he had gained much else in return. Jon had transformed himself into a ruthless, capable combatant. He knew how to wield a knife and how to shoot a gun.

He knew all this, but so far as being with a woman was concerned, it had been quite a long time for Jon.

Actually, Jon had slept with only one other woman in his life. It was his girlfriend, back when he was in his early-twenties. It had been a long time since Jon laid next to a woman but how many men did Kya sleep with was not known. She never told Jon and probably never would, but it was wrong to assume someone who was attractive automatically had multiple sex partners. Still, Jon couldn't imagine Kya's count being lower than his.

"Are you sure you want to do this?" With Kya asking for Jon's permission, she was so close to him now, he could feel her breath on his neck. Chills ensconced Jon's stiff torso, and all the blood left in his body immediately shot down.

Jon didn't have the strength to answer.

In response to Kya's question, the Marine nodded.

Now consenting, Kya climbed on top of Jon and rested on his lap. Putting her hands on his quivering cheeks, she held Jon for only a moment before pulling him in for a moist kiss. Jon gasped after feeling Kya's soft lips against his own. Going deeper, Kya's tongue grazed Jon's and his heart began to explode in his chest. While he fought to stay calm, it was easier than he thought.

Kya was being very, *very* gentle.

She continued to kiss Jon with a certain deepness that felt almost kind in its approach. Jon slid his hands along Kya's back and squeezed. Instantly, Jon was aware of Kya's experience. She knew exactly which buttons to push in order to enhance Jon's pleasure epicenter.

Everything she was doing, she was doing well, and she just kept going.

After kissing Jon, Kya inserted her hands under his

waistband. Her fingers felt so warm Jon exhaled before clasping his hands even tighter. Stroking Jon's throbbing penis, strong as he was, he held on for as long as he could, but things became exceedingly difficult once Kya removed her top. Her brassiere was pink and padded. It was awesome as it fit against her luscious breasts and Jon's leer was so powerful he thought his eyes were going to melt. It would seem that everything he had imagined had heightened into reality.

How Kya looked in Jon's mind did not compare to how she looked for real.

Bra off, Kya's breasts popped and her nipples were hard as baby toes. From there, Jon felt the full impact of uncontainable, undeniable desire. He was so stimulated he could barely see. When he and Kya switched from the sofa to bed, they tore off their clothes and didn't waste a second. As Kya pulled Jon, both fell onto the soft duvet and continued to engulf themselves in a storm of ceaseless, stirring passion. It was a moment Jon didn't want to end. As he sought to extend it for as long as he could, Jon kissed Kya harder and longer, and she did the same.

Now resting on Kya's sweaty body, Jon kissed her on the neck and chest.

Kya gasped.

Whatever Jon was doing, it was working. Kya's eyes popped and she moaned.

Now inside, all that was left to do was engage in the rhythmic pelvic thrusts and read each other's bodies for other cues and signs. Jon was a fairly observant individual. As soon as he penetrated, he surrendered all control over to Kya.

She would guide him the rest of the way.

At a gradual pace, Jon did his best to keep up and to last. Fortunately, he was doing better than he thought. He endured and just did his best to listen to what Kya was saying. If she moaned or her eyes glinted, it meant she was pleased and she wanted more.

Jon followed this direction and Kya did the same. They both moved with grace and ease, and the sensations Jon felt were absolutely astounding. He moaned to express his satisfaction and Kya's sounds were equal to Jon's.

Both were happy, and Jon had forgotten the joy of this kind of human expression, what it does to the body, and the effect it can have on the mind. Sex is the last untouched form of physical engagement—the greatest interaction two people can share. After, Jon's orgasm left him feeling weightless, it was made even more satisfying when Kya shouted louder.

Upon climax, Jon's eyes closed and a cyclone of tingles enveloped him like a shell.

His eyes went glassy and his body became lathered in sweat. The little light displayed in Kya's apartment shined off her body and Jon trembled. They spent almost an entire hour together. Once both had achieved that pinnacle of their sexual joy, Jon lay next to Kya like a deflated balloon. Breathing heavily, Kya's hair appeared disheveled and damp. Both were left empowered and stunned. Jon wanted only to sit in admirable silence.

He turned over and pulled Kya in.

Not saying a word, Jon had dreamed of this moment for too long. He imagined lying with Kya. He fantasized about having her and hoped one day he would, and now that moment had finally come. He would store every fraction of it and secure it into his memory for all time.

"Thank you," Jon said.

These were the only words he could muster. Kya lifted her head from the pillow and gazed. "*For what?*"

"For this," Jon said. "For, you know..."

"Oh, for what, for having sex with you?" Kya replied, so amused she chortled.

Jon was about to tell Kya the truth about how he really felt and why. He never thought he would have sex with a girl like her because girls like her were deemed as being unattainable. They were cut out only for high-value males and not war vets who lived at home with their mothers.

"For giving me the chance to just...be with you," said Jon.

"Uh, you're welcome," said Kya, unsure how to respond. Still, Jon didn't care. He was thankful, and he always would be for sex or anything else rarely given.

Kya placed her hand on Jon's chest. He wrapped his hand around Kya's brittle fingers and held them gently.

"I hope it was good for you."

"What?" said Kya. Sitting up, the sheet once covering Kya's chest slipped off. Breasts bare, she grabbed her bracelet off the nightstand and slipped it on her wrist.

Jon didn't care to get dressed. There was still time left before they had to go back to work.

"You know," said Jon. "The..."

Kya scoffed. "*The sex?*"

Jon nodded. He gulped and felt nervous but also embarrassed. "Yes."

"What are you talking about?" Kya asked. She crawled along the bed, still naked. "It was amazing."

"Oh?" Jon replied. He felt gratified. He didn't expect Kya to commend his efforts, but she had. "Good," Jon said. "Really good, but are you..."

"Am I what?" Kya barked.

"Being serious. I mean, you really did enjoy it... *right*?"

"Yeah, why...didn't you?"

"No, absolutely," said Jon. "Absolutely, I did. It's just...I've been told I'm..."

"You're what?" Kya was begging Jon to tell her now.

Jon looked at his leg. He had removed his prosthetic along with the rest of his clothes before sliding into bed. "Not the best at," he said, "you know, at *satisfying* someone else."

"And who told you that?"

"People," said Jon. "People I've known...in my past."

"People...as in other girls you've been with?"

Jon nodded. "Yeah. I mean, there weren't many," he said. "Actually..." Jon stammered. His level of embarrassment had reached an all-time high now. What he was about to say, he wasn't quite sure how to phrase.

"There was just *one*."

"One, huh?" Kya didn't seem too bothered by this notion. How many guys Kya had slept with, Jon had to assume, was a lot more than one.

"Yeah. Long time ago, and anyway," said Jon, "she said something to me before I left for the Marines, right before we broke up."

"Let me guess?" said Kya. "She said you sucked in the sack, huh?"

Jon's head moved side-to-side and he was recalling everything that happened back then. The girl Jon used to be with was attractive, no doubt, but she had a real mean streak. She knew how to cut people down and she cut Jon bad.

"Yeah," Jon said. "That's exactly what she said."

"Funny how so many think the bedroom is the only place that counts," said Kya. "They always think it's about how good you do in here and not out there, know what I mean?"

"What?" Jon asked. "You mean, you don't feel that way?"

"Well, I mean, yeah, I like sex, sure," Kya said. "I mean, yeah, I like it the same as everyone, and I want it too, no doubt, almost the same as everyone else wants it, but it's like anything else in life, really. You get better at it, you learn, and you figure it as you go, and that's pretty much it."

Jon's head continued to sway and he didn't know what else to say to the woman of his dreams. Kya was right.

"Guess not," Jon said.

"Still, I wouldn't worry about any of that now," said Kya. "We have bigger things ahead of us, as you know."

"Right," Jon nodded. "I do."

"And what better way to get a boost than a good old-fashioned pick-me-up *bang*?"

Jon giggled. Kya was curt, and often, Jon adored just how swift she could be.

"Can't think of anything better, actually," said Jon. Kya sat next to Jon, putting her bra back on. Jon took this as a sign he should get ready too.

He slipped out of Kya's bed, grabbed his prosthetic and shirt.

"Because there isn't anything better," said Kya. "Just use what you got now because tonight, it's going to be our last stand. Are you sure you're ready for it?"

"Yeah," Jon said, enjoying the confidence provided by Kya. "I am. I'm damn ready."

CHAPTER 11
STONE IN STREAM

WORK WAS CALLING TO BOTH KYA AND JON. AND, when he and Kya did arrive at The Conquistador, it was still early.

The parking lot was empty, but neither Kya nor Jon parked in the main lot. After the OverTakers gained control of The Conquistador, club employees were required to place their vehicles in an entirely separate parking lot. It was located across from the others, where there were fewer spaces and even fewer cars.

Jon and Kya both proceeded to enter from the same entrance.

Holding the door for Kya, she brushed Jon's arm and scurried down the steps. On their way to The Conquistador's Annex, this was where everyone was supposed to meet. Hopping along, in here, there was another hallway. It was wider and painted with The Conquistador's unique shade of red, which was carmine. Most of the club was gold, though...gold like a palace. The lights in the stairwell were all off now, but for some reason, the space next to it was bright.

It was bright because it was active, and it was active because it was occupied.

Jon hustled down the stairs without taking the time to look. However, no one's peripheral vision was sharper than Jon's. He'd gained this skill primarily in the Marines. He could see everything in the corner of his eye, and he could see him now.

Jon could see Irons clear as day.

"*Ah-hoi,*" Irons said to Jon, cheery almost to the point of cringing annoyance. "Look who's here, *back in the game*...I see?"

Jon slowly turned to look at the man who was always messing with his head.

"Thought you already knew..." said Jon. "I work here again."

"I did hear," said Irons, "but did you forget, I'm the one in charge of all things now. Sure you knew that, didn't you...Marine?"

"No," Jon glared at Michael Irons. Slowly, he turned to face the deceitful swine who played him and his mom. "You're just in charge of security," Jon said. "You might control who guards, but you're damn sure not in charge of guarding the door, at least not all of them."

"Sure," said Irons. "Sure. Sure."

Jon looked Irons up and down and his lips curled in disgust. If Jon could strike him without consequences, then Jon couldn't count the times he would have chosen to do this to this man. So smug and so confident, Jon couldn't wait to expose Irons for the menace he truly was. Yet, why Irons wanted to talk to Jon now made the Marine feel uncomfortable.

He remembered how Irons was an expert in reading

people. If he did choose to talk to you, it was because he was trying to understand you. He wanted to see what was truly going on inside your head. And, if there was something, then he would no doubt use it against you.

This was his signature. It was his greatest weapon.

"And you're here now?" Irons asked Jon. "So early, it would seem."

"Got some work to do," Jon defended. He stopped looking at Irons and his head shifted as he stared at the stairs. There was no sign of Kya anywhere. The Annex had cleared and what Jon needed was to get downstairs and execute the plan both he and Kya created.

"Do you now?" asked Irons with his arms crossed.

Irons crept closer to Jon, who didn't move a single muscle.

On the surface, Jon's rigid demeanor made him seem utterly petrified. Stiff as a plywood, he couldn't look at Irons and any change to his appearance would reveal Jon's hatred. Jon was fairly good at hiding how he felt, but he was no expert.

No, Kya knew how Jon felt about her within the first five minutes of their initial conversation. The Marines wasn't a place where one fought to keep their thoughts hidden. Such a skill was dominated by the people working in the CIA. Jon was certainly not part of this group. No way he was even close to CIA material.

"Yeah," Jon said, looking down the stairs. "And I need to go now."

"Good," said Irons. "Good to see you're back to working hard. I think Betsy would be proud to know her son didn't desert his duties, even if there was a time when that's exactly what he did."

When Irons said this to Jon, the Marine wanted to drive his fist straight through Irons's chest. "Don't you dare say her name."

"Still bitter, are you?" asked Irons. Jon glowered. Yes, he was still fucking bitter. "I assume...she's well then?" Irons asked again.

"She's fine," Jon snapped, "but then again, how would you feel if you were in love with a man who was only interested in you because he wanted to gain access into a nightclub?"

"Sure," said Irons. "I'll admit, it was a dirty move, but then again, how would your mother feel if she knew her only son was working in a place that was not what it appeared to be? Does she even know you don't work at a nightclub? Well, not *only* a nightclub."

Jon didn't answer.

He didn't because Jon was tired of defending The Conquistador or thinking about the reasons why he'd chosen to return to it. He knew well by now what the club really was, and to say Jon didn't care wasn't exactly true. He did care. In fact, Jon cared so much that he came back to preserve The Conquistador's valued principles and ideology. Most importantly, he wanted to preserve its *abilities* and *truth*.

"She knows only what she needs to know. She knows who I am and now you do too."

"I do," said Irons. "In fact, I know...*it all*."

Jon's impulse was to scoff at this statement. Irons was arrogant. He saw himself as this all-knowing, all-encompassing force. He liked to think he understood the club, the industry, and the truth. Irons believed he knew and understood all things, but what he didn't know was what was ahead of him. No, Irons was not prepared for what the Doormen had planned.

"Guess so," said Jon.

"And I do have something for you."

Irons marched toward Jon.

At this moment, time was everything to the Marine. Jon had to convene with the other Doormen soon, and Irons was interfering in the process. Whether it was intentional or accidental, Jon couldn't tell. What he knew for certain, however, was how much he hated everything there was to know about Irons. He hated this man right down to his fucking core.

"In the next few weeks, there will likely be some changes made to this place."

"Changes as in...you *leaving*?" asked Jon.

Irons grinned like the retched puke that he was. He stood so close to Jon he could see the disenchanting look in his *boss's* eyes.

"Perhaps. It all depends on the decision the Commission makes, whether or not they think that this club would be better as it was or to make some sweeping changes to ensure its future. Either way, The Conquistador will not be what it used to be. Newer things will happen. And, when new things come, Jon," Irons said, "you either jump on the moving train or you get left behind like everything else. Look, I know things have been intense, and I know you came back here because you wanted things to be different. Well, I can help you find something once this is all over and done, something a bit more...*permanent*."

"Hmm. Is this you...making me an offer there, Mike?" Jon never called Irons by his first name. He also never heard anyone refer to him as Mike, not even his mom did this. No, the very idea of doing this put Michael and Jon on an equal playing field. Irons might be the man in charge, but calling him *Mike* was no doubt an insult.

And Jon meant it as such.

"It's me telling you that the horizon is in sight now, the end is near, and it's you who will have to decide whether it stays the same...or whether it changes. You remember what your mother wanted," said Irons. "Don't you?"

Jon shut his eyes. The fact that Irons had the audacity to mention Jon's mom was cooking his very bones. Irons had no empathy for anything or anyone. He had no remorse for all his lying, cheating, and manipulation. Only a fool would believe anything Irons said now, and Jon was no fool.

"She didn't want you to be a bouncer forever," Irons said. "She didn't want you to tango with fools all your life. She wanted something better. And, under these possible club changes, maybe something better is waiting for you, but only *if* you're willing to show the courage your mom knew you had and do what's right."

"My mom knew things," Jon said, "and one thing she did for sure is...if she found out I was talking to you right now, she'd tell me to do only one thing."

"And what's that?" Irons asked, nearly laughing at the thought. "Spit in my face?"

"No," said Jon. "Not her style. She always advised me to be the bigger person in certain, more damaging situations."

Jon glanced at the stairs again so he could look at the Annex one more time. There, Jon could hear new voices. He knew there were other people down there, more Doormen. Now that he was done with Irons's line of questioning, Jon was free to move on.

"No, she'd just tell me to walk away and give you the cold shoulder, and maybe add in her favorite quote."

"Yeah? What's that?"

Jon nodded. "She'd say...kiss my fucking ass, you bastard."

Jon twitched his hips to give Irons his ass in a literal display of demeaning behavior. The quote was clear and direct, and so...Jon's time with Irons was now finished.

He was done.

———

Down below, the space was occupied.

More than this, it was crowded. *Filled.*

All the Doormen were present and Jon could see every last one of them: Danix, Li, Owen, Duncan, even Addison. As soon as Jon stepped into the Annex, everyone looked at him because Jon was the last to arrive. But, once he was here, Addison nodded.

"Shall we get started?"

Jon couldn't be sure if Addison was asking him or telling him. The Marine didn't care either way. He answered anyway.

"Yeah," he said. "*Let's begin.*"

The Doormen brigade was then told of the plan without anyone saying a single word about it. This was Addison's decision. No longer was he sure if their conversations were being listened to or not, but still, Addison outlined the entire plan and used only hand signals when he could.

All of this was done while Owen kept a close eye on the door.

"No one comes down," said Addison. "No one."

Owen did exactly as he was instructed.

None said a word while Addison whispered the rest of the plan. It was pretty simple and straightforward, although there were still a few lingering questions on Jon's mind. The most important detail was how the bouncers were supposed to split into two teams.

Team One consisted of Jon, Owen, and Li.

They were supposed to stay on the floor. They were also supposed to watch Irons and the rest of his Over-Taker clan while Gomez and his team set up the *sting*.

None disputed their roles.

"Okay," Jon said.

"Good," said Addison.

With the plan locked in, everyone took their positions. Addison walked to the back of The Conquistador. As he proceeded, Jon saw him check his watch.

"Keep your eyes open," Addison said to Jon. "You know how plans are. Sometimes, they work like they do on paper, but more often, once they're put into practice, well, you know how quickly things can change."

"Right," said Jon. "I do."

And this was all true.

No one understood how quickly things could change more than Jon. His entire life, he'd been forced to adapt to new settings, new things. Even after leaving the military, none of this changed for Jon. In fact, it only got worse.

"Will do."

"Just be careful, okay?" advised Addison.

Jon nodded.

So often in his life, he wasn't guided by a male figure. He had no father and he never spoke about how he longed for the guidance of one. Someone like Jon yearned for the influence of someone older, someone else he could count on.

Did he want a dad? Most definitely.

Did he cry because he didn't have one? *Absolutely not*.

Jon thought for a time that Michael Irons might fill this role. Part of Jon hoped he would. And yet, when Irons turned out to be a liar, this role went unfilled. Jon hated Irons because of this. He wanted to think of Addison as a father too. He was trustworthy and someone who came through for Jon whenever he needed him to. He let Jon back into The Conquistador. He sympathized with his motives and he understood them.

And yet, as Addison grabbed Jon's arm, he said something so caring and kind that Jon thought maybe he always had this figure in his life. Maybe Jon had a lot more than he thought.

He still had Lieutenant Dan and he still had Kya.

Jon had everything he needed. In fact, he always did.

And he would have had none of it if he didn't work at The Conquistador.

Remembering what Lieutenant Dan said about how a place and a cause are defined by the people who *serve* it, not by the people who *own* it.

America is sometimes owned and controlled by those who don't care about its power or its people. And this is something only people who truly serve their country know to be true.

Those are the people to whom Jon was loyal, not the powers above but the infinitely forgotten people below.

The Conquistador might have its secrets and those secrets might be a weapon, but its cause was the part of it that made incredible sense to Jon. It was something that, in his mind, was worth protecting. To this day, Jon still believed in it. So long as he did, then he would continue to fight for it.

"Careful is the name of the game," Jon said to Addison later.

Doing his best to remain calm, Jon assessed the situation. Grading it as much as possible, Addison tapped Jon on the shoulder.

"Good luck," Addison said. "And remember, hand signals only and minimal communication with the other Doormen."

Jon nodded. He understood. All of this was self-explanatory. The plan was unfolding now and the clock was ticking. Jon knew exactly what he had to do. "Got it."

"See you once the show's done," said Addison.

"Yeah," said Jon. "See you after the show."

"Now, let's show these bastards who runs shit here," said Addison. "This is our club, our kingdom, and no one is going to take it away from us!"

With all the Doormen there, all of them roared in unison. They only had so much time to be together before the OverTakers came to get them. It was to be their final unifying moment.

Jon ended it the best way he knew how.

"*Oorah.*"

Once a Marine, always a Marine.

———

The Doormen proceeded to their assigned positions. At this point, the club was exploding with monumental bursts of equal parts pretentiousness and annoyance. It was a stream of new clientele that left a bad taste in Jon's fucking mouth. The guests were in and everything was getting louder and louder. With the music turned loud, the drinks slinging as the OverTakers dominated the setting.

Poised almost everyone, they were almost double the size of the Doormen.

Still, it didn't mean they were as good. They weren't.

However, tonight, the OverTakers weren't dressed in their usual attire. Every member of The Conquistador's security team wore a three-piece gray suit. This made them stick out like sore thumbs as they wandered about the club, keeping a close eye on everyone.

Jon stayed by his post and looked dead ahead.

The first part of the plan was getting Gomez inside. As of now, he didn't see him anywhere. When Jon looked around, searching for him, Jon saw only Kya. Irons only had control over the club's bouncers because that's what the Keeper said.

This allowed for a swift and prompt return for Kya. Still, she was not working at the bar, not anymore. No, most of those positions were now filled. So, tonight, she was The Conquistador's promoter and its main server because that's all she was allowed to be.

And yet, that was all she wanted.

Kya's status was ideal for the battle ahead.

"See *him*?!" Owen shouted in Jon's ear. The music

had reached such high levels that even from a close proximity, Jon could still barely hear his friend.

"No!"

The *him* was Gomez.

And the only person who could get *him* into the club was Kya. She knew how to use her sex appeal to charm a few of the OverTakers, who didn't see her as much of a threat. This was sexism at its finest. Kya was more of a threat than the other Doormen, no doubt. Her body was a myriad of deception. And, regardless of how reputable or strong, all men eventually cave in the presence of a hot female. This was a truth Jon had witnessed time and time again. For Kya, her ability to get Gomez into the club would be an easy task.

All she had to do was convince whoever was at the door.

Jon didn't see Kya do this, but he didn't need to. He soon saw Kya, and she wasn't alone. She grinned at Jon and subtly jerked back her head. Gesturing behind Kya, sure to Jon's assumption, was Gomez. He wasn't alone either. Kya stood with Gomez and a few of his friends.

All looked exactly as Jon expected them to. Their choice of wardrobe was hardly suited to a place like The Conquistador now. In typical Gothic fashion, Gomez's friends were dressed in black garb. They were wearing thick eye makeup and looking like they were out for trick-or- treating.

None of this offended Jon. To him, it couldn't be more perfect.

"Good job!" Screaming this at Kya, Jon also had to fight to be heard over the music.

Nonetheless, Kya heard Jon loud and clear. She kissed him on the cheek and walked on ahead. When

Kya passed Jon, Gomez smiled. Showing his lip ring and with his hair fashioned into a mohawk, Gomez looked almost the same as when he first met Jon. Among him were other journalists, each one carrying a presumed surveillance device.

Jon couldn't be seen talking to Gomez, so he then chose not to talk to him. As he prepared to go into the club, Jon carefully mouthed the words...*good luck*.

Adhering to this, Gomez nodded.

Then, in an instant, he hopped up the steps and shuffled to the second level. Followed by the others in his company, Gomez made his presence known right away. He abruptly passed Michael Irons and delivered a cunning gaze to the new head of security. And, just as Jon had assumed, Irons noticed Gomez instantly. Jon watched him quickly flag down another OverTaker. Hurrying toward this *new* guest, Irons pointed at Gomez as he walked up the stairs, minding his own business.

"Who the hell is that?" Irons snapped at his colleague.

Jon might have been far, but his ability to read lips was so refined he could make out full sentences without hesitation or error. And this was *exactly* what Irons said.

"Get him the hell out of here! Get his ass out!"

A lightbulb then turned on inside Jon's head as he smirked.

Phase one was now in motion, and all Jon had to do was see how far Irons was willing to go to keep up appearances and seal The Conquistador's stance on exclusivity and elitism. However, brutality and discrimination were his game and so, Jon understood what was to come next. He just needed to sit back and watch as the world consumed Irons and his OverTaker clan.

The trap was set, and Irons was about to fall in.

It would be impossible for him not to. He was, after all, a taker, and takers...*take the bait*.

CHAPTER 12
FACTIONS, FACTORS, AND FALLING

PREDICTING IRONS'S NEXT MOVE SHOULD BE SIMPLE for Jon.

Irons was doing exactly as expected.

He followed Gomez like a dog picking up a scent. Jon, while on the first floor, was subtle as he moved. He wanted to see what Irons would do, but he stayed confident.

With Gomez on the second level, Jon played it cool.

He was calm. He followed the rules. Now, he was just a simple guy going about his business with his head down. He fought to be as non-threatening as he could be, but Jon kept a close eye. He followed Irons up to the second level. Soon after Jon saw him near the railing, he suddenly stopped. He stopped because he couldn't move. He was frozen because just when Jon thought everything was going as planned, he found himself hearing Addison's voice again.

"Nothing is ever as it seems."

Addison was right. Actually, in this instance, he couldn't be *more* right.

"No."

There was a reason why Irons was pursuing Gomez and Jon thought he knew what that reason was. He thought Irons had chosen to follow Gomez because he didn't approve of him being in his club.

However, this wasn't *exactly* true.

What was truer was Irons was walking toward a man who was also on the second floor and who was overlooking the grand space below. Now, Jon hadn't seen Larry, his boss, in some time. Ever since the Over-Takers had taken control, Larry was a non-existent entity.

And yet, Jon was not told the reason for Mr. Thomas's absence. It had to be personal.

Nonetheless, Larry was here with Michael. *Why?*

With no clue as to why, the owner being present changed so much.

It changed everything!

Jon watched Irons cozy up to Larry and place his hand on his shoulder.

Jon glowered.

How dare he put his hand on Larry, their boss and the very man who built this club!

Soon after Irons completed this gesture, he raised his hand and pointed at Gomez.

Jon could see the interaction like he was staring at it through a microscope. Irons was clearly telling Larry about Gomez. Jon read both their lips! And, being such an expert at doing this, Jon could make out every word and each one forced him to shudder. Irons pointed at Gomez and snapped into the club owner's ear. His phrase was abundantly clear.

"Did you see that asshole, see how he was dressed?"

Larry nodded, but his nod seemed different to Jon. For some reason, Larry looked frail. His eyes were empty and his chin moved like he wasn't entirely aware. Still, he reminded Jon of someone who was shell-shocked and possibly disturbed.

Was that the reason why Irons had chosen to bring Larry now?

Did he want to show everyone that Larry Thomas, owner of The Conquistador, was like the Doormen? Was he unfit to serve The Conquistador?

Was Irons working with a setup of his own?

"Shit," Jon snapped. "Motherfucker."

With no radio on his person, there was no way for Jon to communicate what he was seeing. He couldn't tell Addison or anyone about Larry's presence. Right now, the stakes couldn't be higher. But when Jon saw Larry being guided from the railing, he was going after him. He was pursuing Gomez!

The Marine's heart sank.

The goal was never to hurt Larry or to frame him!

No, it was to expose Irons and his fascistic security team. And yet, with Larry being here, he could be potentially caught in the crossfire, get hurt or worse. Given his condition, Larry Thomas was too fragile and too broken to know what was really happening.

Irons knew this and he was prepared to take full advantage.

"Shit, we have a problem," Jon said like he was actually being heard. Despite not being heard, saying it did make him feel slightly better. He spoke again. "We have a big fucking problem."

————

The unexpected arrival of The Conquistador's owner had complicated things to say the least. Like stabbing wheelchair spokes with a broom, his very presence could very well send Larry out of his chair.

Jon wanted to get Irons but not Larry.

And yet, if Jon did anything to indicate his true intentions, he would only be revealing what was at hand. His heart beat faster as he ran. The second floor was exploding. Among the flashing lights, all the booths were occupied and there were swarms of people. Everywhere Jon looked, he saw someone new.

While he could see them, no one noticed Jon.

He was not an official member of club security, he had to remember. He was wearing The Conquistador's usual attire, but the OverTakers' choice of wardrobe was far more elite. As a result of the size of this crowd, Jon did have some camouflage. He blended in well while keeping a close eye on Irons, Larry, and Gomez.

He was still going about his business, and Irons was still following. Along the way, he continued to converse with Larry. He placed his hand on Larry's arm. Michael Irons was not a naturally warm person. He wasn't very tactile or, for that matter, kind. If he was being this way now, then it was but another tool designed for manipulation. It was the classic tool, and it was working.

It was working because, as Jon could see, Larry was not entirely there.

He seemed lost.

Even in this boisterous and active setting, Jon could make out certain details.

He channeled his skills as a bouncer and eyed Larry closely. What Irons was trying to get him to do was unclear at the moment. Irons could be taking Larry someplace, maybe to do something he didn't want to. Jon could still read their conversation. Irons's intentions were clear. Jon made out his words in full capacity.

"Doesn't belong. Get him out of here."

"No," Jon said to himself. Jon thought he was alone. Then he heard Owen shouting into his ear. "What the hell is happening?! Who the hell's with Irons?!"

Jon's head shook. Owen was newer to the club than he was. Owen didn't know what Jon knew.

"It's Larry Thomas! He's the club's owner!"

"Why is he with Irons?!" Owen yelled back.

Jon's head shook and he glared.

"I don't know! But we have to get him out of here! He can't be here right now!"

"How are we going to do that?" A solid question on Owen's part. He was right and Jon had absolutely no idea how he was going to get Larry *away* from Irons.

Right now, Larry was a victim in this game as much as the Doormen. He was vulnerable and if he was caught in the setup, then this would only hurt The Conquistador more.

It would not save it!

"He can't be here!" Jon yelled. He and Owen hustled but were careful to stay hidden. Approaching Gomez were Irons *and* Larry.

Why? What the hell was he doing? Jon gulped nervously, like he wanted to puke but knew he couldn't in fear of drawing too much attention.

Irons's ability to improvise and manipulate was beyond words. No one knew this more than Jon. Right now, he was taking Larry Thomas somewhere. He was taking him because he wanted him to show the same prejudice.

Irons was going to ask Gomez to leave, and he was going to do it *with* Larry! What Irons was really doing was covering himself! And, should Gomez record this altercation, then he would be blowing his own spot and Larry Thomas's too!

It was a trap, *a big trap!*

"Have to move," Jon said. Snapping to, Jon raced after Larry and Irons as they stalked.

"What...what's happening?"

"Just come with me!" Jon yelled at Owen. Owen hustled while staying close to Jon.

Steadying up to Irons and Gomez, Jon studied the expression of the lead OverTaker.

Gomez had seen confrontations before. Now, he was holding his ground. He was not moving. No, Gomez was choosing to stay back near the railing while Irons confronted him head-on. Again, Jon read Irons's lips and made out a few questions.

"What are you doing here?"

"Who gave you access?"

"Wristbands. Show them to me."

Irons commenced the fight with Gomez and did not hold back one ounce of his immeasurable set of deadly kills. His tactic was the same as a racist cop questioning someone based on their appearance, their perceived demographic. He pointed and stood in front of Gomez with his finger right in his face. Jon saw Larry, who was standing there watching.

"We can't move in!" Owen shouted into Jon's ear. "We can't alter the plan!"

Jon understood this to be true, but then he wasn't altering it. The goal was still to set up Irons, but he couldn't stand to see Larry involved. If he was part of the sting, then he would go down too. Jon continued to remind himself of this as he moved in.

"I know!" It was his last response before hustling after Irons. With Gomez's back now against the wall, he refused to do whatever Irons was telling him to do. Gomez shouted as he held his ground. "No! I'm staying right here! I haven't done anything!"

"Who gave you access!" Irons yelled at Gomez. "You don't belong here and you know it!"

By now, Jon was only a few feet away. Irons didn't see him, which also meant he didn't see the rest of Gomez's team as well. With eyes on Irons, Jon hoped Gomez would start recording this clear act of outright discrimination. Then again, Irons didn't care if he was being filmed now. So far, he was only guilty of one thing: *being an asshole*.

However, this one quality didn't last long.

When Gomez refused to cooperate, Irons took it up a notch.

Reaching out, Irons squeezed Gomez by the throat. Gomez, so shocked by the sudden, hostile act, Jon could see him starting to stiffen. As Larry observed this without reservation or pause, Jon knew he was standing idly as this new security team choked out a fucking patron, a guest, an innocent person!

"I said get out!" Irons yelled at Gomez.

"No! Let me go! Help!" Gomez shouted as he waited for someone to come and assist him.

Jon snuck up behind Larry Thomas and pulled his sleeve.

"Mr. Thomas," Jon said. "*Sir.*"

When Larry turned to see who was touching him, the man who owned and operated The Conquistador flinched. He didn't expect someone to show up when they did but at last, they were here.

"Jon?" Larry Thomas looked at the Marine like he barely recognized him.

Jon could see Larry wasn't all too there, so he was not completely aware of what was about to happen. "You can't be here right now! We have to get you away from here, sir!" Jon yelled. By shouting over the music, Larry Thomas nodded to show he was going to comply with the Marine. Although Larry was agreeing with what Jon said, still...he was not entirely aware.

What was wrong with Larry?

Was he sick, broken, depressed?

Was this the reason why he was no longer working at the club?

Why didn't Addison tell the Doormen about this? Maybe he did, but maybe it happened while Jon was away. Maybe.

Did he know Irons, know what he was doing?

Jon witnessed similar traits in some of his old war buddies. They'd come home, but they were not entirely there. It would take time for them to recover, but not Jon. He recovered quicker than others and could see the same thing, this *slowness* in his boss right now.

Irons held Larry by the hand and used his other one to secure Gomez in a headlock while dragging him across the floor. Gomez, who had done nothing to provoke this kind of reaction, garnered stares from all those who were standing too close. While Jon did not have any jurisdiction against Irons, he was not the club's top security anymore. Jon wanted to show everyone that they weren't all like Irons. This was not an attempt to look good when caught on camera. No, what Jon was deciding to do was based entirely on his integrity, on his desire to be seen.

"Let him go!" When Jon shouted at Irons, he and Larry stood in front of the banister. Jon had inserted himself directly into Irons's path and called for him to release Gomez. "What the hell are you doing here?!" Irons shouted at a volume Jon hadn't heard until now. Hearing it made him feel unsafe. Clearly, Michael Irons was adamant about taking Gomez out of this club. He didn't like resistance. He didn't like when little people like Gomez thought they were big or talked back to security. Irons liked the power and the authority that came with having his new title. And, if he had the opportunity to use it, to show who he was and what he was really capable of, then he would use it.

"You're not permitted to be in this section! Back downstairs where you belong! I'm removing this unlawful guest!"

"No!" Jon shouted back at Irons. "You're using force to own another guest! I thought you understood that's not how we do things here! The Conquistador is open to everyone. Now step back!"

Irons scoffed at Jon and then released Gomez from his hold. Standing toe-to-toe with Jon, the Marine wasn't afraid of Irons at all. Jon held his ground, the same as Gomez, and he had no regrets.

"You forget how things are changing around here!" Irons raised his voice. "I'm the one who controls the scene now, not you, not anymore!"

Irons said this while standing in front of Larry, who said nothing. This was his club, yet this was how Irons saw things. He actually believed he was the one in control.

"Now get out of my way and let me do my job!"

"No!" barked Jon. "I'm not going to let you remove a guest who doesn't deserve to be taken out! You stand back! You stand the fuck back!"

What Jon was doing now was *not* part of the plan. Now he was choosing to go off book, he was provoking Irons into relying on excessive force to push him out. However, now he was doing it in a way that re-directed the man's aggression.

Now Jon was the target and not Gomez.

"I won't! I don't stand down to men like you!"

"Men like me? Do you even know what kind of a man I am? You're way out of your league here, bud! I tried to tell you that from the start, and you chose the wrong side!" Again, Irons insisted on saying this in front of Larry Thomas, and Jon didn't understand why. "And now, you're going to suffer!"

"No," said Jon. "I'm not."

What Jon was doing now was wielding the Doorman's ultimate weapon. It was not fist or rage or his ability to fight. No, what Jon had now was direction and truth. Calling upon his ability to use words rather than force, Irons sought this and not much else. And it was only a matter of time before this hurt him.

And this was the Doorman's plan from the beginning.

"I'm just going to do whatever I can to make sure men like you stay out of The Conquistador forever!"

Jon felt so exhilarated hearing this. It was like he was being transformed into an action hero. Often when working here, at this club, Jon had experienced feelings similar to this. He had endured many transformative moments that made him believe there was nothing he couldn't do.

There was no mountain he could not conquer and no enemy he could not defeat. Staring at Irons, he stood in front of Mr. Larry Thomas. Jon was simultaneously protecting a friend and standing up to a bad guy at the exact same time.

"How many times do I have to tell you, little man?" Irons screamed, generating more of a scene. "This isn't your scene anymore and you are way out of your league here! Now get...the hell...*out of my way!*"

Irons attacked Jon with a snapping push-kick. Jon, who was not so fast, was hit by the blow and knocked back. After, Jon raised his fists and crossed his forearms and was set for the retaliation. But Irons's kick was heavy. It knocked Jon into next week, and the Marine felt a pain deep in his chest.

In the face of those watching, Jon was nothing more than a difficult patron who had it coming. Jon didn't have it in him to fight back. There were too many people who shouldn't be involved. And, as Jon came to his senses, he looked at Irons as he stomped. With Jon's hands now beneath his waist, he could see Owen and Li charging forward. The second Owen raised his hand, Irons blocked. Then, he pulled Owen in for a hard knee to the gut. Not even Jon expected this and Irons was not only strong, he was fast.

Irons had tangled with some damn good fighters and his training rivaled almost anyone's.

Irons might be a good fighter the same as Danix. After putting Owen down, Irons returned to looking at Jon. And still, the Marine chose to stand back. He wasn't here to fight. He was here to watch a bad man get what he deserved, and only that.

Jon stepped aside and he could see Larry moving.

In a daze, the elderly owner of the club shouldn't be here now. Still, that's where Larry was. He was in the exact last place he should be. Larry was in a fight. He was not throwing fists or kicking legs, but he was damn well in the fight, and Jon was terrified.

"Mr. Thomas!" Jon reached for his boss but he was too damn far.

Gomez was far too.

When Jon attempted to help them, he felt Irons holding his shoulder.

Irons pulled Jon and was on the verge of putting him in a headlock. While Jon brought his guard down, he did let up on some of his strength. He continued his evasion. Stepping aside, Jon did his best to keep Irons from succeeding. He would not put another hand on him again. During the third attempt to strike Jon, he slipped aside and looked at Gomez. "Get out of here!"

Shouting for Gomez to go, by now, the kid had all the footage he needed. Irons was off his rocker and soon, the Commission would know of the corruption as well as Irons's astounding level of uncalled for brutality.

Jon, who wasn't a patron or a customer, was taking one hell of a beating. He could feel blood seeping from his nose. If this was what needed to be done in order to prove Irons was wrong. If this was true. Then he was going to do it.

"Jon!" Hearing Li move in, more OverTakers emerged.

This new crowd was vast in numbers. In Jon's condition, he could make out only a few of Gomez's friends. Everything blurred into a mirage of misshapen people and faces. Jon did his best to maintain his coherency, but in that moment, the only face he could make out was Larry's.

Springing from out of nowhere, the gray-haired legend of a man stepped before Jon.

Sudden, coherent, and now capable, Irons was so focused on Jon that he didn't see Larry Thomas at all. Absorbed by his willingness to show Jon that he was the superior combatant, Irons raised his fist while Jon held his hand up to block.

"See? That's your problem?!" Irons shouted at Jon. "You can't really endure anything at all! You confuse toughness for brains, kid! A real fighter would've tapped out by now, but you didn't! You didn't because you don't know when you're beaten, and whether you choose to accept it or not...you, Jon... are beaten!"

Irons yelled and then grabbed a handful of Jon's hair. Jon, who was barely able to see or hear, prepared for a new strike. It was probably the last one Jon would receive before he was knocked out. Still unable to see everything, he could see Larry. He could see his boss trying to help, and in that moment, Jon could hear the voice of Lieutenant Dan.

"It's about the people who serve, the people who stay and do not run."

"Let him go!" Larry Thomas suddenly seized Irons's shoulder.

The head OverTaker, still absorbed by his rage, didn't look. No, he only reacted.

Thrusting with his hand, Irons pummeled Larry. So amped, Irons was willing to strike anyone who was standing too close! And, while Larry was the last person anyone should hit, Irons did. He hit him.

He hit Larry fucking Thomas!

"Get outta my face!" Striking again, Irons grabbed Larry's face. Clasping his cheeks, Irons pushed.

Jon felt whatever breath was still left inside evacuate. Everything inside Jon dropped instantaneously. In war, Jon experienced a fear like this whenever he heard the sound of a gunshot. His heart dropped in the same way it did after hearing the whistling of a bullet.

It was in that moment Jon understood exactly what was happening. It was then that the full strength of Irons had revealed itself. Pushing Larry Thomas, Jon saw everything at once. He saw Li and Owen, and down below, he could see Addison, Danix, and Duncan.

They had returned to the club and what they witnessed was the same as what Jon did.

Jon saw this and he quaked.

"Larry!" When Jon shouted his boss's name, Larry stumbled into the railing.

Being a frail man, receiving this level of force from someone like Irons, Larry clattered against the steel. All the blood rushed from Addison's face, he could foresee the outcome the same as Jon.

Addison shouted too, and Larry tripped again.

Larry Thomas tripped and Larry Thomas tumbled, and then...Larry Thomas fell.

"No!"

Realizing what he had done, Irons stopped dead, and so did the music.

The Conquistador's music never stopped, and yet it did now. The setting was suddenly overtaken by ominous silence as well as stunned faces of everyone in terror. Seeing the descending body of an elderly man, those who were close enough to witness fled in fear of being hit.

"Larry!" Addison screamed.

Landing hard, Larry's brittle bones shattered and his body appeared deflated like a balloon. Although Jon was near the balustrade, he heard the abrupt thump of Larry's body hitting the surface. Jon gasped. He couldn't look. He couldn't see. While he was not new to dead bodies, Jon was quite new to seeing a man like Larry so devastated and broken.

"What...I..." Now speechless, Irons was surrounded by his OverTakers.

All were looking down, shocked and scared. What Irons did had jeopardized every one of them too. It hurt the entire security team and was the very last outcome any of them needed now.

Irons knew this, and so did Jon.

Jon's face was so red he could almost pass for a fucking clown. Still, Jon was able to stand. "What did you think?" Jon asked the stunned Irons. "That everyone who works here like to just pound people's heads in the same as you?"

With the music turned low, Jon didn't have to shout to be heard. His bludgeoned face made this beneficial, and for a brief second, Jon was delighted.

"Right," said Jon, "but you didn't learn anything while working here, did you?" Jon asked Irons. Jon gawked as he stepped closer. "This place isn't about violence or power. It's about something more, something real, and the only force that matters here is words.

Real words. And now, the only words that matter for you are: you lose, Irons. *You fucking lose!"*

Looking around all devastated and humiliated, Irons stared at the dozens of hands holding dozens of phones, each one aimed at him. Next to Jon, Gomez leaned in and clapped.

"You're busted, asshole. Busted clean."

Busted Clean was the name of Gomez's channel. Of course, Irons didn't know this, but Jon did. He knew it well.

"Call an ambulance!"

Hearing Danix calling for help, The Conquistador had changed from being a glorious location for fun and freedom to a bleak, dismal setting. Suddenly, Irons had become the center of so much controversy. Among all the ogling faces and phones, the footage captured of Irons making a deadly error was now everywhere.

It was on the screens in the club and playing for everything to see.

It should have been a satisfying moment for Jon.

His plan was successful.

It worked!

Despite wanting to feel gratification and joy, Jon's feelings were overshadowed by his vast feelings of doubt. Jon may have beaten Michael Irons at his own game, but Larry was a casualty of his own success. In war, when someone dies but their death occurs in the name of victory, it is referred to as *collateral damage*.

Jon hated this term but hated more how Larry could be called this. Even when serving, Jon didn't abide by this rule. No one on their own team should die so that others might live. And as he rushed toward Larry, Jon looked at Addison as he sat next to him.

"How's he doing? Is he okay? How's his pulse?" Jon sounded off questions like he was an EMT. Offering these questions to Addison, the cooler was deadpan—broken and sad. He didn't have to answer Jon for him to know exactly how Larry was.

Addison's face said what his words did not.

His statement was obvious and terrifying at the same time.

"Not good," Addison finally answered. "He's not good."

CHAPTER 13
OWNED

FORTUNATELY FOR JON, THE WORDS *NOT GOOD* were not always synonymous with *not going to make it*. Larry might be hurt, but he wasn't dead. And, if he wasn't dead, then still, there was hope.

As long as Larry kept breathing, he would still have a chance to live.

Soon after his fall, The Conquistador was immediately evacuated. Everyone was asked to proceed to the nearest exits and their club fees were to be reimbursed. It was a bad day for the club, but an even worse day for Larry. In a matter of minutes, an ambulance arrived to assist Mr. Thomas and he was loaded into the vehicle and Addison and Jon both joined.

With the OverTakers being the force in charge, Michael Irons had abandoned the scene.

A coward, he couldn't even stand by his mistake.

The only ones who were aware of what happened were the people there. And they were the only people who remained at The Conquistador. They were its most loyal and most valued custodians. They were the very people who had taken control of the scene despite having a lack of jurisdiction.

After Michael Irons fled, Danix and Li took control.

The club was closed and the people evacuated.

There were no police because none were called. It was an accident still under investigation. Jon could see Addison speaking to the paramedics. "No cops," said Addison. He told them quite clearly. "We will take care of this internally. *Absolutely no police.*"

Duncan and Owen were both being very helpful with this. They assisted customers and escorted them out of the club and kept everyone as calm as possible. With the situation evolving into a total shitshow, all the Doormen could do was keep the OverTakers at bay. They still had to prove to people that the club was at its best when it was in their hands. And, based on how a man had nearly fallen to his death, this couldn't be truer than now.

"What do we do now?" asked Li. "What is to become of us?"

Li's questions were million-dollar inquiries. At this point, no one had any idea what happened. Although Danix didn't know the outcome of such events, he knew what *he* was supposed to do.

His purpose was here, at the club, and that did not change.

"What we always do," replied Danix. "We watch and we assist."

Outside in the parking lot, this setting was pandemonium. Everything had descended into chaos and there was no foreseeing tomorrow or the day after. Still, all that would remain consistent would be the Doormen like Danix, Li, Owen, Duncan, and now Jon and

Addison who were present and ready. They would be here for all the days to come.

Nodding and smiling, Li walked on and followed Danix across the parking lot. With so many still in shock, all anyone desired was assurance and assistance. Danix and Li were not the police, but still, this was their scene. They lent a hand and didn't need a badge to do it. The Doormen had their crests and they had their names, and that's all they needed tonight.

———

Bleeding from his face, Gomez had joined his friends in a corner of the lot. The person next to Gomez was another member of his team and someone who didn't look the same as he did.

Unlike Gomez, his friend Mason was spared of any injury.

And yet, Mason sat next to Gomez while tending to his wounds as best he could.

Mason dabbed Gomez's face. He absorbed the blood dripping down his cheek and onto his neck. The assistance he gave to his friend wasn't doing much. Yet, his willingness to help Gomez was enough. Gomez was not alone.

"So...did you get it?" Gomez asked Mason.

"You mean the footage of these assholes beating your ass?" Mason replied. He tapped the cut on Gomez's forehead with a tissue. "Hell yeah, we go it."

"What else?" barked Gomez.

"What else what?" asked Mason.

"What else did you get?"

"From the fight?" asked Mason.

"Yeah," answered Gomez.

"Pretty much all of it," said Mason. "We got the guy hitting you and we got the guy knocking the other guy off the fucking railing. Who was that guy anyway, the old man that fell to his death?"

Gomez snorted and coughed up the mucus lodged in the back of his throat. He thought about who this man might be. Gomez didn't expect to capture this much footage. He got more than he bargained for, and Mason's question was an important one.

"Someone who was obviously a casualty of this fucking place," said Gomez, "but he's not the one on video I wanted us to pay attention to."

"Who else?" Hearing Mason again, Gomez smiled and his bloody face gave him a clownish mien. It was as menacing as it was thrilling.

"Someone else tried to help me," Gomez replied to Mason. "The someone who tried to stop that asshole from going too far. *He's the one we need to show*."

"Why?" Mason asked. "We have all we need, don't we?"

"We do," said Gomez, "but we also might have more. We have to show the difference between the man who tried to knock me down and the one who tried to *pick* me up."

"You mean the *other* bouncer?" Mason inquired.

"Yes," said Gomez. Still recovering from the beating, Gomez remembered what Jon did and how he acted to try and save him.

"Wasn't that the plan all along? We planned to put it all online," Mason said to Gomez.

Shaking his head, Gomez stood tall.

"Not enough," he said. "We need to put it in a place where everyone will see it."

"Well, what did you have in mind?"

"The world wants a story," Gomez said to himself, "they want to know the truth. Well, I'm going to show them the fucking truth."

———

After Larry Thomas was rushed to the hospital, he was secured on a stretcher and rolled into the emergency ward accompanied by Jon and Addison. They stayed with Larry as he was taken into surgery and made sure to stay close to their boss and friend.

"He has a spinal contusion," said the doctor in blue scrubs. "I need a CC scan stat!"

Jon was gentle as he held onto the stretcher. He and Addison, along with Larry, were both barreling through the hospital. A grouping of nurses surrounded the injured Larry while Addison looked at his wounded father-in-law with a pale face.

Although Addison was present, his daughter— Addison's wife —was not.

"We need to get 'em to surgery as soon as possible. Any signs of a concussion?" The doctor asked the nurse. Jon didn't care for the question. No one knew more about Larry's state than Jon.

"Most definitely," Jon said, answering for the nurse.

"Was it a fall?" The doctor asked. He was turned to Jon. Both shuffled into the next hallway and made their way into the surgical wing.

"A big fall," Jon specified.

"Okay," said the doctor. "So, we have to do x-rays

and some tests before bringing him in. You wouldn't by any chance know his blood type, would you?"

When asked this, Jon looked at the doctor with a slack-jawed gape. "Uh..."

"AB positive." Responding to the question, it was Addison's turn to provide this kind of important information.

"Right," said the surgeon. "Okay."

He pulled the stretcher away from Jon and Addison, and Larry was taken into surgery while the two Doormen stayed behind. Both needed a minute. They needed to think, to calm themselves, but really, what they needed was time.

Standing there next to each other, Addison leaned and exhaled with Jon like he was about to submerge underwater. Jon was tired too. He didn't take as much of a breath as Addison, but he sympathized with his boss's need to let it all out.

It wasn't Jon's father-in-law who was in the hospital, after all.

"Son of a bitch..." said Addison, now back to standing. "Son of a fucking bitch."

Unsure who the *bitch* was in this phrase, Jon looked at his boss with a solemn, frail gaze. The most he could say at this point was, "I know."

"Motherfucker," said Addison. "I can't believe what he did."

"I'm sorry," said Jon. "I know...it's bad."

"It is," said Addison, "but then you don't have to be sorry for anything."

Addison was sympathetic. His voice, like always, was calm. Having attained some stability, when Addison said Jon's apology wasn't necessary, the

Marine's eyes fluttered. He was now showing as much joy as he could.

"It worked," Addison said. "Your plan...it *fucking* worked. Irons did go too far, just like you said, and now everyone is going to see him for what he truly is. The Conquistador...it will be given back to us. *It has to be.*"

Desperation clung to Addison's every word. It was like he was demanding this to be part of his reality. But, after speaking his truth, Jon was not so enthusiastic. In his mind, the OverTakers should be removed, no doubt, but still, there were a number of variables to consider.

Therefore, nothing was certain. Jon recalled the old saying heard time and time again.

Nothing is over...until it's over.

"Right," Jon replied.

Remembering the saying, Jon knew there were more important things to discuss. Now in the emergency ward of the NYU hospital, it was an over-crowded and invasive section of the building. Every last person Jon saw was a potential hindrance to Larry's health. No one was in more need of assistance than Larry. Falling from a high place, Jon was surprised Larry was still breathing. Larry was a tough bastard from a long line of tough bastards. He was old-school. In the past, Larry dealt with criminals and had likely endured and survived a whole lot worse than this.

Jon hoped this was true. He prayed that it was.

"How long do you think he'll be in surgery for?" As Jon asked this question, Addison shrugged.

"Don't know. As long as it takes."

"And your wife...does she know?"

Addison nodded. "She knows."

Jon was happy to hear this, but it wasn't the reason for asking the question.

"But now that Larry is hurt," Addison went on to explain, "it's going to be a free-for-all. Everyone's gonna try to get in now that they know our security is fucked. We're going to have to get back to the club as soon as we can and settle this all with the Commission. Like I said, they're likely to rule in our favor, but..." Jon expected Addison to finish and say, *but we don't know.*

This would be the logical response regarding what had happened. It was true because none of them did know. And yet, Jon was adamant about what he was thinking. He spoke up right away.

"I'm glad, but it's actually not what I was talking about," said Jon.

Addison looked sideways at Jon. He was puzzled by the statement and he didn't know what Jon was referring to if not the mission.

"I meant, did you call your wife and let her know her dad is in the hospital? She should know."

"No," said Addison, absentmindedly. "No, I have not."

"Well...shouldn't you?"

"I should," Addison said, "but then again, I don't really need to."

Now Jon was the one who was lost. How could Addison not relay this information to his wife? She was the daughter of the man who was about to have a series of operations to save his life? Now, this made no sense. In fact, it was damn necessary, and just as Jon was about to speak again, Jon received another notification. Checking his phone, Jon opened Instagram, Facebook, and all others. Focusing on only one story in particular, what Jon saw after were people outside The Conquistador reporting on what happened. It was mostly just noise, so Jon switched to YouTube and scoured what was there. Jon found one woman, a reporter, talking about what had happened.

"*I'm standing outside the famous nightclub, The Conquistador, where the apparent owner of the establishment, Mr. Larry Thomas, suffered a terrible accident earlier this evening.*"

A picture of Larry Thomas was shown in a box next to some person's head. Whoever they were, they owned a channel designed to report on club activity and club stories. Right now, they were discussing what happened at The Conquistador and, in that moment, every person watching the program knew what was going on. Struck with an apparent anxiety, Jon gulped and eased toward the screen.

He wanted to know more.

"*Eye witness accounts say the attack was incited by the club's security and they're a new organization brought in to replace the former security after a probation order was issued a few months ago, I think, right? Now, how the assault was incited is still unknown, but what is known is Mr. Thomas is, like, a staple of New York nightlife and has been for many years. He first opened the famous club almost three decades ago, I think, and, honestly, what fueled this aggression is not yet known but...*"

Although the story continued, it switched to footage between what happened at The Conquistador and the reaction to it. Now, as Jon witnessed the changing of this story, his jaw dropped and his eyes opened so wide they started to burn.

"Shit."

While the entire world began to see what Jon had witnessed firsthand, the Marine didn't know what to say or do. Jon didn't think this was how New York would learn about what happened.

Then Jon paid more attention.

He studied the footage playing on Instagram, Facebook, and whatever. He examined all the vantage points, the pristine angles, the professional capturing, and the fact that it was taken *at* the scene. All of this was due to the fact that someone else was there.

And that someone was Jon's friend. It was Gomez. This was *his* footage.

Jon looked closer and he could see Larry, but he could see Irons too. He could see Gomez and he could see the OverTakers and their heavy use of excessive force. Jon could see this, but then he also saw someone else there too. Within the tussle, the other party was Jon himself. He was right there, in the center of the frame, taking a beating so Larry would not!

At the time, Jon believed he was taking one hell of a whooping, but it was for a good reason. On camera, however, it looked way worse.

The brutality was present, but so was Jon's role in the attack. He was the interceptor. He was labeled as a victim according to all the social media hashtags and comments, the same as Larry. Jon refused to be called a victim, but when he listened to the story, the angle they were working was...different.

According to the reporter, Jon *wasn't* a victim.

He was just doing his job. He was just doing what he thought was right.

She even said this word as she continued to explain what happened. *Hero.*

"*Who is this guy?*" Another line was written there too.

"*Looks like he was trying to protect Larry Thomas, living legend, whoever he was.*"

"*I think he was the owner.*"

"*Had to be, maybe.*"

"*Yes, it was Larry. He's great. He was just trying to protect a guest. Given his age, that's, like, super fucking cool.*"

#protector #ConquistadorOldGuard #BringBack-TheOldGuard #SaveTheConquistador.

The shots closed in on Jon and Irons while the tags and stories continued to pour in from every outlet and subscriber. All the best capturing was done at the exact moment whereby Irons was pounding Jon's face while Larry did all he could to try and stop him. Jon continued to hold his gaze, but the entire time, he considered the sheer impact a story like this might have on the nightclub industry. Most didn't know what The Conquistador *really* was, but Jon did, and he didn't expect this to be the way in which he was informed. He also didn't expect to see himself as the front and center of this breaking and highly implicative story.

"Like I said," Addison continued, "I don't need to tell anyone. This entire thing has been blown wide open. Everyone knows now."

"*The Conquistador was one of the coolest clubs ever,*" Jon was watching one story from a famous influencer. He didn't know her name but she was hot. "*Everyone was welcome there! Like, and what these guys have done to the club, has been crazy. And, like, all of this is due to the former bouncers who did their best to stop the brutality of these new guys...I don't know...but it's been terrible."*

Now it was Michael Irons's image that had been revealed to all. Seeing Irons so exposed gave Jon a grin so fat and wide he felt like he was the Joker. The news had chosen their bad guy, and it wasn't Jon.

It wasn't Jon and it wasn't any of the Doormen.

"Holy shit."

"New guy was apparently hired to work at The Conquistador during its probation," shouted another influencer in yet another story. *"The attack on an old man is total bullshit, whoever he was, and I say we fucking boycott the club altogether. Don't return until these new security fuckers are out. They're abusing their power and hurting people. They got to go!"*

What came after shocked Jon. There was a new hashtag and it was everywhere.

#ConquistadorCancelled   #ConquistadorCorrupt #SaveTheConquistador

Jon trembled.

He was physically shaking after seeing all the stories. The last time he experienced tremors like this was back when he was in bed with Kya. Unable to describe these sensations, all of them were growing exponentially. Jon couldn't stand to resolve the incredible waves of gratification he was now experiencing. It was more than gratification. No, what Jon was feeling now was complete and utter satisfaction. He was feeling victory. He couldn't contain himself because right now, everything Jon had tried to achieve was brought into perspective.

Gomez's plan didn't just work, it excelled in ways Jon never could have anticipated.

It exploded into the world of clubbing, and Jon didn't think it would reach such powerful levels. But, the victory he had now was so big Jon still couldn't accept it as true. For Jon, it was only barely real, barely comprehensible, and so...barely there.

Jon had suffered, no doubt, but he was fighting to let the reality of what happened sink in. And the further it sank, the more it weakened Jon in the knees. He could fall to catch his breath, but with Addison standing next to him, Jon knew he couldn't. Addison placed his hand on Jon's shoulder, and receiving the warm gesture, the Marine smiled.

"Fortune favors the bold, my friend. Fortune favors the bold," Addison said to Jon. "And you know how much we believe in that, don't you? Your plan worked. Now the whole world knows what really happened and what needs to be done."

Jon nodded. Everything Addison said was true. Still, Jon couldn't deny what else his plan might have accomplished. Turning around very slowly, Jon looked back to where he had last seen Larry.

He was once in the hallway behind Jon but he wasn't there now.

"It did," said Jon, "but it came at a price, a big one. Maybe, it's a price we shouldn't have to pay."

"If there's one person who would understand a price being paid," said Addison, "it's Larry. Trust me." Jon blinked and thought about what was happening to Larry now.

Was he in surgery, still in repair, or was he in worse condition than before?

"He didn't seem well," said Jon. "When I saw him, he looked...*lost*."

Jon was looking at Addison, but the cooler's head was all the way down. Addison wasn't frowning, but his broken state was notable. He looked like he was in pain.

"He was," said Addison. "There's a reason why Larry wasn't at The Conquistador as much as he was. He was suffering from early Alzheimer's."

"Alzheimer's?" Jon questioned, now distressed and worried.

"Yeah. For the last two years, in fact," Addison explained. "We hadn't told anyone about it. Only his wife and his kids knew. Wife lives in Long Island, and, well, he wanted to be sure we kept it a secret for as long as we could."

"Then why did he come in?" said Jon. He was referring to how Larry Thomas had come to The Conquistador for some unknown reason.

"Probably because he thought it was me who asked him to," said Addison. "Ever since he started fighting the disease, Larry's been struggling to put names with faces and faces with names. He forgets, gets confused, and, well, Irons, being the prick that he is found out about it and decided to exploit that. He wanted to bring Larry in so everyone could see how we were not the only ones unfit to work at this place. Quite a dirty move, but dirty moves are all Irons has. And, fortunately for us, it blew up right in his face."

"Yeah," replied Jon, "but like I said...it came at a high price."

Jon was downcast. Although troubled, Jon didn't want to show his pain or hurt because he didn't have any regrets about what he did. He knew it was the right thing and he accepted the notion like he did back in the Marines.

He did his job, did it well, and it worked. He succeeded.

Still, casualties and risks are part of the job. Reward is never owed or guaranteed, ever. Yet, survival is its own reward. Whenever any mission is done, the goal is to ensure everyone makes it out alive. Everyone goes home.

In Jon's case and in Larry's, home was not here. It was not the hospital.

But Larry's state was not Jon's doing. No, it was his enemy's.

Jon bent his fingers and his knuckles cracked. He could drive his fist straight into the fucking vending machine and not feel a damn thing. Jon wanted to do this. He needed to do this, but he stopped when he heard Addison speak again.

"And like I said, Larry knew the risks, and he would rather die than see his club handed over to a bunch of heavy fists. He would hate to give everything over to men who thought that violence was the answer. What we do...it's always been about something else."

"*Words*," said Jon. He was reminded of this many times before. Addison was good with words but Jon had heard these kinds of words before. Words were good, but never more than actions.

"Not just words," said Addison. "Something much more powerful than words."

Jon's head tilted. Now curious, Jon couldn't help but ask himself, *what could be more powerful than that?*

"*Choices*," Addison stated. "We are defined and commanded by our choices."

Now feeling fulfilled, Jon was amazed at how Addison always knew what to say and how to say it. The fact that he did only spoke to his leadership as well as his experience in this trade. Considering his choices, Jon was still thinking about Larry, where he was, and whether or not he would ever understand what happened. Jon shook his head and regathered his thoughts. Once again, Addison touched Jon on the shoulder.

"And you made the right choice," he said. "You did the *right thing*."

Jon had no regrets, true. He did, however, understand it wasn't just him who did what was needed. Jon mentioned this. He said, "I didn't do it alone," and Jon then thought about Kya and about Gomez, and also... about the other Doormen. All of them were in this together. And yet, Jon didn't think he would see any of them until tomorrow.

But he was wrong again.

"Addison!"

Calling out to her husband, Tanya Krowe—who was Addison's wife—sprinted down the wing. Jon could hear heels pattering the tiles as she approached. With her complexion red from the presumed distress, she looked at Addison as she hurried toward him.

Tanya was a prim lady with dark hair and hazel eyes. Her appearance was something noted for Jon because, to him, she looked drastically similar to someone else Jon knew. In fact, the similarities between Tanya Krowe's appearance and Kya's were not only mind-blowing, they were downright uncanny.

Waving her down, Tanya gasped and Jon took a step back. Although he was aware of how Addison felt about his decisions, he didn't know how Tanya felt about anything yet. Being Larry's daughter, she could react differently.

Jon observed her state. Now sweating, Tanya trembled as she fell into Addison's arms.

"Jesus," said Tanya. "Fuck."

Holding Addison close, Jon gave Tanya the space she needed. How much she required, Jon wasn't sure, so he gave her as much as he could and stayed quiet as a church mouse.

"Do you know how long it took for me to get here? Club is locked down. No police, but the parking lot is packed."

"Okay," said Addison. "I'll call Danix to deal with all that. For now, let's deal with this."

"Right," said Tanya. "You're Jon, right? Jon Haze, the Marine?"

Unaware that Tanya was speaking to Jon, apparently, she knew his background and his name. This was more than Jon thought she knew. They had both never really met each other.

"Yeah," Jon said. "That's me."

"And you're the one that tried saving my father, right?"

"Tried," repeated Jon. Gloom consumed Jon and he now stood there all glum and disappointed. "*And failed.*"

"Not according to the footage circulating online," added Tanya. "Everyone's talking about the club's *good* bouncer, the one who tried to protect the *legendary nightclub owner.*"

Jon's forehead wrinkled and his eyebrows curved.

Being informed of his new reputation, Jon's image now was conjured from the online web and one conceived as a result of Gomez's acute footage. Jon was only somewhat familiar with online presence and *cancel culture*. He did see some of this starting to surface. He didn't know how much the story had spread or how it had changed based on what others were saying.

According to Tanya Krowe, Addison's wife, people were saying a lot.

"Really?"

"Yeah," said Tanya. "And I think what you did was brave. *Really* brave." After receiving the compliment, Jon couldn't help but grin. He blushed as Tanya rubbed his arm with tender gratitude and appreciation. "Thank you."

"You're welcome," said Jon, "but it was a group effort. I mean, Addison helped too."

Addison shrugged at Jon. "Just a little," he said. "Just a little."

Jon didn't agree. Addison was aware of what Gomez was doing and approved of his actions. Also, Jon had not yet mentioned Kya, who was the one who suggested Gomez in the. She was the one who got him inside, and everything Jon said was true about who should receive most of the credit. And, just as he was about to say more, the hand that was once only grazing Jon's arm now grabbed tightly and pulled. Falling forward, Tanya fell into Jon's arms and delivered a solid, rousing embrace.

The last person to hold Jon like this was Kya as well

as his mother. And, when Jon received the warm gesture, he thought about how much he missed both of them right now. Also, he wanted to know where Kya was. She should be here too.

Jon wanted her to be here.

"Thank you," Tanya said to Jon. Her cheek pushed into Jon's chest, which was still sore from Irons's kick. "Thank you so much for fighting to save my dad."

"You're, uh, you're...you're welcome." Jon squeaked out his reply yet did not express any enthusiasm. While his actions were brave, they had not produced the intended result.

"I just want him to be okay," Jon said.

"We all do," said Tanya. "But his fate is in God's hands now."

Tanya's words provided some comfort. Jon looked at his hands. His heart thumped and he felt a rousing sensation growing from inside. The coincidence—or maybe it was synchronicity—that emerged from this situation was undeniable.

Jon had heard these words before, including and especially the term *in God's hands*.

Jon hadn't really thought about James since his return home. James was Jon's best friend back in the Marines. He was his brother and the one whom he served alongside. The last time they were together, they were raiding a building. During their search, they were attacked. There was an explosion and the roof collapsed, and James died in Jon's arms. Racked with some survivor's guilt and trauma, Jon bounced back to life after he became a bouncer ironically, but he didn't have time to think about James or, maybe, he just refused to. And yet now, tonight, the way Jon felt about Larry was *almost* how he felt about James. He felt hurt, shaken, responsible. Jon's heart ached, like everything was happening too fast for him to process or understand. Jon couldn't contain the feelings of struggle or uncertainty, but it was an endless stream of new thoughts and peril.

Here, it was Tanya who told Jon about God's hands.

But then, it was Lieutenant Dan who told Jon the exact same thing. He assured Jon that what happened wasn't Jon's fault. It wasn't his fault, and there were things that Jon lost too that he didn't talk about but should have. He lost his leg, he lost his purpose, and he lost his best friend.

And yet, as Dan also assured Jon, his duty was not the problem.

Jon did his job, and although it didn't end the way he wanted, still...he fought and kept fighting.

"So...what do we do now?" After a moment of mediation, Jon looked at Addison. He was now with Tanya, his wife, and both were looking through the surgical wing. This was the last place where they had seen Larry before he was rolled away.

"Do we go back? Does Michael now have to leave? What about the Commission and the Keeper? Will they return to The Conquistador and give the club back to us? Really, like, what are we supposed to do now that the truth is out there and everyone knows about what happened?"

Addison swallowed a sizable gulp.

Was he nervous or, like Jon, was he too having a

moment? Jon waited for Addison to clear his throat and his mind. He responded once he was all done.

"Revealing the truth is only *part* of the plan."

"And the other part?" asked Jon. He hoped this next part would be easier than the one they had just completed.

"Getting other people to believe it."

"But," said Jon, "they saw the footage, didn't they?"

Addison nodded, and Jon looked at Tanya. Biting her tongue, her long nails tapped the base of her chin.

"How could they deny what they saw?" Jon asked.

"They, as in the people of New York?" asked Addison.

Jon's nod was so unyielding it was almost military. Right now, Jon was thinking of everything done and what else needed to be done going forward. Jon believed this was what Addison was thinking too. Jon hoped it was.

"Yes," said Addison. "And knowing Irons, I'd say he's got a long list of excuses he's going to work his way through. Guilty as sin, still, you can goddamn guarantee he's got himself an alibi. Mark my words."

Despite Irons's back being against the wall, so to speak, he was no doubt prepared to defend himself and his clan. And he would do this purely because he could.

"He will not go quietly," said Addison.

"Then we'll make him leave," snapped Jon. "We'll do whatever we have to in order to shut his ass down." Jon now burned with determination. All Addison could do was grin and chuckle.

"Is he always this hard?" Tanya asked. Addison's reply was a rueful chuckle.

"More than you know," said Addison.

Seeing Addison so amused, Jon felt like maybe he should be the same way. Maybe he could let his guard down and be more relaxed. Jon tried to be, and then he felt his phone vibrating in his pocket.

There was a message. It was from Kya.

Coming to hospital.

Reading the text, Jon was confused. Kya might be on her way, but how did she know where Jon was now? He never told her.

"Is that Kya?" At first, Jon thought it was Addison who was asking him this. As it turned out, it was Tanya, which was also strange.

"Yeah, it is," Jon said to Tanya. He was glib, almost to the point of coming off as rude. How did Tanya know it was Kya texting Jon?

"Yeah. How'd you—"

"I told her," said Tanya.

"You...told *her*?" asked Jon. He couldn't grasp how or why Tanya would tell Kya about Jon. Granted, he wasn't displeased by this fact. No, Jon wanted Kya to be here, at the hospital. However, he didn't know Tanya and Kya were close.

How were they?

"I did," said Tanya.

"You know her?" asked Jon.

"Do I know *her*?" said Tanya, scoffing at the comment. "Of course, I know her."

Jon's question seemed dumb. Tanya responded like it was silly, and so, what Jon needed now was clarification, and lots of it.

"No," he said, "I mean, do you know her *well*? Like,

I didn't know the two of you actually texted each other."

"Well, we do," said Tanya. "We text all the time, actually."

When Tanya said this, she was behaving the way Addison had earlier. She was gleeful and was practically enamored with Jon's question. So far as the Marine knew, he hadn't said anything funny. Apparently, it was enough to cause Tanya to chortle.

"Really? I didn't know you two were close."

"Oh, we're *very* close," insisted Tanya.

Jon bent his head and had one more question worth asking. *How close?*

"I didn't know that," Jon said.

"Yeah, we go way back. Actually, we go right back to the beginning."

With Jon's interest piqued, he thought he didn't know what Tanya meant when she said this. Now he came to see he knew exactly what Tanya was talking about. Before he could say anything else, Tanya spoke for him. "She is, after all, *my sister*."

Hearing this, Jon choked on his own saliva.

Even under such difficult circumstances, it was a weird fact to be informed about now. There was really only one way for Jon to react to this information. Seeing now how obvious Kya and Tanya's relationship was, even their names sounded similar. And, when Jon first saw Kya, he thought she was beautiful. Tanya Krowe, Addison's wife, was also beautiful, just like Kya. Now Jon was thinking he only saw Tanya in this way because she looked similar to someone else he knew.

Tanya and Kya had more in common than Jon realized or maybe he had just not paid enough attention to the now incredibly clear similarities. Now, he began to see that it was such an easy comparison. Why Kya didn't mention this to Jon was beyond baffling.

Jon found himself shaken by the lack of transparency as well as the lack of honesty. Then, and Jon thought about it more, Kya did give her full name once. Kya told Jon it was Garner. She said it was Kya T. Garner, and Jon made no other queries about this after, but then he most assuredly should have.

The T might have stood for Thomas, but the rest was made up for some reason.

Why did she lie? Why did she refuse to tell Jon she was Larry Thomas's fucking daughter?

Now, Addison rarely talked about his personal life.

"*I'm a private person*," he once said to Jon. Oddly, Kya said the exact same thing.

Larry didn't speak much about that either, but now it was a giant web of interpersonal relationships: Addison was married to Kya's sister and so that made her and him brother and sister-in-law. As well, it was Kya's father who owned the club, Larry, yet she never once mentioned this to Jon. It was odd, although it did explain a lot about her, about him.

There were always these moments between Kya and Addison, like they knew each other but didn't provide any details. Suddenly, all these moments dawned on Jon in one huge picture, and he found himself considering all the obvious things which he had never *ever* mentioned.

Weird. Wild. Out there? Wow!

Kya was very involved and was also incredibly capable under the right circumstances. She was the reason why they beat the Fallen Sons and why they had taken down Michael and his OverTaker bodyguards. There was so much attributed to this, but still, Jon wanted to know why.

Why didn't she tell Jon the entire truth?

Perhaps it wasn't relevant and maybe it was, but Jon couldn't see how, though he should have.

"Right," Jon said, laughing now too.

"Oh, and she likes you," added Tanya.

"What?" Jon replied. "But why? Why didn't she tell me she was Addison's sister-in-law?"

Jon didn't think Tanya would reply or make a comment, or that a comment like that was even necessary.

"Private person and not relevant. Nepotism. Secrets, and Addison. He didn't want her to say anything."

"Why?" asked Jon. It was a good question.

"It's all business at The Conquistador," Tanya said to Jon. "Thought you knew that."

Jon said nothing. Tanya's father, Larry, was still in the hospital and now was not the time to have this conversation. He was in a fragile state, and mentioning Kya now was not the best time. Considering how they had just slept together, Jon had felt something he never felt before with anyone ever. He was now guided by this feeling and, as Jon looked at Tanya, he did his best to appear pleased.

He didn't want all his emotions to show. Here, he wanted to be respectful to Kya and Addison. A way of thanking Tanya for what she said, Jon snorted and his lips squiggled into a crooked smile.

Thanks.

Now gathering all of Tanya's attention, Jon also

knew who the person was. It was exactly who Jon hoped it would be. Kya arrived the same as her sister said she would.

Now here, Kya roamed the halls and marched straight after Jon.

"Where is he? Where's Dad? Is he okay?"

Dad. Until now, Jon hadn't heard Kya say this. However, what other connections were there to make if not this? If Addison was married to Larry Thomas's daughter, and his daughter was Tanya, and Tanya was Kya's sister, then obviously the two had a relationship.

After arriving at this conclusion, Jon was here not as a colleague or as an employee. No, he was here now as a supportive boyfriend and friend. And, as Kya fell into Jon's arms, he held her close. Tenderly. "He's in surgery," Jon said. "He's in..."

Kya kissed Jon's cheek before she broke into a sob. She held Jon close, and this proved that he'd made the right decision to intervene when he did.

He now had the full support of everyone here.

"What about Gomez?" Jon asked. He recalled how Gomez was just as involved as Larry. Kya pulled her face so she could look at her boyfriend.

"He's okay. The story hit pretty fast," said Kya. "I'm assuming you know about it."

Jon nodded. "I know a little."

"Well, it's flooding everywhere," said Kya. "I mean, it's online and hitting people's feeds harder than a cross from fucking Tyson. People everywhere are now aware of the brutal security that once had control over New York's famous club. It won't be long before a change is in effect."

"Right," said Jon. "And when is that change going to happen?"

Jon's question was meant for Addison.

He didn't know where the changes would lead or how this entire conflict would end. While Addison was prepared to answer, Jon was unsure if he was being disrespectful. The owner of the club—Kya and Tanya's dad—was now in a hospital, and all Jon could think about was his future. Part of Jon wished he held back more. He didn't ask the right question right away. Giving it a second thought, what Jon said wasn't uncalled for, but then his future was uncertain. If the OverTakers weren't taken out of The Conquistador, then what happened to Larry would have all been for nothing.

Jon would rather see himself run over than to see this come to pass. Now waiting for Addison's answer, a surgeon in black scrubs exited the wing and marched toward the four.

"Is there a family member present?" the surgeon asked. He still had on his gloves and scrub cap. When the surgeon came forth, Addison did too.

"We're all family," Addison confirmed. He was choosing to include Jon in this statement, which was awesome.

"Well," said Tanya, "I'm his daughter, and so is she..." Tanya pointed at Kya. Jon could see a thin layer of tears accumulating there now.

"I am," said Kya.

"Right," said the surgeon.

"Is he going to be all right? Is he going to make it?" Addison spoke up. Standing so close, he was practically towering over him. As Addison demanded an update, the surgeon began rubbing his jaw. Jon felt instantly sick. If it was good news, then the doctor would have said it right away. If it was bad, then they usually stalled. To Jon, it felt like this doctor was stalling.

"He sustained serious injuries, but he's stable for now, it's just..."

"What?" said Tanya.

"His spine was severely fractured. Falling as far as he did, he didn't just suffer a concussion, he also broke both legs and one shoulder."

"Jesus."

"But he's going to make it, right?" said Kya. "I mean, he's going to be all right?"

It was then that the surgeon's eyes began to close and he pulled off his cap. "Like I said, he's badly hurt. He'll be okay, but..."

The room fell silent and everyone's level of shock reached considerable heights. Jon could feel the tension brimming. Everything was so thick with tension it was unavoidable, and Jon could sever it with a knife. Despite this, Jon held out for as long as he could.

He couldn't wait. Jon assumed no one else could either.

"Is he going to be all right or not?" Jon barked at the surgeon like he was back at the club. When the doctor realized Jon was about to lose his temper, everyone glared. Clutching his cap, the doctor looked at Jon and then at Addison, Tanya, and Kya.

Jon was so close to knocking the surgeon out, he wanted his damn answers.

Soon, Jon had them.

"He'll never walk again," the doctor uttered.

The first sounds Jon heard after were hard exhales

coming out of Tanya's. The news hit her the hardest. And when Jon turned his head to examine the reactions from everyone standing there, it was Addison who frowned and shook his head.

"So...he's *paralyzed*?" asked Kya.

Jon felt like this was an obvious fact by now. Then, he thought maybe Kya had to say it because once something is said, it then becomes real. It lives!

"Yes," said the doctor. "I'm sorry."

Jon bowed his head. Like any good boyfriend would do, or should do, he held Kya and listened to her cries of agony. With her head resting on Jon's chest, he rubbed her back and wanted to give her all he could. Caressing his partner, Addison did the same. But, unlike Kya who bucked was crying gently, Tanya was broken.

Sobbing profusely, she wailed in the middle of the dense hallway and Jon continued to stroke Kya's hair while Tanya cried.

"Can we see him?" Addison asked later.

The doctor nodded and began to take a step back toward the door.

"He's resting now. We had to give him a lot of medication, as I'm sure you can imagine, but yes...yes, you can see him in just a few minutes."

The doctor left the room and Jon let go of Kya. She needed to be with her sister now. She scurried after Tanya, who responded by taking her sister's hand. Pulling her in, the two hugged and Jon stayed still. His time for comforting Kya was done. It was time for her to be with her family, *her actual family*.

However, Jon did stand with Addison as Tanya and Kya were consoling.

While the two of them were now quiet, Jon waited

for Addison to speak. Jon hoped Addison would tell him what to do. Although Jon was capable of giving his own orders, when he heard Addison say this, it gave Jon some reassurance.

Often, it was Addison who could give Jon this. He was the one who gave Jon the approval he often craved.

He granted Jon with the belief that he could be better, be stronger, and confirmed that he was on the right path. And yet, Jon was just starting to embrace his new path without Addison. He couldn't wait for people to give permission or to put his mind at ease. Jon had to trust himself and he had to believe he was right and no one else.

Once he believed he was, then he would be.

The law of attraction, Kya once said to Jon, is to believe that something is certain, and then you do all you can to make it so. If you work, believe, and summon the energy required, one day, this outcome will come to fruition. It will be true.

"We have to go after them. Irons is still back at the club. He's hiding. We have to find him and we have to get him before the police arrive," Jon said. "Can't keep the situation contained forever."

At first, Addison was silent. Then, as he turned slowly to look at Jon, he glared back at his friend who was almost family.

"They won't go quietly," said Addison.

"I know, but the Commission will be on our side, no? I mean, they know Irons and his band of assholes did not make The Conquistador safer or better. They're not part of its future. In fact, they couldn't be any more caught up in its past." Every word out of Jon's mouth was the truth. "They only wanted the *ciphers* and nothing else."

Jon was bold to mention this. None talked about the ciphers—*the great keys of the world of clubbing*—but then again, it was a topic worth mentioning. It needed to be said.

The OverTakers were a nefarious force and should be removed from The Conquistador once and for all. What Jon didn't know at this point in time was how were they to do that?

How were they, the club's first and only Doormen, supposed to get rid of Irons and his syndicate? How were the Doormen supposed to win this notorious and ugly battle now on the horizon?

"The Keeper needs to order them to be removed for them to be. The code dictates they go."

"Okay," said Jon. Now he knew what the step was, all he and Addison had to do was take it. "Then we'll bring in the Keeper. How do we do that?"

"We have to wait," said Addison. "Once what's happened is presented to the Commission, they'll send the Keeper back, and he'll tell the OverTakers what to do. Hopefully," Addison said, "he'll them all to go straight to hell."

Jon smirked. He liked the sound of that.

"Okay," Jon replied. "But how long will that take? How long will it be for the Keeper to come to The Conquistador?"

"Too long," said Addison. "Too long."

Marching down the hallway, before Addison was gone, Jon caught a glimpse of his expression. Addison was scornful—filled with hate. Jon had rarely seen Addison appear this way. He was mostly a calm, assertive, and watchful kind of guy. He said more with his vocabulary than he did with his tone of voice. Now fired up and eager, Jon followed his boss. Wherever Addison was heading to now, Jon wanted to go with him.

"Where are you going?"

"Going to check on Larry, and then I'm going back for them! Can't afford to wait," said Addison. "Can't afford to hold on."

"But the Keeper, the rules..." said Jon. Suddenly, he was remembering the code of ethics that held the world of nightclubs together. Jon began asking himself all questions he felt pertained to these rules: the regulations, the creed, and the laws.

Was Addison permitted to move before he had the Keeper or the Commission's blessing?

What was his goal once he got back to The Conquistador?

How would Irons respond, and could Jon...could Jon go too?

"We have to follow them," Jon said.

"Yeah, well, some rules are meant to be broken," said Addison. "And it's time for Irons and his brigade of fools to know that. When you cut down a king, you better make sure he's dead. Otherwise, a Doorman will come and chop off your fucking head."

"Shit," said Jon. "We're going back and we're going to do what?"

"Make 'em leave," Addison said to Jon. "What else? We're gonna make 'em *all* leave."

"And if they don't?" Jon asked, hustling next to Addison and staying with him every step of the way. "If they *decide* to stay?"

"Then we do what we were *trained* to do."

"Use words?" Jon inquired. Immediately, the Marine knew this was not the best method under these difficult circumstances. Addison smiled with relish.

"Not this time," he said. "This time...we cut them down and chop off their heads, like I damn well said."

After this, Jon didn't say a goddamn word. In the end, it was all he needed to hear.

In fact, it was all Jon *wanted* to hear.

CHAPTER 14
THE TAKEDOWN

ONLY TEN MINUTES AFTER BEING INFORMED OF Larry's condition, Jon, Addison, Kya, and Tanya were all given permission to go and see him. While Jon didn't know exactly what to expect, in his mind, he pictured Larry Thomas resting on a stark bed, bandaged, bruised, unconscious. And, as it would turn out, that was exactly how he looked when he stepped into the room. Walking alongside Addison, Jon gazed at his boss and legendary proprietor, Larry Thomas. Now asleep, Larry was tucked in under a big blue blanket. His heart monitor beeped, and so, he was alive, but how much?

Jon gasped at the thought.

"Oh, my God...Dad." Tanya raced to see her father and Kya joined in.

The two sisters fought to each put their hands on their father. Though unconscious, Jon hoped Larry would feel them standing close. More than this, Jon wanted Larry to know that he and Addison were there with his daughters. They didn't love him as much as they did, of course, but still, goddamn did they ever care.

"Careful," Tanya advised. Being the older sister, she touched Kya's arm and made certain she was gentle. As of now, Kya was laying on her dad's chest. With arms opened wide, Kya held her dad very close.

All of this seemed strange to Jon. Never had he ever seen Kya with Larry before. Then again, Larry rarely was at The Conquistador, and Jon and Kya were only just starting to get close. Still, when watching how Kya was with her dad, it reminded Jon of his own mother.

Right now, Jon missed her. He missed her so very much.

If she was where Larry was now, then Jon's reaction would be the exact same as Kya's.

"He seems so weak," Kya said to Tanya.

"I know," Tanya replied.

At this point, it was impossible to ignore. Larry was an elderly man, but the injuries he sustained were substantial. They were critical. Jon also considered how he and Addison could explain to Larry what happened and what was going to happen now.

He had never told someone they wouldn't walk again.

Although Jon understood it wasn't his place to do so, the onus would fall under either Kya or Tanya or maybe even on Addison too. Nevertheless, there was no one in the room who could sympathize more with Larry's position.

It was almost a year ago Jon had been told something similar.

It wasn't long ago whereby Jon himself was lying in a hospital bed. He had awakened only to realize he lost a part of himself. He remembered looking ahead. Jon was now seeing his mother, her face all sweaty and her hands clutching a wad of tissues. Jon remembered the doctor standing in a white coat, the one who finally told him *no*.

He said, "*No, Jon Haze, you will never have full use of your leg ever again.*"

It was not the same as Larry, no doubt, but it was close. It was so close, in fact, Jon could feel his boss's pain as he lay still before the Marine. Jon could feel it, and he hated damn near every second of it.

"When do you think he'll wake up?" Addison stood next to Tanya after she asked this. Unsure if Tanya was asking Addison *this* question or if she was just asking anyone. Even still, Jon didn't have an answer.

He had no idea when Larry would wake up or if he would at all.

"He'll wake when he's ready." Addison always knew what to say. A man careful with words, Jon liked what was said.

"He will," Jon said to Kya. "He's going to wake up."

Despite this being a certainty, the waiting period between would be difficult. So, no one said a word until Tanya sniffled and stepped up to the bed.

"I want you to finish this, do you understand me? I want you to find the people responsible and beat them, do you understand?"

Addison didn't verbally respond to his wife's demands. All he did was nod.

"We're going to," Jon took the liberty of speaking now. "Believe me, we're going to."

"When?" Jon thought this next question had come

from Tanya, but it was Kya who asked it. Like Tanya, she too had a taste for revenge.

"Right now," said Addison. Jon was prepared to answer again, but instead, the answer came from his boss.

None of this mattered. Jon would have answered the same way.

"Right fucking now." Bringing an end to their conversation, all Jon and Addison needed was a little more time with Larry, *just a little*. Observing their lord for the last time while in this hospital bed, what was done was done.

All that was left to do now was stand and fight.

———

Back at The Conquistador, the remaining Doormen did not move or vacate the premises. No, they chose to stay and were all following Danix but the main doors were locked as Irons fought to keep the situation contained. Yet, that was simply not going to take.

The Doormen were gathered in one location, in a place known only as the Corner. It was distant from the epicenter of the club and was, in fact, not inside the complex as much as it was at the *corner* of it, *hence the name*.

Now, Jon hadn't ventured to this *corner* before. In spite of not seeing any of it firsthand, Jon was aware of its existence. He would describe it as a *secret corridor* because it was formed into a narrow passage separated from a very large house. The Conquistador was that house. Actually, it was more like a castle. And, like the Annex, only a few were made aware of this new place.

According to Addison, once he said it used to be a *private café* but was abandoned years ago. Oddly, it was once owned by Larry himself. And so, those who had been employed at the club the longest knew about it.

They knew about this place, but thankfully, none of the OverTakers did.

After Addison and Jon arrived, the Corner was the first place the Doormen were using as cover. Addison sent Danix a few texts. He asked where they were and what they were doing, and to this, Danix's response was simple.

C.

According to Addison, this was all he received and all he needed to receive.

"I know where they are," Addison said to Jon. "They're there and they're waiting."

Jon nodded.

"Let's go and get them."

Addison parked his BMW in the alley where the limousines had pulled up and where the smuggling had taken place. As it was a success, Jon could only assume Irons and his OverTakers were oblivious to what was happening. Scampering toward the Corner, Addison looked over his shoulder and Jon did the same. While they might feel alone, there was always a chance they might not be. Delivering a hard knock, Jon stood by and waited. Not long after, Addison's fist clashed with the door's panel. It opened, and Jon looked up and saw Danix standing there.

"Hey." Danix greeted Jon and Addison before stepping aside.

Unwilling to stand in Addison's way, even Danix understood the sheer urgency of the situation. The clock was ticking, and there was no time to waste.

"Addison, you're here. Glad you found us," said Danix.

Inside the Corner, Jon followed Addison into this new space. Although it was *new* to him, the room itself did look quite old. The Corner did appear like an old café with its black walls and quaint little shelves. Jon didn't only see Danix in this place known as the Corner.

He saw everyone. All the Doormen were there, and it was a glorious sight to behold.

"Yeah," said Addison. "I figured you'd be here."

"Figured right," said Danix.

Jon was near Addison but was not as noticeable. He was standing in a corner near a broken-down shelf. Jon could see Danix, obviously, but also saw Li, Owen, and Duncan too. In total, there were six Doormen and that was only from the main team. Where the other bouncers had gone was unknown, but only the main guys were aware of the Corner's existence. Jon knew they were here because they were going back, back to The Conquistador. And there was only one reason to *go* back.

Only the *real* Doormen stayed. The real Doormen had returned to fight.

"Status?" Addison asked.

"Club's closed, obviously," said Danix, "but cops are gone."

"Gone, *why?*"

"Well, they were here to question," Li replied to Addison, "and they did, but they don't have sufficient evidence to place Michael under arrest. So far as he's concerned, he operated clear within his rights. What happened to Larry was an accident."

"An accident, really?" asked Addison. "Is that what you're going with?"

Jon scoffed. To say what happened to Larry was an accident was completely absurd.

"Ridiculous," Jon said. "Absolutely ridiculous." Jon thought he was only talking to himself. He wasn't.

"Yeah," said Danix. "Fucking dumb, but still...the fact remains, without a warrant and without a goddamn attorney, Irons and his OverTakers are going nowhere. And we can't go in because the club's locked down. We won't be able to do anything until the Keeper gives us the all-clear, and given what's happened, he damn well should."

"Yeah," said Owen. Jon looked at Owen. There was a table in the middle of the room. It had chipped legs and a cracked center. Owen was using this to sit. It was not like Owen to speak up, but he was doing precisely that now, and it was great.

"Come on, this must have found its way back to the Commission. They saw what Michael did to Larry, how he pushed him off the balcony! I mean, come on, they attacked us! They fucking attacked us! We have every right to stop him right here, right now!"

Jon had never seen Owen this furious. He was a top-notch guy who could do some top-notch shit, but every word out of his mouth was real and honest.

"It's still our club," Owen said.

"Owen's right," said Addison.

"What?" asked Owen. Clearly, Owen was shocked to hear Addison commending him. Jon felt the same way too, except it made sense because Owen was. He was right. "I'm right? Did you say I'm right?" Owen snapped.

"I did," answered Addison. "We can't afford to wait for the Commission or the fucking Keeper, and the goddamn situation calls for something a little more enticing."

"Well, what did you have in mind?" Danix asked Addison.

The cooler grinned. "If they're not going to leave, then fuck 'em...we're going to have to make 'em leave."

"Make 'em leave?" Danix was positioned next to Addison as he replied with a slow, methodical voice.

"Yeah," said Addison. "Make 'em."

"Are we...even *allowed* to do that?" Li hesitated to ask this. Jon had the same concern back at the hospital.

Could they disobey the Commission if they had a good reason to do so?

Apparently, that's exactly what the Doormen were about to do.

"We have grounds to defend our club," said Addison. "They crossed the line and they attacked our king. Like the knights that we are, we have an obligation to avenge him, avenge him and protect our castle."

"Shit," said Owen.

Jon smirked at his friend, who smirked right back.

"And no one's going to stop us?" Owen asked Addison.

"In the state we're in, only one person would be stupid enough to even try."

"Oh yeah? Who?" Duncan was the one speaking now.

Upon asking this, he received only a batch of hard-ass stares from everyone who was present in the Corner. With all the eyes on him now, Jon thought Duncan understood just how silly the question was. The only person who could and would stand in the Doormen's way was the same one they were going to knock the fuck out.

"How many OverTakers were in The Conquistador tonight, including Michael?" Jon wasn't sure who Addison was asking.

Maybe it was for one person or everyone inside the Corner.

"Based on what we remembered seeing..." Danix held his hand to his chin, and Jon could tell by his long pause that Danix didn't know. "I'd say around..." Danix shrugged. He really didn't know.

But few did.

Jon didn't know either. Then, he remembered that he did...he did know. He remembered back when he had his conversation with Irons. This happened when Jon was considering whether or not to work for him.

Irons said he had a place for Jon.

One spot left. *Just one.*

"Ten," said Jon. Everyone was now looking in Jon's direction because he now had their undivided attention.

"What?" Danix asked.

"Ten," Jon said again. "There are ten of Michael's men on duty, maybe, possibly, at least...from his core group."

"And how do you know that?" Owen was the one asking now. Jon looked at his friend, inched himself out from a corner in the Corner and moved across the room.

"Let's just say one of those spots was almost mine,"

Jon said. "But I can guarantee you that's how many there are."

"Shit," said Owen. "That's a lot."

"Six versus ten," Danix added. "B-Team is out. It's not their place and they're not Doormen, not really. So, it's only us now. Can't say the odds are in our favor."

"They never are," Addison replied. "And that's what makes it so much more raw, doesn't it?"

No one said whether or not it did. Jon looked around the decrepit room. He stared at all the faces of the Doormen. *His friends and his brothers.* So inspired, Jon had no problem replying in the only way he knew how.

As well, it was the best way to respond. *"Oorah."*

"Do we go now?" asked Danix.

Jon watched Addison look around the room the same as he had done earlier. Wasting no time, Addison tugged the lapels on his jacket and glanced at Jon, who was standing closest to the door.

"Right now."

————

Wasting no time, Addison led the Doormen back to The Conquistador like calvary.

Although moving as one impenetrable unit, everyone stepped to the beat of their own entry music. Moving in complete unison, Jon felt like he was walking on air. He saw almost everyone in the Corner, with the exception of the only person who was missing.

Jamal—the club's main man at the door—was not included for some reason.

Where was he? Jon wanted to ask but chose not to

now. If Jamal wanted to rumble with 'em, then he would be welcome always. The Doormen, now heading toward a formidable enemy, were still outnumbered, so they would need all the help they could get. Approaching the door, Jon stopped because the area surrounding this area of the club was almost mostly cleared. There were a few people still lingering, yes, but of all the people Jon could see, the police were not one of them.

With no cops, that's exactly what Jon wanted to see.

"Where's..." Jon was on the verge of whispering something to Addison. Before he could, he stopped talking because now Jon did see Jamal.

After the changes to The Conquistador, Jon had rarely run into the gargantuan teddy bear who was his buddy. At this moment, however, Jamal was exactly where Jon wanted him to be.

In fact, he was exactly where Jamal *needed* to be.

"Yo!" Jon's face lit up like a Christmas tree.

Almost glowing, he stood near the door where Jamal was positioned with his chest out and looking fucking ready to go. Actually, to Jon, he looked like Brandon Gleeson in the film *Gangs of New York*. In the movie, Gleeson's character was a member of the gang called the Dead Rabbits. He was their ace-in-the-hole— one last add-on for the gang who was competent and could deliver—which was exactly what Jamal was about to do.

"Jamal," Addison said to the heaviest Doormen. "You're here."

"Of course, I'm fucking here," said Jamal. "What, you think I was going to fucking bail on you boys now?"

"Never," said Jon. He gave Jamal a brotherly grin.

Jon hoped his man knew how happy he was to see him now.

"Just didn't see you in the Corner," said Danix. "Didn't know where you'd gone to."

"Yeah, well," said Jamal, "after the fucking club cleared out and everything got locked up, I needed to get out of sight from the other OverTakers who were guarding the door. Difficult for a guy like me to do, you know? But I went where no one expected me to go."

"And where is that?" asked Jon.

Jamal didn't say anything after Jon spoke. Rather than speaking, Jamal looked both ways to make sure he was alone. Then, he waddled from the door and moved along the sidewalk. Now heading toward a sewer grate, Jamal stopped over the cage and tapped his boot against the perforated steel.

"What, didn't you forget about this or *what*?"

Jon looked down and so did everyone else. Based on the Doormen's shared silence, Jon assumed none of them knew what Jamal was talking about. None did, except for Addison.

"*Greta's Way*," Addison said.

"What?" asked Jon.

Addison's grin broadened. He tapped Jamal's big-ass chest. "Son of a bitch."

"What the hell is *Greta's Way*?" asked Owen.

While it was Owen who spoke, Jon wanted to query as well.

"Back in the day," said Jamal, "VIPs were brought in through an underground tunnel. It was the best way to move The Conquistador's more, shall we say...*shady guests*."

Jon's eyes opened wide. He looked through the cage and down into the space below.

"Fucking Gotti used this shit back when he came to The Conquistador in the old days. Hasn't been used in a really long time, but yeah, still works."

"How do you know about it?" said Duncan. Jon understood how—out of all the bouncers—Duncan was the least familiar with The Conquistador's history.

"Fuck do you mean?" asked Jamal. "I'm the fucking door guy. I know every which way in and out of this damn club. I know what you're supposed to know and everything you're fucking not supposed to know either."

"So that's what you used to get out then?" Danix asked Jamal.

"Yep," said Jamal. "Now it was a little tight, no doubt, but it's what I used to *get out*, and it's exactly what we're all gonna use to get *back in*."

"Well, where does it lead?" asked Li.

Jamal slid along the grate and shifted to its corner.

"Goes through the kitchen, but straight through the VIP," said Jamal, "and right up to the dance floor. If we take that route, the OverTaker bastards will never see us coming. It's the best plan, if you ask me."

"It's the *only* plan," Addison specified, the same grin still evident on his satisfied face.

"They're guarding the doors," said Jamal, "the fucking assholes who took our club from us. They'll be expecting us. They know we're coming for their asses. You want to send the pukes a message, this is the best way to do it." Jamal nodded and his head swayed side to side. "Not on our fucking grounds. Not on our fucking turf."

Among more inspiring words, the Doormen

nodded. They delivered a form of communication only they specialized in. It was the jerking of heads and chins. It was more than just a simple command. It was a display of truth and obedience.

It was also the best way to say the most gratifying phrase any one of them could speak.

We're in this together. We fight as one.

The similarities between being a bouncer and being a soldier were undeniable for Jon. While they weren't exactly the same, Jon still couldn't deny how often the two duties intersected. Right now, Jon was with a squadron of Marines about to enter an enemy-occupied building. Although stealth wasn't the signature of Marines, it was a hard one for the fucking SEALs.

Danix was proud to say he was one. Jon felt more stealthy now, he felt more like a ghost than he ever had before. Jamal opened the door. He was the first to pass through. He crept past the sewer grate and beyond. A dark tunnel and another secret passage to The Conquistador.

Jon shuddered.

He didn't mind the shadows. What he didn't enjoy was the damn smell. Reeking of sewer, there are few things that smell worse than this. Jon followed Addison, Jamal, and Danix into the passage that ran under the club. It had been some time since anyone traveled through it.

Like the Corner, this secret hallway contained so much history.

Along the walls were pictures, some dating as far back to the fifties, and crinkled autographed pictures of people who, at one point, were pretty famous and revered.

Jon stayed close because the corridor felt like it was being lit by candles.

What really gave it light was what shined from inside the club itself. Not far ahead, Jon saw what little light was still gleaming from the floor above. Last Jon could recall, The Conquistador was a castle made of perpetual light. Now, however, it was settled into something else, something abysmal and drab, like a black hole conjured where light used to be.

As of now, Jamal was leading a brigade of bouncers into battle.

At the very end of this dimly lit corridor was yet another set of stairs. In this case, the set was not like other stairwells. Jon had seen so many stairs throughout the club. Therefore, it was automatic for him to assume there would be more. Looking at the one ahead, Jon was instead previewed to what appeared to be an elevator, yet...not a traditional elevator.

No, it was a portable passage but what it lacked was the perceived doorway and any switches required to operate it. What Jon was seeing now was actually a rectangular prism with a low ceiling. Therefore, the Doormen were crammed to the point where they were shoulder-to-shoulder. Although claustrophobic, at this point, Jon wasn't exactly sure about where he was standing...or where it was going to take them.

"Everyone *in*?" asked Addison.

Jon was shocked to see how Jamal was able to fit. He did, but only just barely.

"Yeah," said Owen. He was barely audible when trapped inside this cluster.

"Where the hell is this taking us?" Duncan asked.

He stood beside Jon. He wanted to know as well. *Where were they going?*

"You'll see," said Jamal. "Just...hold on."

Jamal said this to the other Doormen. Then, he reached out and uncovered a movable rod located beneath a hidden panel. Like those classic elevators seen in the fifties, this tool was something Jon had observed only in movies. Jamal torqued this rod and flicked a switch. Suddenly, the box they were in screeched like a freight car.

"What is this, like an underground fucking vehicle?"

"Yes, you could say that?" replied Addison. Being the man he was, Addison understood how this mode of transportation worked. It shifted along an underground track and motioned like a tram.

"So...this is how you moved the VIPs back in the day," Jon said to Addison.

"Don't ask why," Addison replied. "It was all Larry's idea. He thought it would be cool to transport celebrities by giving them an actual ride into the club. He would pull up in *this* car and drop them right off in the VIP section without anyone seeing. You can imagine how long that lasted."

"Not long, huh?" Jamal said.

"Would you ever get into one of these things?" Addison asked.

Jon snorted and grinned. *Fuck no.*

Jon said this to himself as the cart began to slow near the end of the rickety track. Jamal stood and waved everyone along but was cautious. He pressed his finger against his lips and urged everyone to stay quiet and to move slowly.

The Doormen responded as they should.

Creeping up behind Jamal, where this mode of transportation was taking the Doormen to was not yet known. Now, Jon *did* see a door. It was a dummy door that Jamal pushed aside and peered in with his giant head. Obviously done to make sure the coast was clear. When it was, he waved the Doormen again.

Jon followed Jamal but didn't say anything as they entered. Now in another secret room with more tables and chairs, to Jon, this looked like a dining room fitted with candelabras and folded wooden seats. Like the Corner and the underground corridor, this room was also abandoned. It was but another facet of The Conquistador's *older days*. It was a remnant of what the club used to be. One by one, the Doormen went with Jamal. Beyond this minuscule room was another dance floor, which was not the main dance floor but a space not far from a stage. Then, after moving into another narrow passage, whenever Jon thought he had viewed nearly every section of the club, he encountered a part of it completely new and unseen.

Through this door, all the Doormen dispersed.

Despite moving in a loose formation, Jon searched Michael Irons and his fake bodyguards.

But club was empty.

It was dead silent.

"Stay close," Addison advised. "Stay close and keep your eyes open."

Jon sniffed; a reflex and something Jon did whenever he was trying to *sniff* out an ambush. Undoubtedly a possibility now, as soon as the Doormen managed to enter, they were addressed by the booming voice of

Michael fucking Irons. "That's far enough there, gentlemen."

Stopping dead in his tracks, Jon gawked at the OverTaker leader.

Looking across the dance floor, Irons stood dead center. Like a statue, Irons posed with his legs opened and his arms flexed near his chest. He was not entirely unaccompanied. Throughout the setting were more OverTakers. Everyone had taken their positions, and all were dressed in their signature gray suits. The specialists Jon saw here were bigger than he recalled. However, the Doormen were big too. All of them varied in size but most were younger than Irons and his brigade. Jon considered himself to be a younger man. Addison and Danix were sort of young men too. The majority of The Conquistador's original bouncers were far younger than any of the OverTakers, and this was their advantage, at least it was in Jon's mind.

After Irons made his presence known, everyone stopped and stared.

The tension brimming carved Jon's face into a rictus. In his mind, he was already fighting. In his mind, he was already beating Irons to a pulp and listening to his begs and pleas.

"Hold and do not move." Irons provided this warning as he switched hands.

Now gripping the lapels of his jacket, the leader of the OverTakers gave his collar a tug and tightened the garment against his back. He secured his jacket before things got messy.

"I see you found your way back," Irons said. "But in case you haven't noticed, the club's closed until further notice."

"See that," said Addison. "In case you haven't noticed, your way of doing things is done. After your little stint of brutality, you and your psychotic gang of mutts have now been completely exposed. The club world now knows what you are, and they also know who The Conquistador really belongs to."

Jon smirked at Addison. He couldn't have said it better himself.

"Please." Irons brushed aside everything Addison had said like it was a feather flailing in front of him. "An old man was in the wrong place at the wrong time," Irons declared. "We were just doing our jobs like we always do. We were making sure someone who didn't belong in our club, someone who snuck in actually, was escorted out the door. You know what happens when a club just starts letting anyone in, don't you? It loses its truth. It loses its identity. Besides, in case you haven't noticed, your Larry Thomas was a man who was outdated and worn out from years of working too hard and spending too much time worrying about *keys* instead of planning how to revitalize and recreate a club for a new generation. But then, as you know, only with keys is any of that possible."

Irons cackled, but Jon did know what he meant.

It was like the keys—the ciphers—of The Conquistador could be used for something bigger and more important.

"Therefore, if you ask me, he got what he was always going to get. It was only a matter of time before he stepped too far too quick, and well...you know what happens when a person does that."

Irons's explanation was total bullshit. Every word spoken from his flapping trap was derogatory and dumb. Jon knew it, and so did the other Doormen. None were here to discuss what happened, only to take action and take back the club that was invaded and being destroyed.

"And if you think people actually give a shit what's said online these days, then you really need to grow up. Face it, Addison, we're going nowhere. This club is still ours, as is what it's holding—all its secrets."

"You sure about that?" Addison snapped back. "Or maybe...you forgot something too."

Addison pointed at Irons and squinted at the powerful cooler. What Addison said hinted at a truth Irons had not yet embraced. The secrets he referred to were the very reason why he'd taken The Conquistador in the first place.

Irons wanted what it had, and what the club had... was *treasure*.

"What?" Addison's voice beckoned. "Do you think we'd start a war on sacred ground if there was even the slightest chance that we'd harm what we've worked so hard to protect?"

"Are you saying—"

"Fucking right, we are," Addison cut off Irons before he could say anything more. "You're not going to get your hands on anything you want, Irons. So, maybe now you can explain to the Commission how you managed to nearly end the life of a customer when it's your job to keep them safe."

Irons, now gobsmacked by Addison's claim as he spoke as The Conquistador's main protector, twitched as he nibbled on his lips. He was unable to contain his malice, and so Jon grinned, knowing that the Doormen had in fact beaten the OverTakers at their very own game.

They might be bigger and more equipped, but the Doormen were smarter.

They were wiser, and so, they were deadlier. More than this, they were better. *Much better.*

"You're not cut out for this trade," Addison continued to taunt Irons, something which Jon loved. "You never were, and you never will be."

"Is that what you think?"

"No..." Despite most of the conversation happening between Addison and Irons, Jon felt the need to abruptly insert himself into it too. He wanted to speak so that he too could participate in showing Irons how he was unfit to be here.

"It's what he knows," declared Jon. "It's what he *fucking* knows."

Addison glanced at Jon, who gave his boss and friend an agreeable nod. The tension between the two teams was clearly on the rise and Jon could smell things starting to heat up. Yet, Jon was fueled by it and was ready to let it wash over him, for the Marine could feel the ferocity and wanted only more. He wanted a war and a victory. He wanted everything!

"It's over, Irons," Addison said. "Relinquish control of The Conquistador, revert it back to us, and stand down. Do this now and you might still walk out of here in one piece. We can do this the easy way or—"

"*The easy way?*" Irons glared at Addison. The easy way was not his way.

Jon wasn't surprised by anything he'd seen or heard. The chances of Irons going quietly were about as likely as the Doormen surrendering. Since they never would, then the OverTakers never would either.

"You really think the Keeper is going to let you take us out? You know as well as I do that a verdict has to be reached for us to disappear. I don't know about you," Irons said, "but I don't see the Keeper around here. I don't see anyone except for you and your band of merry trespassers."

Jon found no sign of the Keeper as Irons said. The purpose of Irons saying this was only to poke fun at Addison, to make him feel worse. Irons wanted to make it clear that they had no right to be removed. This was only what Irons knew to be true. However, it wasn't *exactly* true.

"No," Addison said a few seconds later. "You don't see him."

"We do," said Jon.

After he said this to Michael, the nemesis's eyes popped like someone was shining a light into his gaze. Addison was surprised to hear Jon's reply. Honestly, Jon was too. He was told the Keeper was a representative of the Commission. He was also told he would not be present here, at the club.

But Jon was wrong.

Sure to the Marine's satisfaction and surprise, the Keeper had miraculously appeared.

As if manifested out of thin air, he was standing by the bar in his classic uniform: a long black trench coat as well as the weird but surprisingly cool bowler hat. The Keeper glared.

"Mr. Keeper," Irons acknowledged.

Jon observed Irons now. He was never one for

showing fear. Jon never saw a man like Irons afraid. Nevertheless, when Jon saw the Keeper now, a noticeable tremor snaked across Irons's lips.

"What brings you here?"

"Pretending like you don't know," the Keeper replied to Michael Irons. "Well, I might look like a man who reads more than he watches, but the footage of a bouncer knocking over one of the city's most famous club leaders is unavoidable now."

Jon gawked. Irons held the lapels of his jacket so tightly the fabric crinkled.

"I know what you did," the Keeper continued.

"What happened was an accident," Irons insisted. "Nothing else, nothing more."

"Well, it would seem your rivals beg to differ," said the Keeper. "After all, it was one of their own who was almost killed."

Jon heard a whimper scuttle through the crowd. It came from one of his fellow Doormen, but Jon didn't know who. He didn't want to know.

"Larry was weak and past his prime," said Irons. "What happened to him was his own doing. He shouldn't have been present, and yet, he was."

"And one has to wonder...*why?*" said the Keeper. He presented a solid question. Jon wondered the same.

"Well, we're perfectly willing to cooperate," Irons said to the Keeper. "Still, make no mistake about it, sir, this club is still in the best hands. See our quarterly profits and illustrious series of guests. We've upscaled. We've made this club better than it ever was before. One mistake does not negate all the success that has come before."

"No, it does not," said the Keeper. "But it does present us with an interesting circumstance."

"In what way?" Irons snapped like a spoiled child. Though a man, he had more in common with an infant than he did with anyone else. Jon realized this. In fact, he realized it well.

"You want to maintain control of this club while others seek only to take it back," said the Keeper. "It leads me to why I'm here now."

"Aw yeah?" Irons barked as he bit down on his lip.

In Jon's opinion, he was oblivious to what was really happening. Jon, however, already knew this. The Keeper wasn't here to provide more about this decision. No, he was here to see what unfolded now that a decision was made.

"And you're here to hand over the reins finally to better, more experienced men."

"Not exactly," said the Keeper.

He responded to Irons with a sharp tongue. The Keeper continued to maintain his distance as well as his position. Jon watched like he was on the edge of his seat. Granted, he was always captivated by the Keeper's persona. He was a fascinating man. His status within the Commission was thought worth thinking about.

The Keeper was, in many ways, without fear.

"What we have here are two forces who refuse to back down. One was the force who once had their hands on this institution and another who seeks to take it back. While rules were broken, relationships were shattered, and people were hurt, order still needed to be maintained. And so, there is only one way to end this conflict."

"Aw yeah?"

Jon could see Irons's tongue moving about in his clamped, overly tight mouth. He gripped the lapels of his jacket like he didn't want to let go, but then Irons had no choice. He was going to. One way or the other, he was going to let go.

"And what's that?"

"The way it was meant to be solved," said the Keeper. He didn't waste a second answering. Always, the Keeper's words fired out of his mouth like gunshots. "One on one, team versus team...*man against man.*"

Jon squinted again. He was not confused, only captivated.

Surges of rage and adrenaline spiked inside of him and the whole man versus man possibility gave Jon a rush like no other. In the end, this was *exactly* what Jon was here to do. He was here to throwdown as were the rest of the Doormen.

"A fight," said Irons. "What, like the fucking Showdown, the very contest that put them all in this position?"

Jon remembered the Showdown well. He didn't like it, but Irons was right. The Doormen did participate in a Showdown. It's where they faced off against the Fallen Sons and won. It was also a competition that sent them into a spiral and into the exact position they were in now. As well, it pushed Jon to the brink of his honor, his malice and his rage. Another Showdown was not what Jon wanted to do today. It wasn't what any of the Doormen wanted.

"No," replied the Keeper. "Not another Showdown. I'm afraid this calls for something a bit more...*drastic.*"

Jon liked drastic. It was synonymous with insanity. Jon was ready to get nuts right here, right now.

"*A Rumble*," said Addison.

"What?" Jon asked.

"An old school, no-holds-barred fight to the end."

Jon looked at Addison, who was now grinning. Jon was hoping he would be smiling and he was.

"I was hoping you'd say that," Jon said. He stared at Addison with the very same smile. A Rumble was straight from pages of *The Outsiders,* which was Jon's favorite book growing up. It was a story about two rival gangs, the Greasers and the Socs, as they fought each other for supremacy. It was an epic scene, both in the novel and in the film, and for Jon, it was wicked. And right now, Jon was down for an old-school Rumble and there was no better time for one than tonight.

"A Rumble?" asked Jon.

"Precisely," said the Keeper.

"And the cops?" Jon was also thinking about the police.

"Without a warrant, they have no jurisdiction in a place like this," said the Keeper. "So long as they're not present...*it will just be you.*"

"Unless, of course, you're afraid of cops," Jon said to Irons.

Now, the deadly head of an elite security unit turned slowly. Now insulted by Jon's claim, Irons's reaction was exactly as the Marine intended. Unless Irons was afraid, Jon imagined he wasn't. So, there was no reason for him *not* to throwdown. For so long, Jon wanted a piece of Irons. He was a tough bastard and a deadly fighter, and Jon had faced him once and lost. Jon desired to face him again, and what better place to do that than here?

"The last thing I am is afraid," Irons said to Jon. "In fact, at this moment, I couldn't be less fucking afraid."

Jon glowered. His image of Michael did not change. He was a big guy but was also quite the skilled guy. He had extensive knowledge of many things: face control and combat. And yet, whenever Jon was in his presence, he was a rival that towered over almost anyone else. Due to this fact, Jon could not imagine a deadlier enemy standing before the Marine than now. But, being the beast Jon was, he also waited to get beaten or to get eaten.

However, Jon found himself prepared for both.

"Are you sure?" Jon coldly replied to Irons's question.

When he said this, Irons gawked at Jon like he wanted to take a bite out of his ass too. Jon didn't shudder. He did not relent.

"A Rumble cannot happen," said the Keeper, "until someone throws the first punch. Is there anyone here who would like to do the honors?"

The Keeper scanned the entire level of The Conquistador, not one had chosen to step forward to respond to the Keeper's offer. Jon glared at Irons. He wanted to hurt him, badly.

"No one's gonna go first, huh?" Jon turned to face the person speaking. It was the last person whom Jon had expected. Duncan, who was new to the club, had shown some serious brass balls these last few weeks. As a man willing to stand up for himself, Duncan stepped toward this enemy.

Fist back, Duncan targeted the OverTaker who was

standing the closest. Jon appreciated his willingness to strike but even he could see the punch coming.

"Let's do this!" Duncan shouted.

The OverTaker defended himself, just as Jon had expected he would. He blocked with his right hand and then swiped it down. Then, this Taker booted Duncan in the knee and finished him off with a brutal hook to the jaw.

Duncan plummeted shortly after. The OverTaker Duncan hit was no easy handle.

While he was a lot bigger than Duncan, this Over-Taker glared after he put the newest Doormen down on the ground. Duncan might have lost the upper hand, but his willingness to throw the first punch was exactly what the Doormen needed at this point. By striking first, it distracted the rest of the OverTaker brigade and gave The Conquistador's loyal guard the chance to start.

After Duncan kicked off the Rumble, the Doormen stampeded toward the OverTakers in a brutal clash of well-trained and well-prepared soldiers. The charge mimicked the enraged rush of two armies colliding at the pinnacle of battle. Jon, who dropped to the floor, targeted his OverTaker by kicking him in the ankle. The man dropped and Jon responded with a throw. He pulled the Taker's shoulders and forced him down. As the Rumble continued to erupt, it became a sensation of new smells, sights, and singes.

The Keeper, who sanctioned the fight, placed his bowler hat back on his head and walked away slowly.

"Rules of a Rumble go to the last man standing," said the Keeper. "The last man standing wins. When it's done, it's done. Good luck."

He drifted into the background, for the Keeper's place was watching, not fighting. He observed from a floor above and stayed in a safe space, but no space was safe now.

Jon knew this, and because he did, he felt even more ready.

Now fully absorbed into the fight, Jon watched every Doorman enter the brawl while every OverTaker did the same. Having been in fights before, Jon had never been in one of this magnitude. He was unable to comprehend what was going on, and though Jon fought in a war, those battles were modern and thus dictated by modern warfare. There were rules, targets, technology. With none of this available to him now, all Jon had was the man standing in front of him and the hope it would stay that way.

Eyes up and body set to fight, Jon glared at yet another OverTaker. He stared down a man with slick hair and black gloves. He was taller than Jon...but stronger, more skilled than him?

Most definitely not.

"Let's see what you got, Marine!" The OverTaker shouted.

Jon raised his hands and, keeping his distance, watched the Taker stomp directly into Jon's space. Without hesitation, the man was keen on striking back hard and fast. Jon wasn't. If he was in Danix's gym right now, then this was the part of the spar where a takedown would be his main strategy.

And, based on where Jon was now, it was the easiest one to do.

Jon lunged, wrapped the man's legs up nice and good, and hooked in with his back heel. Pushing his opponent to the floor, Jon had him exactly where he wanted. Jon's hands latched the Taker's neck and was later pulled into a choke. The attack happened faster than Jon had anticipated.

Jon squeezed and waited for the man to go nightie night.

Just as Jon wanted, the man became unconscious in a matter of seconds. This was one fighter down, and there would be another one up right away. Up as easy as the enemy went down, Jon stood and looked around the room. There was little time to waste, but what was once a cluster of exchanging bodies had now spread throughout The Conquistador.

Jon didn't spend much time checking, though he felt like he should.

From what Jon could see, Danix was doing the most damage.

Smackdown between two OverTakers, the brute of a man was exchanging punches like he was in the middle of a zombie raid. He pounded one with his fist and the other with his elbow. He jabbed and hooved.

While the OverTakers were skilled, they still couldn't put a hand on Danix. He was always the bigger, stronger opponent.

Jon grinned. The Doormen were still kicking ass!

After seeing Danix, Jon saw Li too. However, while Danix and Jon were on the dance floor, Li was in a fight near the railing. Quick-handed and agile, Li chopped one OverTaker and deflected the others. Jon was always envious of Li's agility as well as his mobility. He always knew how to use his environment to his advantage. Li snagged the railings and gripped the bars. Then, pulling himself forward, Li propelled around the balustrade and then delivered a series of epic kicks in mid-air.

It was quite a glorious sight to behold.

Not every Doormen who was in the fight was so nimble. The OverTakers were not like most enemies. Even if a few of The Conquistador's bouncers seemed to be doing well, not everyone was. Addison didn't fight as much as everyone else. Jon had seen him in action in the past. He knew what Addison could do. No doubt, Addison was a fighter, but then, so was the man he was up against.

And that man he was facing...was Irons!

A raw fighter, Irons didn't know how to relent, back down, or cease.

Now, Addison was suitable but his strengths were better for defending than attacking. Irons assaulted Addison with everything he had. He deployed a series of fast kicks and Irons's legs faded together in one blur as he struck Addison two to three times. Although Irons was formidable, so was Addison. He blocked a few of Irons's hard snaps and parried what he could. And yet, wherever Addison decided to move, Irons was there waiting for him. Irons shot a back-kick and then another side one, and Addison deflected one and then another. He could not stop the third.

And Irons's third hit was the deadliest.

It sent Addison flying back, and the cooler landed hard on his back. Racing after him, Jon could hear his friend moaning after he hit the floor. Jon glared. He hurried to Addison so he could help him up. They would take Irons together!

What Jon knew for sure? Two...is always better than one.

"Addison!" While screaming for his friend, Jon was halfway to Addison when he was hit by a new OverTaker.

Jon felt the full force of the strike and tumbled into a post. Rattled, Jon's head ached. His neck felt like he'd been hit with a mallet. The OverTaker was built like a Viking—big, burly, and battle-hardened. Jon shook his head to regain focus. By the time he did, the same striker was now in front of him. He was there, and he was just as furious.

"*Ah.*" Although Jon's vision was still blurry, he refocused before continuing the fight.

His senses returned slowly, but Jon refused to be hit again. He swung his elbow and Jon clobbered the next OverTaker directly in the mouth. The strike was messy, hard, and exactly what Jon wanted. While anyone else who would have been hit this hard would have fallen down, this OverTaker absorbed the hit like a champ.

Jon hopped about to get a little loose. His opponent gasped while shaking his head. Jon could hear him smacking his lips as he recovered. Although he was hurting, he was far from done. As soon as this man regained consciousness, he glowered at Jon.

"Fuck you, kid." Jon hated being referred to as *a kid*. Some saw it as a compliment, but Jon couldn't stand it. Since when was a twenty-four-year-old about to be twenty-five Marine a fucking kid?

"Not a kid, grandpa." Jon torqued his body and delivered a spinning hook-kick.

He didn't think this was a possible move in this fight. However, Jon's prosthetic made kicking harder. It was like he was wielding a weighted baton on his shin, but it also provided no encumbrances whatsoever.

It was fast and delivered right on target.

Jon watched the OverTaker fall. Jon didn't stay to see if his opponent was unconscious. Instead, he scoped the rest of the battlefield for more fights.

As of now, everyone was holding their own.

Danix had put two men down so far and was now tangling with another. He was engaged with a much bigger opponent now and Jon could see Danix bleeding, as was the man standing in front of him.

Jon spat and moved on.

Li was facing down another opponent as well. And this new fighter was really making Li work for a living. The OverTaker was trying to grab Li but failed each time. Fighting Li was like fighting a ghost, and no one ever won a fight against a fucking ghost. Once again, Jon spent only a brief amount of time watching the fights. He liked to observe because, from what he could see now, everyone was still in the fight. Jon would say that the Doormen were winning, but this was a Rumble. And, like the Keeper said, *nothing was over until it was over*.

Jon shivered.

Looking around for the last time, Jon eventually realized he could not see Addison. No, the cooler was missing. And, when Jon scoped the scene in search of him and Michael Irons, he looked up. The fight was not taking place on the second level of The Conquistador. This was where Jon had originally thought it was going to go down.

Instead, this one altercation was occurring in a place that had slipped Jon's mind. Rarely did Jon ever look in this section, but now he could see it.

Jon could see it and he didn't like it.

He had no idea why Addison would go here. Then, Jon thought maybe it wasn't Addison who decided this. Maybe it was Irons. Sometimes when fights do occur, one doesn't know where they are going or why. Sometimes, both fighters are so keen on winning that they become unaware of their surroundings. They have to use their environment as well as their skills to keep themselves protected.

Addison was in a place that was not only unprotected, it was also dangerous.

Along the ceiling of The Conquistador's dance floor was a steel balcony that ran perpendicular across the squared section below. Positioned above this was a set of strobe lights and just below a set of viewing windows. This was the place where the club technicians and lighting experts would frequent. It was to replace bulbs, change lighting, or rig foam or mist so it fell down from the ceiling.

The location was only accessible by ladder, and yet, neither Jon nor Addison had one.

No way they were going to do this now.

Jon wanted a piece of Irons, yes, but he also needed to help Addison. Despite the fact Addison was doing well, like Danix, he too was bleeding. Irons had taken hold of him good. He was using his superior fighting skills to take Addison for one hell of a ride. It was for this reason that Addison ended up where he was now.

Jon believed Addison was determined to beat Irons in a fight. He was willing to go anywhere he must in order to win. It just so happened that where Addison was being led to was a ceiling balcony. It was one of the highest and most dangerous parts of the club.

"No," Jon uttered to himself.

Right now, Jon considered how Addison and Irons ended up there. Jon looked to his left. There was an elevator built between two pillars that no one ever used. The Conquistador was booby-trapped to shit, with so much Jon still didn't know about, and while he should have known about this, apparently...he did not.

In the past, Jon had certainly come across the section. He passed this elevator too, even though it was hidden and far from the confines of The Conquistador. However, throughout most of this hidden section of the club, none would notice unless they were given the opportunity to.

Jon didn't have any opportunities. He didn't because he never understood exactly what he was looking for. Jon didn't know what was there until he actually took the time to look. And yet, all Jon could see now was Addison fighting a person who might actually be better than he was. Addison was skilled. He never required any backup. Still, what Jon was giving Addison now wasn't just backup. He was giving him friendship, support, and another set of hands to bring Irons to the ground.

Again...two is always better than one.

Moving up to The Conquistador's roof, Jon boarded the elevator and pushed up.

Following his friend, Jon cracked his knuckles. He was prepared to help Addison in the biggest fight of his life. He wanted to help Addison because, well, Addison was now...fucking family. "Hold on, Addison! I'm coming!"

The platform moving up was not slow like Jon expected it to be.

No, before stepping onto it, the flat plank didn't

look like much. Then, the movable platform shot upward and Jon watched the Doormen fight the remaining OverTakers. With more gray suits appearing across the floor, Jon was hesitant about leaving his brothers to fight on the field below.

But from what he could see, they looked to be okay.

"I'm almost there," Jon said to himself. "Almost."

And the elevator continued to climb up, up...*up*.

CHAPTER 15
THE HEAVY HANDS

LIGHTS CUT ACROSS THE CONQUISTADOR'S CEILING, and below, Addison and Irons exchanged blows like McGregor and Mayweather. Throwing jabs, both refused to stop until the other surrendered. None were the surrendering type, so all that could stop this match was if one of them fell and died.

The Rumble was, as the Keeper said, *a fight to the bitter end.*

"Not me," Addison said to Irons as he delivered another punch.

"And not me!" Irons replied.

As both men had been fighting for some time, they were both bruised and bleeding. Irons had a nice shiner along his jaw. Both Addison's eyes were blacked out like someone had dabbed them with black paint. Addison's lips were bleeding and his shirt was torn around the arms and shoulders.

He had never been in worse shape.

Addison spat and hit back at Irons with a push-kick. The capable killer blocked low and fast. After Addison kicked, Irons did the same. While Addison's was a straight-kick, Irons had curved his leg and struck with a hook. He popped Addison in the face and sent him into the railing.

Addison coughed and staggered.

What he needed was a time-out. Unfortunately, there was no time-out, only time-in.

Addison exhaled while the elevator stopped. Sprinting off the steady platform, Jon raced after Addison. The space above, which was narrow and rickety, not once did Jon feel balanced or, for that matter, safe. Still, he was willing to do away with all of this if it meant helping Addison, and that's exactly what he planned on doing.

"Addison!" Jon quickened.

When he saw Addison kneeling, Jon knew he couldn't fight anymore. Immediately, Jon pictured the scene from *The Dark Knight Rises*. He recalled how Batman fights Bane in the cavernous underground of Gotham City. It was the scene where Bane and Batman fought their first fight. Here, both characters continued to punch the other until one of them seceded. It was here where Bane broke Batman. He lifted the Bat high above his head and dropped him hard onto his knee, breaking the Dark Knight and debilitating him in one devastating, crushing blow.

Jon would rather have his back broken than see Addison get hurt like this.

Someone like Michael Irons was strong enough to lift someone like Addison over his head and then break his back like he was a two-by-four. This was what scared Jon most. Absolutely, Michael Irons was strong enough, and absolutely he was the type to do something this brutal. Yet, when Addison cocked his hand back for a solid punch, such an attempt to strike at someone like Irons proved futile.

Addison could barely lift his arm.

The strike he delivered was so weak even a child could block it.

Irons swept Addison's fist aside like it was nothing. He deflected the blow and then responded with another. Jon watched Irons elbow Addison's chin and then knock him down with a spinning back-kick. It was actually messy. Jon could hear Addison's body colliding with the rickety steel. Addison lambasted the metal and Jon unleashed all his fury and rage onto Irons. He'd been aching for this moment. Jon was so fired up that he felt like he could fly. It was because of this reason that, as soon as Jon saw Irons deliver the strike, the Marine decided to take flight.

Pushing off his back leg, Jon soared across the balcony and initiated a flying knee that hit Irons dead center. Jon had relied on his prosthetic to land the blow and gasped as he landed.

"Nice hit there, kid," Irons said to Jon with a grin.

"Thanks," said Jon. "But I ain't no goddamn kid." Jon then threw a distraction punch, to which Irons flinched at the phony blow. Due to him reacting to this fake out, Jon was able to hit back with the real one. He smacked Irons's right temple and popped him hard in the skull. The punch hurt Jon's knuckles, but it was exactly what he needed to be done.

After landing the first hit, Jon hit back with another, then another, and another, and another. Jon punched Michael Irons and kept on until he achieved the final knockout. Jon landed seven clean shots to Irons's body but not once did the big man fall.

No, he wasn't even fazed by Jon's countless punches.

Jon readied himself for yet another hit to Irons's bruised mug. And, before he could land one more, Irons returned to his original fighting position. He returned to being the bigger, better fighter. Then, blocking Jon's strike, Irons snatched the Marine by the wrist and yanked. He pulled Jon into his tough body and then Irons elbowed Jon square in the face and rattled the Marine. Now, Jon knew Irons was a damn good fighter. He thought he had prepared himself for this level. And yet, every time Irons hit Jon, he was reminded about how none were prepared to face a man like this.

When Jon did get back on his feet, he widened his stance and gawked at Irons.

"You're not backing down," said Irons. "Your mother would be proud of you. Look how brave her son is now. Look just how far he was willing to go to protect his own."

"A man who doesn't protect his own," said Jon, "isn't a man at all. Like you," Jon said to Irons, "the only person you fight for is...*yourself*."

"No," Irons replied. "I fight for the truth too. I fight for resources and reach, the same as any other man does. It's why I decided to come here, see? It's why I convinced Rex and his rebels to come too, because I knew they wanted what's buried deep beneath this place! What they want is the ultimate access! And, once my men are done beating yours, we're going to walk right in and take all of it! We're going to do this so we can finally get the chance to operate a club of our own within the secret guild that Larry still thinks he's a part of! And once we do that, we'll then be free from all the stress and pain that comes with protecting people who have never cared about us! And when we're done with that...well, who's going to stop us?"

When Irons said this to Jon, he laughed. The truth that Irons was here to uncover—the secrets buried beneath The Conquistador—was not where Irons thought it was.

"What?" asked Irons. "You think you'll actually be able to stop me from taking those keys, do you? Do you think after coming this far I would not take the greatest thing this place has? The Conquistador doesn't deserve it," Irons said. "It never has, but then that's the thing about Conquistadors. They might try and discover new things, new worlds, but in the end, whatever they find... it's always something taken by someone else. Eventually, all of them were replaced, and it's time for you to be replaced too."

"You can try," Jon said, "but should you go ahead and do that, well...then you're going to have to go through me, because I'm standing right here, in front of you, and I ain't afraid. Never have been. Never will be."

"You might not be afraid," said Irons, "but you sure as shit are all alone. You're alone, just like your mother was alone and just like you made her feel whenever you left and walked out the door. Face it, Jon, you're not a good son. Never were and never will be."

When Irons mentioned Jon's mother, the Marine fists became so hard he felt like his knuckles might crumble.

"She was alone, and you're gonna end up just as alone as she is. And that's what you're really afraid of,"

Irons said to Jon. "Not me, but what's going to happen to you once you're all finished with this place. You're gonna have no friends and no future. You're just gonna end up a washed-up Marine who could never find his way because he wasted too much time serving the will of others. Amazing. You left one war only to join another. But there's a problem, see? Back in the desert, you were actually winning, but here? No, here, you've already lost. Here, you lost the moment you started serving *them*! When are you going to accept it, Jon? You're the bad guy! You're the fucking bad guy!"

Jon gritted his teeth and squinted until his eye muscles began to throb. He battled the terror boiling inside because all of his fears and struggles had now been put into words. All of them were spoken by the man whom Jon Haze despised. Everything Jon had to overcome was being expressed by Irons, and it was for these reasons he had chosen to leave. Jon had come back because of what Lieutenant Dan said. He explained the meaning of service to Jon and fighting for a cause, even if there are imperfections and uncertainties, is noble.

Creed is honor and loyalty matters.

"It's not about the people who salute the flag, it's about the people who sew it back together whenever it's torn."

Jon remembered the phrase all too well. It was true. For Jon, it always would be. In the end, we all have to take a side and we all have to protect and care for something. Jon didn't just protect The Conquistador because it was a nightclub, no. What he protected were the people in it, because people are real. People are worth fighting for.

Tonight, Jon fought hard to protect Addison, Danix, Larry, Li, Owen, Duncan, Jamal; all his fellow Doormen who were his brothers. He fought for Kya because Jon loved Kya. He fought so he could keep her and everyone else safe and unharmed. He protected his people from all the forces that sought to destroy them. Forces like Irons and his brigade of OverTakers would never ever understand.

They wouldn't because they couldn't. They were incapable of caring.

"No," said Jon. "I'm a soldier. I'm a fighter. *I'm a motherfucking Doorman!*"

In a rage, Jon sprinted across the steel balcony and didn't think or consider the consequences of his bold yet daring act. Jon didn't care if Irons punched him out cold or if he kicked Jon off the balcony. It would be impossible to hurt Jon. Whatever significant damage Irons could do to Jon had already been done. The most harmful weapon in Irons's arsenal was not his fists or his strength. No, it was Irons's words that cut deep like a knife. Jon had now been stabbed straight through his heart, and it burned Jon as if salt was smeared across a gushing wound. And yet, Jon didn't care. No, what he did was he stampeded across a rickety bridge twenty-five feet above The Conquistador's dance floor. Then, he drove his shoulder into Irons's gut, and pushed him down onto the steel. Jon's anger had gifted him with incredible power. He was able to knock Irons onto his back, and Jon felt solid as a statue.

No doubt, Irons knew how to strike hard and fast, but then so did Jon. Another notable skill Jon possessed was his timing. It was impeccable. Once Jon had Irons exactly where he wanted him, Jon wrapped him up like a spider crawling along strands of a very fine web.

Michael Irons was big. Although not as big as Danix, Jon had sparred with Danix many times in the past. Each battle was brutal but each time Jon learned. Still, Irons's mass was substantial. Jon felt like, in many ways, he was wrestling with a tree. At the time, Jon was ready to lock up this tree of a man and squeeze him until his bark—which were his bones—splintered.

Now, at this moment, Jon summoned all his remaining strength and he grabbed tightly and then tried to execute the perfect rear-naked choke. Irons's response to this attack was swift. He reached up and grabbed the railing and hoisted himself up. Jon knew Irons to be magnificently strong. Up again, Irons twisted as he tried to shed Jon off his body.

Still, the Marine fought to hold, and he did. He did *hold*.

"Ah, you son of a bitch!" Jon roared. He continued to throttle until Irons tapped. Suddenly, Jon was back to learning from Danix at his gym. Some people would rather die than tap out. Jon imagined that Irons was one of the few who fell into this category.

He'd rather die than give up.

Irons gripped Jon's forearm and clenched. Although Jon maintained his choke, the setting itself was another opponent. Jon, now high above the ground, wrestled with Irons on a plank so narrow it could barely fit one person let alone two. The entire time, Jon was reminded of the potential fall. And, due to always seeing what was beneath, Jon was distracted and frightened. This compromised his grip on Irons's body.

Jon was unable to hold him as tightly as he needed to be held.

With a fraction of Jon's grip now loosening, Irons jerked his elbow and popped Jon in the chin. From there, he ruptured Jon's chokehold. Once the Marine lost to the OverTaker leader, the powerful man flipped Jon over and dropped him onto the hard steel.

The balcony clattered and wobbled.

Irons snapped three kicks at Jon. And, while Jon did what he could to block these blows, every attempt to protect himself was pointless. Jon was hammered by Irons and already felt way out of his league.

"I warned you, boy," Irons said. "I warned you that this fight is beyond you, but still, you wouldn't listen. Still, you couldn't see what was right in front of your weak, pathetic eyes."

Jon rolled along his shoulder and rose up slowly.

"You couldn't put aside your foolish pride and just go home. Why?" Irons was now raising his voice as he addressed Jon. Wounded, Jon glared. "Why couldn't you just go home?"

In that moment, Irons was hoarse because he was bogged down by his rage. Jon was hit hard by the change in Irons's tone as much as he was struck by his blows. When being asked such a foolish question, Jon felt the need to answer. He felt the need to answer as well as the need to bring his hands up to his face.

Doing this, he was in fact showing Irons he was not done fighting, not yet.

Still, Jon refused to back down.

"Because," Jon replied with stoicism and fortitude, "here, I am home."

Jon grunted the last syllable and felt a grumbling sensation cutting at the back of his throat. After expressing his loyalty to The Conquistador, Jon was ready to go head-to-head with Irons, even if it meant falling to his death. And there was no worse way to die than this.

"Are you?" snapped Irons.

Jon's mouth was opened. Though he was about to say more, before he could do any of this, someone else decided to speak for him. And this someone was the same person who had not left Jon's side since he arrived. Still, they were there. Still, *he* was there.

"Yeah," said Addison. "Yeah, he is. *He is fucking home.*"

Addison glowered at the ferocious leader. Irons, who stood at the opposite end of the rickety bridge, was positioned between Jon and Addison. Now, with Jon set to fight and Addison standing to his left, the liar turned bouncer turned supposed Doorman was now completely surrounded.

He was facing two opponents instead of just one.

"What?" Michael Irons said, looking at Addison. "What, you don't think I can take the both of you? I had you down and I can keep you there if I wanted."

"So?" said Addison. "So, what are you waiting for then? Move!"

Irons spat and turned to look at Jon. Right now, Jon looked back at Irons with a grim, no-nonsense expression because it was at this moment, he could foresee the end to what was an epic fight. Before, Irons was only facing Jon or Addison. Now, he had the added struggle of fighting both at the same time. Jon and Addison were skilled, no doubt. Never had they teamed up on a single opponent, though. And yet, there was no better time to do that than now.

"You're not ready for this," Irons declared.

"Oh, we are," said Jon.

"You're not!" Addison shouted at Irons and then cut himself loose.

Addison leaped head-first into the fight, stomped after Irons, and gallantly entered the battle by throwing not one but three punches in rapid succession. Addison hit Irons in the chest and then twice more in the face. Jon scampered to join Addison. Irons responded instantly. He punched Addison with a hook and then knocked him back into the railing. Clattering the same as before, Irons could not see Jon flying through the air as he delivered a stunning flying knee.

"Ah!" Jon drove his knee hard into Irons's back. He banged up Irons's spine nice and good and the blow was spot on. It forced Irons to scream, "Goddamn it!"

Jon then spun and executed a spinning hook-kick. He was never good with this move, but he had been practicing it for some time. Also, the space to perform the kick was limited. Jon barely had enough room to lift his leg let alone turn and lift it.

And yet, Jon performed the hook-kick and whacked Irons furiously in the jaw. It was a tough kick to deliver, but with Jon's prosthetic acting like a cudgel, he smoked Irons and shook him to his bones.

Irons gasped.

Drool spilled from his wobbling mouth as Jon glared. The kick, which was satisfying and fun, also gave Addison an opportunity to respond with an attack of his own. Executing a sidekick, Addison clobbered Irons's ribs and forced him to stumble into Jon.

From here, Jon slipped into Aikido.

He squeezed Irons's wrist, bent it back, and then around. From there, Jon had obtained control of the joint. Bending the wrist again, Jon manipulated Irons's arm and flipped him over. With Irons now down, Jon and Addison had the upper hand—something both bouncers greatly desired.

Jon kicked while Irons blocked.

While Irons deflected, Addison punched in what was a constant and relentless battle. Still persistent, Jon booted Irons upside in the chin. He was tough and Jon understood this about him more than anyone. He wouldn't surrender even while blind in one eye.

Jon felt the best way to beat him was to blind him in two.

He caught Irons on the swing. Then, Jon remembered Danix's words:

"If your enemy persists, you can either fight harder, or you can fight smarter."

Danix had expressed this to Jon when he had him in a triangle choke. Then, Danix reached out and gouged Jon's eyes with his thumb. Danix didn't push his thumb into the socket all the way, but he did introduce this attack to Jon without actually delivering it.

"And sometimes fighting smarter is fighting uglier... messier."

At the time of the instruction, Danix was also holding Jon by his Gi.

At the time, Danix had Jon exactly where he wanted. And Jon had Irons exactly where he wanted.

To see this through, Jon reached out and plunged his thumbs deep into Irons's eyes, just like he was taught to.

Pushing down as hard as he could, Irons squealed like a baby.

Always, this man underestimated Jon. Men often do underestimate the power of boys, except Jon was no boy. He was one before he joined the Marines but left the unit as a man, as a brutalist and someone who knew how to get a job done.

Jon hoped he would never have to again. Things changed.

Picking Irons's eye right out of his skull, Jon came again in to hit with a swift elbow. Jon's strategy for taking out Irons's eye was similar to Danix's, though it was not quite the same. Jon had seen Danix do some crazy shit, but never had he seen him do anything like this.

He was now armed with a pencil, one of the many tools a cooler like Addison had on his person. Jon had removed a pencil from his pocket and wielded it now like a knife. And, with a quick jab, Jon pierced Irons's same wounded eye, and the liar of a man squealed.

"*Eeee!*" From down below, all the Doormen stopped to look up. Against the Doormen, no one stood a chance against them.

The Rumble was over and victory was taken.

And that victory belonged to them, to the Doormen yet again!

After stabbing Irons in the eye, Jon slumped onto the railing but did not fall. It was a thankful break. While the pencil had penetrated Irons's face, it did ruin his orbital cavity.

Jon imagined some of Irons's eye remained intact.

Later, Irons reached up and snagged the pencil sticking out of his skull. Still, with the strength to pull it out, Irons grabbed the shaft. With a yank, he tugged it from his bleeding face.

"Ah-ha!" Irons's shouts echoed through the club like a church bell.

Again, Jon was reminded of Irons's sheer toughness and the absolute brutality a man like him could distribute. It was an ugly sight to behold, but at the same time, it was also quite pleasing, quite pleasing...*to the eye*. If Irons didn't think he lost now, then he never would.

"It's over, Mike," said Jon.

Jon rarely referred to Irons by his first name let alone the common short form of Mike. Still, Jon waited for Irons to throw his hands up and surrender. Though he was not the type to do this, there truly was nowhere for him to go now. And yet, Irons continued to stand and hold on but Jon had to ask himself if this was how he wanted to go out?

Was this how Irons wanted to die?

"The Rumble is done and all your men are down. We're all that's left," said Jon.

Irons dropped the pencil and spat up blood. A hard strip of red appeared streaked across Irons's doleful eyes. Still, Jon could make out his glower. He could still listen to his brutal screams of agony as Irons replied. "Never!" His yells reached new levels. "I've come this far, done more than you could possibly imagine to get here, and I'm going to stay...stay until I get what I want! I want the ciphers!"

The ciphers.

Until now, Jon didn't think Irons would say these

words or make this demand, but he had...he did! He knew about The Conquistador's precious keys, yes, but he had never heard Irons speak about these immensely valuable tools that granted so-called unlimited access to its users.

"What? What did you say?"

"Fuck you," said Irons. "Doesn't matter now. There's only one way to beat this club, and I'm going to do it. I'm gonna burn this place to the ground! I'm going to end it right here, right fucking now!"

Again, Jon wanted to know more. What was Irons's plan for doing this?

Was he belligerent or was he just furious? Maybe Irons was insinuating bigger plans for the future of this club, all pertaining to the *real* secret being kept inside The Conquistador?

"It's over," said Addison. He made no further comment about anything Irons mentioned.

"Nah," said Irons. Blood from Irons's bludgeoned eye spilled down his battered face in one single streak.

A clownish grin made of curdled blood oozed between Irons's bent teeth and he reached into his pocket. "You know the old saying there, buddy boy... ain't nothing's over...*till it's over*."

From Irons's left pocket, the fearsome manipulator removed a chrome cigarette lighter that glistened in the dark environment. Jon stared at the lighter and scoffed. "What the hell are you doing with that?"

"Surroundings, friend?" commented Irons. "You're not good at knowing what's around you. You never were."

Jon's gaze hardened because no, he didn't know, but apparently, Irons did.

"Look beneath you, see what your Rumble has done."

Jon glanced at the aforementioned space below. He didn't see much, nothing except for pockets of liquid scattered across the dance floor. If Irons hadn't told him to look, Jon wouldn't have done so. Now that he did, he detected a smell. As of now, it reeked of alcohol. In fact, it smelled of a lot of alcohol.

Jon flinched after smelling the fumes.

"Glasses broke, drinks spilled during our little fight," Irons explained. "And soon as I drop this shit, the entire place goes up in smoke. All I have to do is get close enough to that flame and poof!" Irons made an exploding gesture with his hands. "You're dead, and this whole place is about to turn to fucking ash!"

"You really think one lighter is going to burn this entire building down?" Addison snapped. "You really have lost your mind there, Michael. Like I said to you before, it's over."

"No," Irons grunted, "it might not be enough, but it's still a start, and that's all I've wanted. All I wanted was a good goddamn *start*!"

After this, Irons tossed the lighter and Jon watched the flame fall down to the space below. As the light grazed the floor, a fire erupted. Therefore, Irons's plan for lighting up the entire club was a pointless attack. No, it wouldn't work, but then Irons knew it wouldn't. Once he finished tossing the lighter, Irons hopped over the railing and landed on a swinging set of lights.

"Shit!" yelled Jon.

How Irons managed to pull off this mad stunt had very much shocked the Marine. And yet, while Irons stood on the metal beams, he held the bracket and glared at Jon and Addison. What he was doing, in Jon's mind, was complete and utter madness. The man could barely see and he now purposefully thrust himself into a place where sight was everything. It was necessary! Therefore, how could Irons still willfully jump onto the most unstable section imaginable? Now, Jon knew Irons was a tough bastard. Still Jon didn't take him for stupid or reckless.

Everything he did now pointed to this.

"All it takes is the smallest spark to bring an entire army down to its knees. One tiny spark and one person brave enough to create it," said Irons.

"What the hell are you doing?" Addison continued to scope out Irons, like saying any of this would change the cooler's mind. Jon wanted to ask the same question. However, knowing Irons, there always was a plan. Always, he had a reason for doing what he did.

"Starting the fire," Irons said. "Ending your time here, because if I can't take your club, then no one will! Fuck The Conquistador, and fuck its old ways! You're done, do you hear me?! Done!"

Jon's head bent and he continued to look even more confused by Irons's barking statement. Eventually, this feeling did settle. It began to dwindle as soon as Irons grabbed hold of a cluster of wires attached to one of the lights. He tugged the thick cord, which emitted violent sparks. Speckles of fire flashed in front of Irons's now partially blinded face and tiny flames peppered the ground. And yet, Irons continued to seize the wire.

"What are you doing? Are you fucking crazy?!" Addison yelled, but Jon knew the reaction was pointless. By now, it was apparent that Michael Irons was anything but sane. He responded to Addison's howling with a cheap, unimpressed smile.

He raised his free hand and saluted the two Doormen.

"See you on the other side."

Like the furious man that he was, Irons gripped the burning wire so taut his bicep trembled. Then, jumping off the bracket, he pulled the sparking wire down toward the wet dance floor. Swinging like Tarzan, Jon could already see how this was going to pan out. It would go down exactly as expected. Sparks from the ripped wire doused the alcohol pool and—igniting the flames—gave birth to a fire capable of engulfing all of The Conquistador!

It was messy and crazy. It was this but not impossible.

A fire was building and Jon could see it escalating to near uncontainable levels. However, a fire like this *could* be stopped. Still, Irons was escaping! Jon refused to accept him leaving this scene. As Irons swung on the wire spitting out flakes of searing sparks, Jon hopped over the railing. Then, he looked back at Addison.

"What are you doing?" Addison asked Jon. "Jon..." Addison's tone changed. Once addressing Jon Haze like a boss, he was now speaking to him like he was his parent. Voicing his concern to the Marine, Addison's voice was fractured. Jon could only make out the last words before he did what he never thought he would do.

Jon jumped.

A long time ago, Jon lost a friend and a brother because he failed to act. He lost so much he loved because he was too afraid and too worried. Now, Jon was about to leap without looking. Though he was looking only slightly, Jon understood this was the only way to stop Michael Irons from getting away.

Someone had to chase him, someone who wasn't afraid, and Jon was done being afraid.

He was done thinking about what *might* happen instead of what was certainly going to. And, what was happening was Jon learning to fight without hesitation or any signs of fear. When he fell toward Michael, Jon latched onto him as well as the wire he was holding onto. Now secured, Jon grabbed the sparking tube before it could create more flames. And, once Jon had Irons in his grasp, he battled him while holding on tightly to the dangling sling. Irons, who could barely see, felt Jon's body colliding into his own. He knew Jon was there but he had not yet fallen. Once Jon managed to take hold of his wire, he pulled it against himself. Then, Jon gawked at Irons for the very last time.

"You wanna start a fire?" Jon invited. "Well, why don't you try starting with one that's supposed to happen, the one burning inside your ugly-ass self?!"

Jon pulled the fiery tip and glared. What he was about to do to Irons, Jon didn't think he was capable of doing. He didn't believe he had such malice or brutality in him, but a lot had changed for Jon this last year. And so, Jon throttled the sparking tip and, with vicious intent, jammed it deep into Irons's throat—plunging it as far in as it would go.

Jon listened to the vomit-inducing gargles and watched as Irons's throat lit up like the Fourth of July.

After this, Jon took the other dangling wires and wrapped them tightly around Irons's twitching body. Jon roped him there so he wouldn't fall but would instead be left hanging over the dance floor while on fire!

He was to be a trophy dedicated to the Doormen's victory—*a symbol for all to see.*

Jon let go. Jon fell and Irons coughed, gagged, and convulsed. Still holding on, somehow, the sparks were continuous. No, they were relentless. Few lights still managed to shine inside the broken club, but as Jon landed, he began to see just how much the fire had spread.

Looking around, heaps of flames scattered about the area. Some were big, others were small. Jon was expected to be greeted by his fellow Doormen. Instead, he was only greeted by one.

"Come on!" yelled Danix. The flames crackled and Jon was encased in heat so intense it burned his eyes.

"What?" Jon looked past Danix and toward where the Doormen had last assembled.

Before, Jon could only see Li, Owen, and Duncan. Now, all he could see were walls of smoke and the faint silhouettes of people fleeing for the nearest exit.

"The club is on fire! We have to move!" Jon's head continued to turn in all directions. The fire Danix was referring to now only touched a portion of The Conquistador. Still, a fire spreads. And according to Danix, it was spreading fast.

"I thought I stopped it!" Jon yelled.

"Nah," said Danix, pulling Jon's arm. "There was no stopping this."

Jon's head shook in disbelief.

Watching the fire, Jon realized he had no choice. He sprinted with Danix toward the door and pushed through the smoke and heat. Now coughing uncontrollably, most of what Jon could see was compromised. He held on tightly to Danix and he guided Jon out of the club and into the parking lot outside.

Still in the midst of a coughing assault, Jon grumbled while also standing reunited with his fellow Doormen. He counted everyone who was with him. All were assembled and all were now free.

Although Jon was glad to see all the bouncers, they were not the first details Jon had come to notice. Watching the raging fire gobble up Jon's place of work—his home—in a perennial blaze of flame and ash, Jon blinked to regain focus. When smoke hits—and this was something Jon had learned back in the army—it hits hard.

Jon rubbed his eyes and sniffled.

Then, turning to face Danix, Jon asked his friend about the whereabouts of Addison. Jon struggled to speak. Eventually, he managed to squeak out a barely audible question.

"Where..." Jon coughed and continued to press his wrist deep into his eyes. "Where's...*Addison?*"

With The Conquistador on fire, the whole building...*was burning*.

Jon swung into Irons while still holding onto a long cable. Based on what Jon could remember, he didn't know where Addison was or if he was coming back. He only assumed Addison had escaped the same as the rest. He didn't know this for sure until Jon glanced at the door again.

"He's..." Danix was about to answer Jon when suddenly he didn't have to. There was a lingering haze beyond where Jon was standing. A silhouette of Addison began to take shape. Now lumbering along,

Addison wobbled, but soon, he managed to clear free of the smoke and debris. Evidently, Addison was the last one to escape the fire.

Jon hurried after his friend. He called Addison's name until he answered.

"Addison! Addison!" Like a child calling out to his father, The Conquistador burned, and Jon put an end to Irons and his OverTakers, but in the process, he couldn't imagine losing someone he cared about.

When Jon came to Addison, he touched his shoulder. "Are you...are you all right?" Jon asked Addison, who looked at Jon soon after. Addison's eyes were shaped like acorns. It was obvious he was pretty far from okay.

Addison nodded. "Dandy."

Addison knew how to lay the sarcasm on so thick that Jon let out a piggish snort. There was no way anyone could be real after what happened. Still, Jon stayed with Addison and touched his shoulder.

"The club," Li said, "The Conquistador...it's...it's..."

"*Burned*," said Danix. When he stared at what was left of The Conquistador, the rest of the Doormen did the same. Watching the flames as they continued to consume the place they all knew as home, The Conquistador was their whole world. There really was nothing left to say or do.

"It's gone," said Jon, awestruck and hurting.

"Shit," said Duncan.

"Fuck," said Owen.

"What do we do now?" asked Duncan.

"We..." Jon looked at Duncan, jaw dropped and eyes acquiring the same fiery shade as the conflagration itself, he was about to say something but stopped when he heard Kya calling out to him. As soon as Jon caught sight of Kya, she instantly fell into Jon's arms and held him tightly. Jon kissed her neck and cheek.

"You're okay," Kya said to Jon. "My God, you're okay."

"Yeah," said Jon. He held Kya close too. "I'm okay."

"I can't believe the club!" shouted Kya. "It's gone! On fire! How did that happen?"

Jon looked up while, at the same time, waiting for someone else to say something. When none did, Jon had no choice but to speak for them. "We won," he said. "We won."

Though this was not entirely true, in the end, the Doormen were left standing and the OverTakers were not. To Jon, this marked a clear victory. In fact, it was all the victory the Doormen could hope for under the circumstances.

The Conquistador was gone, but they were not. *They were still here.*

"Doesn't look like we won anything," Kya said, "if you ask me."

"We're still here," said Owen. "They're not. Isn't that right?"

"Whatever," said Duncan. "The club is gone. Who knows what's going to happen now. Where's the Keeper? What does he have to say about all this? I mean, shouldn't he have something to say?"

Duncan searched for the Keeper. Soon after he did, the cloaked man arrived from the darkness and crept toward the remaining Doormen like the Grim Reaper that he was. Though he was not death's emissary as much as he was the emissary for the hidden truths regarding the world of nightclubs, it was a world Jon was now familiar with.

"Doormen of The Conquistador, the Rumble victory is yours. You have won. The club will return to you pending the approval of the *Ancients* as well as receiving a Forge Form, which can only be accessed when you've returned to the *Old Guilds* to complete your *Trials*."

Jon squinted. New concepts and titles were being introduced to him now: Ancients, Forge, *Trials*?

What did all of this mean?

Was it real, made up, or something new, maybe something dark?

Jon coughed and looked again at Addison.

"What does that mean?" he asked. "What's he talking about?"

Addison didn't say anything to Jon. The Keeper still had more to say.

"Do you still have yours?" Addison reached into his shirt and removed a chain around his neck. One of the ciphers from the vault dangled from a thick necklace comprised of linked metal. And, when Jon saw this one *cipher*, he remembered when Addison first recovered it. At the time, he didn't know what it was used for, only hints about them, the door, *what they opened, and above all else...what they could do*. Now that Addison showed it to the Keeper, the cipher was the tool necessary to begin the *rebuilding process*—the Forge...whatever that was or foreshadowed.

When the Keeper saw this, he commented. "I suggest you take it to the *Ancients* then," he said. "As soon as possible."

"To do that, we would have to go far, to where it all began...*to the original five clubs. Old Guild*"

"Indeed," said the Keeper, "but such is the only way you will be able to rebuild. You must reopen the old doors before you can walk through any new ones. You know the rules put forth by the Commission. Every club is to use their own ciphers to *enter*. No club, cabaret, or bar can stand unless they have *access*, and the *ciphers* are all that can grant that. And, given the state of things, I'd say that's the best you can hope for now, if you still want it. This is my assessment, and I wish you all the best in the next phase. Goodbye and good luck."

The Keeper tipped his hat to Addison and then walked off into the night. Without context or reason about anything said, it all sounded as though the Keeper was reading from a textbook. Jon didn't have a clue about any of this, only that Addison did have The Conquistador's ciphers with him now, at least he had one.

Apparently, this was the *key* needed going forward.

"What the hell's he talking about?" asked Owen. "Trial...for *what*?"

Owen's question was the same as Jon's, who gazed at the Keeper and watched him closely as he vanished.

"Where are we going, Addison?" Jon asked. "Where do we go in order to resurrect this place?"

Silently, Addison squeezed this key. Eyes up, the flames had reduced The Conquistador to a burned skeleton. Jon stood next to Addison and thought about the words now plaguing his mind.

Ciphers. Ancients. Guild. Forge. Door. Access.

Who, what, where, when...why?

"Like I said, it's far," Addison said. "Very far."

"Well how far," asked Danix, "is *too* far?"

Addison snorted while the light from the dwindling flames reflected off his sweaty mug.

"Further than we've ever gone before," said Addison. "Deeper than we've ever gone before, and we would have to pay a visit to other clubs, different clubs, with different rules and *very* different Doormen."

"Deeper?" said Li. Now deepness meant something to Jon. It meant wherever the Doormen were planning to go next might very well force them into new territory, unveil new secrets, and encounter new powers.

Deadlier powers.

"The deepest?" asked Addison. He turned to face the remaining Doormen. "I can't ask you all to go, but to resurrect The Conquistador, we have. We—" Suddenly, Addison stopped talking. His head was shaking in distress. Addison gulped back all his booming anxiety. Jon never saw his boss in such a state. He didn't know what to make of it. What he was thinking about now was the *Forge* mentioned only by the Keeper, whatever it was.

"Have to go back?" Jon asked. "Back to where it all started?"

Jon inserted his question right away. He didn't care. He had returned to unite with his fellow Doormen, and now that he had, he was here to finish. Just like he did back in the Marines, traveling was in Jon's blood, and so was war.

"Never," said Addison. "For now, we stay here."

"Stay?" Jon barked. "But what about what you just said, the war, the ciphers, the access, the trials, and everything else we need?"

While Jon was amped up and excited, Addison was everything but. Although the Doormen were looking for more advice, Addison had none for any of them. Instead, Addison ended their time together with a simple nod and lent Jon another gentle hand on the shoulder.

"There will always be another war to fight, Marine. Always another door to protect and always another Irons. For now, we stay, and we figure out tomorrow when tomorrow comes," Addison said this to Jon, who was reticent to accept such advice. "And if tomorrow asks us to suit up and go on a new journey, then we will."

"And what is tomorrow asking of us now?" This question was Danix's.

Looking at the giant Doormen, Addison stepped along. "It asks for us to go the hospital," he said, "to go and visit a man who needs us now more than ever."

"And what about the club?" asked Jon. "The Conquistador's future?"

"Later," said Addison. "Not now. Not today. Now, we all have somewhere better to be."

Not a single bouncer could argue with this. In the end, how could they?

Addison always had a way with words and articulating certain truths, revelations, and lessons. Although Jon was prepared to do battle, maybe this battle was not prepared for him.

Jon liked having a war to fight, but then, he wasn't sure if that's what this was.

Doormen weren't soldiers, *or were they?*

In truth, Jon couldn't comprehend tomorrow or the next day. He couldn't, and he didn't want to. The

Conquistador was gone. And, though there was a way to get it back, Jon couldn't help but ask...*was this really what he wanted?*

Jon watched Addison skulk through the smoke. Where he was going, Jon assumed, was the hospital. It looked as if he was simply walking away from everything, and Jon wasn't going to lie to himself, none of this looked good.

With The Conquistador gone, maybe this was how Jon's journey ended.

Maybe he was done fighting, and maybe all he wanted was to go home and never look back. His instinct was to follow Addison, but the time for following him was over. Jon would stay a Doormen for as long as he was needed. No matter what, he would stay loyal to his kin. And yet, with Irons gone and the OverTakers defeated, Jon found himself feeling surprisingly fulfilled.

For now, he was at peace. He won the fight, got the girl, and discovered the truth.

"Addison?" Jon gazed through the smoke and tried to see where Addison was walking. Holding his gaze, the smoke rose, and the sirens blared in the distance.

Jon looked around for more Doormen. They were gone.

Where?

At this point, nothing was known or certain. All that was understood was Jon's next step, where he would be granted a new path, a new challenge that would test him the same—or perhaps—worse than he already was. But now he had Kya by his side.

Jon glanced at his phone. There were six missed calls, all from his mom.

With another enemy gone, another day lived, it was time to go home. Jon was grateful—grateful that another day would come and then, he would wait to decide.

He had all the time he needed to consider, all the time he wanted.

In fact, Jon was destined for this war. He was built for it.

He just didn't know it yet.

ACKNOWLEDGMENTS

There are many people I need to thank for helping to publish this novel, and I think the best way to do that is to start at the very beginning. First, I would like to extend my warmest and most sincere gratitude to Jake Bray, Mike Bray, Patience Bramlett, Rachel Del Grosso, Ellie Folden, and everyone else at Wolfpack and Rough Edges who has worked hard to bring this book to life. It has been a long road, but you took a chance on me as well as on this story, and I am immensely grateful for everyone's patience and understanding. You have allowed me to improve upon this book in ways I never thought possible and long have I wanted to share stories about the enigmatic club, The Conquistador, as well as former Marine turned bouncer Jon Haze. And, because of your courage, these stories can now be told. I am also thankful to my fellow Goddardites, my Heebie Jeebie pals from Goddard College, for providing community and sanctity to a writer who was rejected by other MFA programs, and yet, you gave me a path and a voice when I thought I had none.

I would also like to thank my writing teachers: John McManus, Douglas Martin, Jan Clausen, Melodie Campbell, and David Bergen, who—though they did not assist in the creation of this novel—still, nonetheless, sculpted me into the creative artist I am today. Next, I would like to thank writers Brian Drake, Mark Allen, and Michael Black—gentlemen who have generously donated their time and their knowledge and who provided feedback to someone who was once a complete stranger. If not for your wondrous input and generosity, this book would not be where it is today and I would not be welcomed into such a glorious family of talented men and women. I also thank local writer friends, including Brent Van Staalduinen, who gave time and encouragement, and my great friend and confidant, Mark Jordan Manner. Mark, you guided me through this vast literary landscape, and without your help, I could not have navigated, conquered, or, for that matter, endured the many changes and challenges that come with this industry. I would also like to thank a man who is more than a friend but a mentor, Mr. John Corr. Candid and kind, receptive and lethal, you throw me on the mats, and still, you also help me both in and outside the dojo. I am thankful I met you when I did. I hope I might continue to train and learn alongside you in the years to come. I thank Naben Ruthnum, Lucy S. Snyder, Andrew F. Sullivan, and Amy Jones—writers who have taken time out of their busy schedules to look at my work and who have given me strength during tough and difficult times. I offer my gratitude to all my family and friends, including my teacher friends—good and decent colleagues. I thank my alma mater buds, Greg Zavitz, Brent Duguid, and Andrew Francella, someone who spends more time respecting my opinion than he does his own. I thank Dave Franciosa, Steve Legge, Christopher Barrett, and other like-minded geeks, and finally, all the Mazza-Anthonys. However, I owe an extreme debt of gratitude to Sharmaine Gobind, not just a reader but a guardian angel. Sharmaine, you came to my aid when I was at such a low point and you quite literally brought me and my stories back from the dead. I could not have done this without you, and because you were there for me, I will always be there for you.

I thank the people on both sides of my splendid family:

My brother, Cody, my bud and coolest cat going. My best friend and sister, Jenna, a relentless voice of concern. My father, a decent man. My Bentley, my whole world. And above all else, my mother, Sheila. You are an amalgamation of encouragement, power, strength, and truth, which is often inconvenient, but most importantly...of love. Thank you for being my greatest fan, a great friend, and everything else in between. I thank you for following me on my many journeys. I always know where I'm going, and because of you, I am never lost.

IF YOU LIKED THIS, YOU MIGHT LIKE

GENOCIDE: AN ACTION-ADVENTURE SERIES (THE GODS OF WAR 1) BY BRENT TOWNS

Kane and Jensen are hauled before an intelligence committee bent on finding out the truth no matter the consequences...

They are called The Gods of War: Russian Generals who were given birth in the old days of the USSR. They live in the shadows. No one knows their faces. Over the years they have evolved into one of the most dangerous entities in the covert world.

Until they cross the wrong people...

"John 'Reaper' Kane and Raymond 'Knocker' Jensen have been pulled into a new clandestine mission by MI6 to investigate a mysterious gas attack in a Northern Syrian village. As they delve deeper, they unravel a complex conspiracy beyond their wildest expectations. The gas attack is just the tip of a bigger iceberg. And before the two are done, death and destruction will follow them across the globe in their relentless pursuit to expose the truth behind the ominous plans of The Gods of War.

AVAILABLE NOW

ABOUT THE AUTHOR

Jarrett Mazza is a graduate of Goddard College's MFA in Creative Writing Program in Plainfield, Vermont as well as The Humber School For Writers.

Before completing his terminal degree, he studied writing at the University of Toronto School of Continuing Studies and comic book writing under Ty Templeton and Andy Schmidt. He has had stories published online in the GNU Journal, Bewildering Stories, Trembling With Fear, Aphelion, The Scarlet Leaf Review, and Toronto Prose Mill, The Fictional Cafe. His work is featured in anthologies by Silver Empire Publishing, a best seller, Zimbell House Publishing,NBH Publishing, MuseWrite Press, twice by Dragon Soul Press, Gypsum Sound Tales, Hellbound Books and The Ginosko Literary Journal. All are available on Amazon for purchase. He was also an Honorable Mention for the Freda Waldon Award for Fiction, nominated for an Indie Book award, and was featured as a visiting author for the nationwide We Read Canadian event in 2020. His mystery short story was published in an anthology under the editorial supervision of Michael Bracken and was published by Down and Out Books.

He lives in Hamilton, Ontario. You can follow him on Twitter @JarrettMazza